THE CEDAR TREE

A novel based on the popular ATV
series created by Alfred Shaughnessy

The Cedar Tree

a novel by

Michael Hardwick

based on the television
series created by
Alfred Shaughnessy

SEVERN HOUSE

First published 1976 by Severn House Publishers Ltd of
144–146 New Bond Street, London W1Y 9FD with the
co-operation of Corgi Books, Transworld Publishers Ltd.

ISBN 0 7278 0300 X

Printed in Great Britain by litho at The Anchor Press Ltd
and bound by Wm Brendon & Son Ltd
both of Tiptree, Essex

The Cedar Tree

The ATV series was created by Alfred Shaughnessy, who was also its Script Editor. It was recorded by ATV at Elstree Studios, Borehamwood. Ian Fordyce was its Producer. In writing the book the author has drawn upon material from scripts by Felicity Douglas, T. E. B. Clarke, Michael and Mollie Hardwick, John Harrison, Angharad Lloyd, Deborah Mortimer, Jeremy Paul, Alfred Shaughnessy, Arline Whittaker and David Pownall.

CHAPTER ONE

No one knew – and if it knew itself it could tell no one – that in the year 1934 the cedar tree reached its 200th year of life and its full maturity.

No one knew, because there was no mention of it in the household papers of Larkfield Manor. The matter had been speculated upon amongst succeeding generations of the house's occupants, and the concensus of opinion had been that the tree would have been planted when the building work was done. And that was known to have been in 1729.

The deduction was not far out. When old Squire Eldon had had the new house built, to replace and incorporate parts of its decaying predecessor, he had ordered a lawn to be laid at the front, in the fashionable style with a carriage drive looping round it towards the house from two gateways. The grass had remained unadorned for five years, until a nephew, an enthusiastic traveller and botanist, had returned from Asia Minor. It was at his urging that of the specimens he had brought back with him the seed of the *Cedrus Lebani* had been planted in the very centre of the front lawn.

Cedars of Lebanon had first come to England in 1650, so that by 1834 there were enough well-matured examples to give proof of the admirable qualities of the type. With its sturdy trunk, its firm horizontal boughs, its refusal to yield the green of its foliage to any change of season or excess of weather, and its promise of perhaps three hundred years of life, it seemed to justify completely its Scriptural symbolism of strength, well-being and longevity.

The original Squire Eldon had not had enough more years to live to see the tree do more than pierce the ground. His son's children had been able to chase one another around it; but the cedar tree's prime had been reserved for the members of another family.

Larkfield Manor had passed into the ownership of the Bournes in the reign of the last of the four Georges. At no stage had they been a grand family. They were of local, Herefordshire, stock, a good solid county breed which had produced a lawyer or two, a doctor or two, several farmers, clergymen, with perhaps an overall majority of Naval officers. But the female line had consistently outnumbered the male. The daughters had more often than not been pretty, good natured and high spirited, happy to contemplate marriage, child-rearing and an easygoing, undemanding existence.

This ascendancy of the female genes in the Bourne species had not been without its effect upon its males, either. With the single exception of one of the clergymen, who had got himself into deep enough disgrace in the 1860s to have necessitated his being shipped off to New Zealand, never to return, none of the men had ever been what might be termed effeminate. But almost without exception they had borne some such feminine characteristics as gentleness and ready understanding and sympathy for the plight of others, which tended to contrast them with the harder, harsher tendencies of most men of their station in life.

As country gentlemen, they had dutifully ridden to hounds, but had seldom relished the prospect of the kill. As serving officers they had behaved well towards their underlings and acquitted themselves well in action. At home, they had permitted their womenfolk to dominate them quietly, while believing that they were the decision makers and the steadfast rocks for a weaker, more dependent sex to cling to.

The cedar tree's symbolic qualities would have seemed to anyone a fair enough reflection of those of the Bournes.

In 1934, when the tree's bicentenary passed unnoticed, the head of the family was as typical a specimen of the male line as could have been picked from any genealogical identity parade. Arthur Bourne was 48, but a combination of early greying of his hair, wartime strain, and a tendency to worry, had between them added the appearance of a few more years to his features and movement.

There had been a time in his childhood, in fact, when there had been doubts that he would survive to be an adult at all. A hint of tuberculosis had kept him from being entered for the Naval school at Osborne, to prepare him for Dartmouth and the footsteps of his father, Admiral Sir William Bourne, whose knighthood for his services in Far Eastern stations had been one of the few titles ever bestowed upon a Bourne.

Arthur had been kept at home at Larkfield, educated by a private tutor, until he was fit and old enough to be able to enter Eton in 1902. He had done well there and had won an Exhibition to Oxford. A better-than-expected, though by no means brilliant, degree in Law had whetted his appetite for that profession. After going through the requisite motions in the Inns of Court, he had been called to the Bar in 1911 and taken into the chambers of a moderately fashionable K.C.

If his father had been disappointed he had not revealed it – except perhaps in private to his wife. When they had returned together on leave from the East shortly before Arthur's summons to the Bar, there had been a quiet dinner at a Naval club in London, a tentative suggestion by the Admiral that it would still not be too late for Arthur to enter the Service – in a legal capacity, if he wished – and a hinted offer to pull a few strings at the Admiralty. Arthur had expected this and had debated the matter with himself in advance. He declined politely, was relieved to read no overt disappointment in his father's expression, and went away with a weight off his mind.

Three years later he was in the Royal Navy, after all, and without the necessity for any string-pulling. The day after the outbreak of war he volunteered. To his relief he passed the medical examination A1 and was inducted as a cadet.

Whether his father's name and rank on his enlistment

papers had any influence on his behalf, or whether indeed
the Admiral had written any letters to administrative colleagues, Arthur never knew. He had wondered, and hoped
that neither was the case. But his promotion was as swift as
any eager young man could have hoped for. He had been
given his first small command within a year of joining; had
been drafted to destroyers in home waters six months later;
and had taken part in the Victory March through London in
1919 with the stripes of a Lieutenant-Commander on his
uniform sleeves. On his chest had been the ribbon of the
Distinguished Service Order, awarded for his bravery and
devotion to his duty, his ship and its company in a North Sea
action against two German cruisers when he was captain of
the destroyer H.M.S. *Mansard* in the last year of the war.

Like so many of his generation, Arthur Bourne was faced
with major decisions at the war's end. He was better placed
than many. He could return to legal practice, with every
prospect of steady advancement. Or he could stay in the
Navy. The offer had been specifically made to him of a permanent engagement and confirmation of his present rank.

It was Helen to whom he went for a decision. He had
married her when the course of his life had seemed set steady
for a lawyer's. Their first child, Elizabeth, was born a year
later; the second, Anne, a year after that; and the third and
last in September 1918. Her name, Victoria, was no pun on
the victory. Like her sisters, she was named after a queen of
England. And, as though deliberately true to the Bourne
traditions, Arthur had produced only girls.

All three were born at Larkfield Manor, where the by then
retired Admiral and his wife had insisted Helen go to have
her first child and subsequently to live with them while
Arthur was away at the war. Before that Arthur and Helen
had been renting a flat in London, postponing the decision to
buy a house until he could settle into a permanent practice,
possibly in his native county. And so the cedar tree had cast
its benevolent shade on the infants from their earliest days,
shielding their tender skins from hot sun and letting the

breezes whisper soothing reassurances to them through its leaves.

'You must decide, darling,' Helen told Arthur one afternoon at Larkfield. This was not long before the war's end, while she was still expecting their third child's birth. They were alone in the hall-sitting-room.

'No, no,' he answered, characteristically wanting her to take the decision that would swing his evenly poised mind one way or the other. 'It's up to you.'

'Why ever?'

'Because it's you who'll be most affected. As a peacetime Service wife you'd have to live abroad a great deal.'

'But I'd love that. I've only travelled on the Continent.'

'It's a very unsettled life. Two years there, one year there, then back again. Father and Mother would tell you.'

'They seem to have come happily enough through it.'

'You'd be on your own a lot, while I was at sea.'

'I'd have the girls.'

'Ah, I don't think so. You might not mind about having any fixed abode, but it's very unsettling for growing children. Most families put them into boarding schools at home and only see them in the long holidays.'

Helen wrinkled her brow. 'I shouldn't like that. But, darling, it's your career. You've come to like the Navy so much. You're . . . you're so *good* at it.'

He laughed. 'I'm tempted, certainly. It's you and the children I'm concerned about.'

'I'm sure we'd manage. You'd probably find yourself at Portsmouth half the time.'

'Half the time – but where the other half? Malta, Gib., Hong-Kong . . .'

'Ooh!'

'It's all very well you getting all starry-eyed about it. One place can be as boring as the next when you're alone and the newness has worn off. And from some of Mother's stories, peacetime Naval wives aren't necessarily the cosiest society unless you're a dyed-in-the-wool one yourself.'

'I might turn out to be.'

'In that case, it's definitely off.'

Lady Bourne, it had been remarked with varying degrees of supplementary irreverence in many of the Royal Navy's stations overseas, was a bit of a battleship herself, outgunning considerably her mild-mannered Admiral husband. She had mellowed considerably in widowhood.

Helen said, 'Well, it seems to me you've decided it's no go.'

'Not at all. I'm just showing you the implications. You . . . we have to balance them against what'll happen if I resign. A settled home, a place for us all to belong to, a decent enough living standard . . .'

Helen interrupted, 'And a pretty humdrum existence for you, compared with these last few years. Helping people buy and sell houses, sueing each other over straying cattle . . . Darling, be honest. What would you do if . . . if you were single? Completely free to choose?'

A startled look came into his eyes. She smiled. It was always his way to look for a serious implication before seeing a joke. His smile in return showed relief.

'I must admit I'd stay in,' he said.

'Then that's it.'

'Oh no. You said *if* I were single.'

'I wanted to know what you really want. For yourself. You've got to put yourself first sometimes, you know.'

'Not at all.'

'All right, then. I'll put myself first. You stay in the Navy.'

He stared. 'But you said . . .'

'I said I shouldn't like to be without the children for too long at a time, that's all. I'm sure things will work themselves out. And I *should* like to travel. It's what you'd prefer, anyway, and I vote we make the most of it. Besides . . .'

She hesitated and looked at him more seriously.

'What?'

She lowered her voice instinctively, even though she knew they were alone in the house.

'When your father ... when he dies, you'll inherit this place.'

'Yes.'

'You wouldn't want to let it go.'

'Of course not. What do you mean?'

'That you'll have to leave the Navy then, won't you? So, why not stay in now, and do our wandering while we're free?'

'And wait for Father to pop off! That'd feel a bit calculated.'

'It is, in a way. We know that wherever we are and whatever you're doing when it does happen, we'll have to uproot and come here. Your father's only in his seventies. He might live to a hundred – I hope he does, bless him. All I'm saying is that sooner or later we'll be forced into our groove – this groove – and that'll be that. So while we're out of it, let's stay really out of it. You do what you really want, and I'll see a bit of the world before I'm altogether too decrepit.'

Arthur hesitated for the last time. 'But the girls?'

'You were happy enough without your parents to cling to all the time, weren't you? In any case, they're only infants. They'll have to be with us wherever we go for a long time yet. They and' – she patted her stomach gently – 'perhaps their brother.'

So Arthur had remained in the Royal Navy. The 'brother' for Elizabeth and Anne had turned out to be Victoria, though none the less loved for that. And the question of Helen's separation from her daughters never arose, for Admiral Sir William Bourne lived only four years more, during which time all three girls were too young to be implanted into boarding schools away from their mother.

Arthur duly left the Royal Navy as a full Commander in 1923 and with Helen and the girls moved into Larkfield Manor, his mother having transferred herself into the more compact surroundings of a cottage on the estate, and subsequently to London. No major reorganization or redecoration of the manor proved necessary: the elder Bournes had left its traditional features alone and had had the simple decor renewed regularly. The impact of three female children on the place made for more change than any other influence. It was not long before old Scottish Nanny Benson, who had inhabited her attic room for half a century, was telling Mrs. Gates, the cook, that it was quite like old times again to see the place 'cluttering up so'.

From command of a Naval shore establishment at Plymouth, Arthur had been translated to command of a household and an estate. The difference was surprisingly small, except that, apart from Frank Chapman, the bailiff in charge of the farm and the sixty acres of land, and Gates, the gardener and man-about-the-house, the personnel for whom he was now responsible were all female. The broad day-to-day routine was essentially the same: organization, supervision, administration, victualling, welfare, recreation, and all the rest of it. Discipline came last in the order of priorities. The staff did what they had always done, as they had always done it, and no one would have dreamed of trying to change it. As for the girls, Arthur left them to Nanny and Helen, only putting in a judicial warning or rebuke when asked to do so or when irritated by some interruption in the midst of the paperwork, of which he found a surprising amount in connection with so modest an estate.

Besides looking after his own affairs, he found himself involved locally as a swiftly elected member of the parish council, of which in a few years he would be elected chairman; as president, in his late father's place, of the village cricket club; as a sidesman and frequent lesson reader at the parish church; and, in due course, as a Justice of the Peace.

He had considered briefly returning to some sort of legal practice, but had come to the conclusion that it would involve him in too much absence from the estate, which it was his duty to run as efficiently as his father and grandfather before him. After ten years of owning no home and living off furnishings, few of which he could call his own, he was satisfied to drop anchor in the place of his birth, amongst

16

long-loved objects, and simply to carry out his responsibilities to his family, their servants and the surrounding community. Service on the local Bench enabled him to make use of his experience of the law and of dealing with minor human misdemeanours, and this proved a boon to his lay colleagues, who had all too often had to reach judgments more by instinct than through their sketchy legal knowledge.

Larkfield Manor itself was neither vast nor grand. It stood on the edge of a small village, Winchley, and a few miles from a small town, Halbury, in Herefordshire, close to the borders of Gloucestershire and Worcestershire: quiet, little changed country, once much raided by the Welshmen from across the Severn but developed by shrewd Norman barons into one of Britain's richest agricultural regions. The crops and herds of the Larkfield estate were too limited to offer any chance of profits. It did not take Arthur long amongst his late father's papers to realize that three daughters' school fees would more than wipe out the small credit balance the estate had been enjoying with only a retired couple and the staff to support. He had inherited no fortune from his father, and Helen, whose widowed father was an Eton housemaster, living at Datchet, in the Thames Valley, had no money of her own. There was no question of trying to buy more land and increase productivity. It was a case of keepings things going as efficiently and economically as possible, saving a little regularly in order to pay for essential repairs and purchases and in case of unforeseen emergency, and enjoying themselves more as a family than in county society.

It was enough for Arthur and Helen. Five years in Naval circles had satiated her appetite for social life and she had never cared much for it anyway. Unambitious for any further change, happy to devote themselves to their children's upbringing, they settled thankfully into the welcoming embrace of the cosy old house.

And twelve years after they had moved in, the cedar tree, unknown to anyone, attained its 200th year.

CHAPTER TWO

THERE was, of course, slightly more to the year 1934 than the bicentenary of one cedar tree.

Germany's aged President Hindenburg died and Adolf Hitler was appointed Reichsführer. 'The Night of the Long Knives' was the term coined for his ensuing purge of his followers.

Another purge, in the form of a series of 'treason trials', was conducted in Russia by Joseph Stalin, following the assassination of the Leningrad Bolsheviks' leader, Serge Kirov.

Amongst others who died violently in a violent year for 'peacetime' were Engelbert Dollfuss, Chancellor of Austria, King Alexander of Yugoslavia, French Foreign Minister Louis Barthou, and America's 'Public Enemy Number One', John Dillinger. Death came also to King Albert I of the Belgians, Raymond Poincaré, Marie Curie, and – not very many miles from Larkfield Manor – Sir Edward Elgar, whose fellow English composers Frederick Delius and Gustav Holst also died that year.

Among the many lives which commenced were those of the Dionne Quintuplets, of Callender, Ontario, and, less sensationally noticed, of an Italian girl who would in years to come be world-famed as Sophia Loren, film actress.

Films shown in the little cinema at Halbury included *It Happened One Night*, *The Thin Man*, and *The Private Lives of Henry VIII*, while the shop which combined the functions of stationer's, newsagents and toyshop did a pleasingly brisk Christmas trade in J. B. Priestley's travel book *English Journey* and Robert Graves's novel *I, Claudius*, as well as in a new table game, *Monopoly*, and a new line of miniature model cars labelled Dinky Toys.

It had been a year which many people, especially on the Continent of Europe, were not sorry to see end, but which many more elsewhere had found profitable, interesting, even exciting.

Victoria Bourne – Vicky, as everyone called her – didn't quite know what to feel as she stared out of a window of the train carrying her homeward, and began to recognize familiar features of landscape. She was coming back from school for Christmas, and she was coming home for good. She loved the old manor house and everything around it. She loved her parents and could have asked for no better girl friends than her own two elder sisters. Yet she had cried all through the singing of 'Lord, dismiss us with Thy blessing' at final Assembly, and there had been more tears at parting from some of the friends and teachers amongst whom she had lived for the past five years.

Less happy pupils would have felt profoundly relieved to have been released from boarding school at the age of only sixteen and a half. Vicky would not at all have minded another year or more there, and the news that she was to leave at the end of the Christmas term, instead of carrying on to the end of the school year in summer, had come as a surprise. She knew, though, that Daddy wasn't exactly made of money. If she had been a real 'brain', he would certainly have made sure that she stayed on and got to university, like Liz, whatever the sacrifices he and Mummy would have had to make. But she knew that her school record had been more like Anne's than Liz's, worthy but undistinguished.

She sighed, and told herself that, really, there wouldn't have been much point in staying on. She tried to cast her mind forward to the future, but saw only vague outlines there. A few years around the house, she supposed, giving Mummy a hand, riding with Anne, keeping up her piano practice: *would* she ever be able to play really well? Then, she supposed, marriage to someone she'd probably not even heard of yet, or perhaps had already met, all unknowing.

This little fantasy pleased her and she indulged it for the rest of the journey to Halbury, where she found Gates waiting for her on the platform, with the Wolseley car outside.

At four o'clock in the afternoon, only three days before Christmas, it was already dark. It was cold, but there was no snow. The Christmas tree in the hall of the manor and the greenery and other decorations with which the stair banisters had been entwined were the first visual symbols Vicky had encountered since leaving London, where the stores had been ablaze with light and seasonal colour and the shoppers had been scuttling about with that special air of excitement which precedes Christmas.

The lights were on, but no one was about to greet her. Vicky frowned disappointedly at the tree.

'They might have waited for me to help,' she said to Gates, already climbing the staircase with her trunk.

'You know you're in the attic now, Miss Vicky,' he paused to say.

'The attic? No, I didn't.'

'All on your own now.'

'But I don't want to be all on my own.'

'Mrs. Bourne's orders,' he said dismissively, and plodded on.

There was an edge of annoyance to Vicky's voice as she called out, 'Anne? Liz? Mummy . . .? *Anyone* at home?'

Her mother came in hurriedly from the kitchen region, leading off the spacious hall which served also as general sitting-room. The drawing-room proper was deeper into the house and only used for rare formal occasions.

'Darling, you've arrived!' Helen was exclaiming unnecessarily as she leant forward to accept Vicky's kiss on her cheek. 'I didn't hear the car.'

'Only just got here,' Vicky said, the pleasure of the reunion completely eradicating the little feeling of anti-climax at not having found a welcoming committee. But she frowned again. 'Gates has taken my trunk upstairs. Is it true I'm having my own room?'

'Yes, darling. In the attic.'

Helen had expected a pleased reaction, instead of, 'but I like sharing with Anne. We chatter together in the night.'

'You'll have plenty of time for chatter in the day. You're old enough to have your own rooms now – both of you.'

Vicky knew better than to argue the point. It would have been decided well in advance, furniture and linen distributed accordingly, all arrangements made.

'Anyway,' her mother was smiling, 'How was school? Glad to leave?'

'In a way. A bit sorry, too, though I cried a bit last night, to think it was all over.'

'I know how you felt. You probably will again, the night before your wedding. I must admit I did.'

'Oh, Mummy!'

The little joke had broken the thin ice which had formed over their period of separation.

'No, it's lovely to be home,' Vicky said. The implications were only beginning to sink in. 'No more school! Where are the others?'

'Liz went upstairs to read in her room. I'm afraid she's in for a cold.'

'Oh, no. Not at Christmas!'

'Nanny's laying tea in the dining-room. Anne and Daddy were going over to the farm to look at the pond. They thought they'd be back before you came.'

There was the sound of the door opening, and they were back, both enveloped in thick outer clothing: the tall, slightly stooped man and the pretty, pink-cheeked slim girl who rushed at once to embrace her sister.

'Sorry we weren't back,' she cried. 'We've been sliding. I mean, I have. The pond's frozen solid.'

'Welcome home, Vicky,' their father said, kissing her formally and shaking her by the hand.

'I know we've got some skates somewhere,' Anne was saying excitedly to Vicky. 'D'you know where they are? I'm going to search high and low for them after tea.'

'You won't be able to skate now, darling,' Helen reminded her. 'It's dark.'

'Well, tomorrow.'

'If it hasn't thawed,' Arthur said. 'The glass is going up.'

'I've got my own room,' Vicky said matter-of-factly to Anne.

'I know. Where Granny's maid used to sleep when she came here.'

'I don't remember.'

'Looking out over the front lawn. You can see the top of your beloved cedar tree from the window.'

'Doesn't that cheer you up?' Helen asked, a trifle anxiously. 'Come on and see.'

Gates descended the stairs, puffing heavily, as Helen and the girls went up.

'You've got an old pair of pinky chintz curtains Nanny found in the ottoman,' Anne chattered. 'And Mummy's given you a lamp for your dressing-table. A china nymph with nothing on. Quite pretty, really, only her behind's got chipped. Liz bought her at the church fête last summer for three and six.'

They had climbed the two flights to the attic level. Helen pushed open the door of a room and she and Anne stepped aside for its new owner to go in first. She entered tentatively as her mother reached round the doorway to switch on the electric light. Vicky had not often been in the room, but she remembered its cosily sloping ceiling, the flower-patterned wallpaper, the little metal bed, the wardrobe, the dressing-table and the built-in cupboard. Amongst items unfamiliar to her, bought specially for her, was the table lamp in the form of a naked, green-skinned female, flinging up one arm in a gesture of wholly respectable abandon. The one really familiar item of all, her school trunk, lay unopened on the carpet.

Vicky's first impulse was to cross to the small window and peer out, hoping for a glimpse of the tree; but it was too dark and all she could see was the reflection of the room behind her and her mother and sister standing watching her. She bit her lip.

'Oh, Mummy – must I?'

'Darling, you are nearly seventeen.'

Anne put in, 'And we can always pay each other calls and have chinwags whenever we want.'

'Yes, but it won't be the same.'

Helen said more firmly, 'You're not a schoolgirl any more, Vicky. You're a young woman now. Tea will be ready by the time you've washed your hands. Your trunk can wait till after.'

She went away downstairs. Anne put her arm round her sister.

'I think your room's jolly nice, don't you?'

'I suppose so.'

'You'll like it.' And Anne went, too.

Vicky turned to look at herself in the dressing-table mirror. The same features, the same school uniform, rather more rumpled than usual, but all made somehow unfamiliar because of the unaccustomed background of colour and bright light. The door of the built-in cupboard was slightly ajar and she could see some of her clothes piled there. She wondered whether she ought to change before tea and took a step towards the wardrobe, to remind herself of what dresses she owned. But she withdrew her hand from its door without touching it. Just for a little longer she would remain a schoolgirl. One more hour or so – and then a 'young woman'.

'Hello, Vic,' she heard the voice of her eldest sister from the doorway. Elizabeth, tall and slightly prim-looking, despite her fine bones, stood smiling at her. She was flushed a little about the cheeks. Vicky moved quickly to kiss her, but Liz fended her off with an outstretched hand.

'No, don't kiss me, I've got a stinking cold.'

'Mummy said. And at Christmas!'

'Oh, I'll be all right. Not at all prone to bacteria. 0.3 to 1 gramme of acetylsalicylic acid at bedtime, and I'm sure I shall be fine.'

Liz, the clever one of the family, was given to using medical terms as readily as her father would Naval ones. She had spent several years at Lady Margaret Hall, Oxford, and had only recently come down, with her Bachelor of Medicine degree. She was now in her early twenties and at a time of pause in her life. Whether she wanted to advance her studies and commit herself to medicine she was not quite sure. Intellectually, she was attracted by the notion. She was a fastidious girl, especially in her relationships with either sex. No young man of her acquaintance had ever matched up to her unconsciously-set standards, so that there was no incipient romance to hold her back. Yet for some reason or other she hesitated to plunge into a career which she knew she would wish to absorb her life if she were to settle for it. For all her cleverness, she was unable to examine her motives objectively and understand that the reason she was holding back was that she was, first and foremost, a woman, and a striking-looking one.

Just now, though, she was dabbing a running nose with her handkerchief and glancing round the room.

'What a rotten little room,' she remarked unmaliciously.

'It's not!' Vicky was surprised to find herself already defending the little piece of territory she had resented being imposed on her. 'It's cosy.'

Liz shrugged. 'Long as you don't brain yourself getting out of bed. I'll bet you're jolly glad to be shot of St. Mary's.'

'Not as much as I thought I would.'

'Don't tell me you've got the education bug.'

'No fear. You can go on being the family genius.'

'Oh, thanks. We'd better go down for tea. Grandpapa, and Granny, and Aunt Phyllis are here, did you know?'

'Aunt Phyllis already? Oh, goody! You go on, Liz. I must

24

just wash and comb my hair, or Granny'll be giving me her look.'

Elizabeth went, blowing her nose. Vicky scuttled along to the bathroom. When she came back to her room to put out the light before going down it already seemed welcomingly familiar to her. She flicked up the switch and paused a moment, looking through the darkness to where the window was, imagining the cedar tree beyond. Then she turned and went happily down.

They were all in the hall as she came down the decorated stairway, to a general chorus of greetings. Dutifully she went over first to her grandmother, Lady Bourne, who sat alone on the settee. At seventy-three, the Admiral's widow was still very much the high-ranking officer's wife, proud and commanding. But she welcomed Vicky almost effusively and demanded the first kiss of the several there were to be bestowed.

'You've lost weight,' was all the criticism she had to offer as she surveyed the slightly untidy, slightly awkward girl in the unflattering uniform. 'Yes, you look distinctly thinner to me.'

'Two helpings of turkey and plum pudding will start putting that right,' said Charles Ashley, Helen's father, coming over to give Vicky a hug and a kiss. He was not quite seventy, tall and well made, with attractive silver hair and engaging smile-wrinkles around her eyes. Since the loss of his wife he had acquired a certain vagueness of manner which often irritated his opposite number, Lady Bourne, whenever they found themselves together at Larkfield; but beneath it the sharp mind and the quick wit still lay in instant readiness.

Vicky moved on from him to her Aunt Phyllis, Arthur's sister.

Phyllis Bourne had been a favourite with all the girls for as long as they had been old enough to be conscious of her. She was twelve years Arthur's junior, a spinster, but quite the antithesis of what is generally implied by 'spinsterish'.

She was more the sophisticated lady-about-town – town being in her case London, where she lived in a flat and practised as a music teacher. She was pert in appearance, chic in dress and inclined to a bluntness of speech, common to the artistic people amongst whom she was accustomed to moving and faintly shocking to the ears of the insular and more staid community at Larkfield Manor. She alarmed Arthur, amused Helen, scandalized Lady Bourne, astonished Charles Ashley, and filled the girls with wonderment and envy of her independence.

'At any rate,' she said, looking Vicky up and down and then up again after they had kissed, 'you're filling out in the right places.' Vicky blushed violently as Aunt Phyllis's meaning registered. 'So far as the rest is concerned, it's as well to start Christmas a bit skinny. Bags of scope for absorbing rich food. Glad to be home, then?'

'Oh, yes,' Vicky replied, convinced of it by now. 'No more school ever again. No more packing trunks to go away – anywhere. Just long days and months at home, doing all the nice things.'

'But I thought you were ...'

Vicky looked curiously at her aunt as she heard the sentence break off, almost, it seemed, at the signal of a sudden cough from her mother. She glanced round them all. There was a distinct uneasiness about them.

'What, Aunt?' she demanded. She was surprised for once to see even her self-possessed aunt disconcerted about something.

'Never ... never mind,' she heard her say. 'It doesn't matter.'

Vicky turned anxiously to her mother and recognized wide-eyed anxiety.

'Mummy ...' She began; but at that moment Nanny Benson came through from the dining-room, saw her, and enveloped her in warm embraces and Glaswegian-voiced endearments. Everyone seemed to begin talking at once, as if released from constraint by some cue.

'Tea?' her father was asking. 'Oh, good. Come along, everyone, before the scones get cold.'

'Good idea,' Granny Bourne agreed, lifting herself by his proffered arm. 'I'm ravenous.'

'So am I,' Charles Ashley beamed, and rubbed his hands expressively. 'After battling over the Arctic wastes of Larkfield this afternoon I could eat a roast ox.'

'Well, you're just getting hot scones and paste sandwiches, Father,' Helen smiled. 'Now come on, girls. You must help Nanny pass round.'

Vicky glanced at her Aunt Phyllis once more, but failed to catch her eye. Throughout teatime, with its commonplace, jovial chatter, she couldn't help wondering once or twice why it was that whenever she approached her aunt that lady seemed to move on from whomever she was talking with to join someone else in uninterruptable conversation.

After tea, when everyone had dispersed to work, or read, or rest before dinner, Vicky went alone to her room. She switched on the light and shut the door. She went to the dressing-table and looked at herself long and hard in the mirror. Slowly she took off her uniform jacket and stood regarding the twin bulges under her jumper which Aunt Phyllis had so blush-makingly drawn everyone's attention to. As though caught in some guilty act, she hurriedly went to draw the window curtain, though even the most shameless exposure could not have been visible except by a watcher from the topmost branches of the cedar tree.

Then she went to her wardrobe, opened the door and riffled uncertainly amongst the dresses hanging there. All were old familiars, worn briefly during school holidays and in some cases remembered as hand-downs from Anne. She selected one at length, a short, light blue one, and laid it on her bed. She opened a drawer of the dressing-table and found underclothes, laid in neat piles by Nanny, no doubt.

Once more she stood in front of the mirror, regarding for the last time the reflection of the schoolgirl. Then, with sudden, determined movements she stripped off everything

27

she wore, no longer pausing to fold each garment neatly as she had been disciplined to do, but throwing everything into a pile on the carpet. When she was naked she dressed again in softer underwear and slipped on the blue dress before allowing herself to look in the mirror again.

The transformation was disappointing in a way. She had seen herself in that dress often enough before, and this time it looked somehow childish on her more mature body. The hoped-for feeling of emancipation would not come. She let her shoulders sag and began languidly to brush her hair. There was a tap at the door. It opened, and a made-up Anne looked round. Vicky thought how grown-up she looked.

'Mind if I come in?' Anne asked, and did so.

'*You* needn't knock.'

'Oh, yes. You're entitled to be private now. With your own room.'

Anne was wearing a long evening dress. Her hair was carefully done. It was hard for Vicky to imagine the tomboy Anne of the jodhpurs and roll-necked jersey.

'Don't you look beautiful!' she exclaimed. Anne looked down at herself with some surprise.

'Do I? It's only an old dress Liz had and Nanny altered for me.'

'Terribly glamorous. Oh lor', I'll feel terribly awkward going downstairs for dinner. Look at me!'

'I like that dress. When your hair's done . . .'

'I just don't feel right. Everyone's . . . grown up and used to it all, except me.'

'Cheer up. You're sitting next to Grandpapa. You know how fond he is of you. Anyway, Christmas spirit! Aren't you excited?'

'Of course I am. It's just that . . .'

'What? Is anything wrong, Vicky?'

'It's a feeling – that there's something I'm not supposed to know about. Aunt Phyllis nearly said something at teatime, I'm sure, only she just stopped in time.'

'You're imagining things. What should there be?'

Vicky regarded her sister closely. *Was* she imagining that Anne was finding it hard to return her gaze steadily?

She asked, 'It's not ... no one's ill, or anything, are they?'

Anne shook her head firmly.

'Daddy and Mummy ... There isn't any sort of trouble? A row going on?'

'Honestly,' Anne assured her emphatically. 'Everything's perfect.'

She began to speak more rapidly. Vicky could not help feeling that her sister was seizing the chance to steer an awkward conversation her own way.

'There are all sorts of Christmas plans. I'm going to a fancy dress party at Roxburgh Park on New Year's Eve. We're all going to the Boxing Day Meet. And on Christmas Eve, tomorrow, you're going to the Pony Club dance at Halbury Town Hall with the Baileys.'

Vicky's attention really was distracted by this.

'A dance! Oh, no, I couldn't. I'd be terrified.'

'By a dance? That's ridiculous.'

'No, it isn't.'

'You've been to dances before.'

'Yes, but I ... I feel different.'

Anne looked at her in bewilderment. The passing of only a few years had obliterated her own memory of the difficult transition from schoolgirl to woman. The gauche figure in front of her was just the old familiar Vicky, awkward as ever in her first hours of return from school.

'I don't want to go,' Vicky was saying, with almost a tremble in her voice. 'I haven't got to, have I?'

'Of course you have. Mummy's accepted for you.'

'But I'll be a wallflower. Nobody'll dance with me. Anne, I can't go. I won't!'

'They'll make you.'

'I'll be ill. I'll catch Liz's cold.'

Anne flushed crossly at this petulant outburst.

'You're nearly seventeen now,' she said coldly. 'Don't be so silly. And come on, or we'll be late. You know how punctual Granny expects everyone to be for dinner.'

Vicky seized the hairbrush again and began to tug at her unstyled hair.

'You go,' she said unhappily. 'I'll be as quick as I can.'

'Well, don't be too long,' Anne said, and went out.

In the hall, Arthur Bourne was handing sherry to his mother and sister Phyllis. He wore a smoking jacket and the ladies were in long dresses. They were joined almost at once by Charles Ashley, in a well-worn dinner jacket, soft pleated shirt with stick-up collar, and velvet slippers, an early Christmas gift.

'Am I last?' he asked, accepting his glass.

'Far from it,' Alice Bourne said pointedly.

Arthur looked about him apprehensively. 'I'm afraid I must apologize for my wife and all three daughters,' he told his father-in-law.

Phyllis drained her glass and held it out for a refill. She said cheerfully, 'I know Helen's down. I heard her talking to Mrs. Gates as I came out of the bathroom. Oh, I did enjoy my lovely, lovely long soak.'

At that moment Elizabeth and Anne came bustling down the stairs together, each accusing the other of having used up all the hot bath water. Phyllis made a wry face at Charles, who grimaced humorously back.

Helen came in, dressed for dinner but slightly flushed from the kitchen heat.

'It's not quite ready yet,' she told them all.

'Time for a glass of sherry, then,' Arthur offered, but she refused.

'I've put you at the head of the table, as we're eight, Charles.'

Her father gave a little bow. 'Anywhere you say, my dear.'

'Sorry we're so many females for you.'

'But I adore the company of females. I've spent years surrounded by scruffy boys and almost as scruffy masters, some of them.'

'Well, I've put Vicky next to you. Ah, here she is.'

Vicky was coming slowly down the stairs, holding the banister as if for support, strangely shy in her own home.

'Sorry I'm late,' she muttered and hurried instinctively to her mother's side. 'My hair wouldn't stay,' she said, *sotto voce.*

'Your hair looks nice, Vicky,' Phyllis said loudly, making the comment sound spontaneous. The girl gave her her thanks with a look.

'How's the piano, dear?' Aunt Phyllis went on, recognizing her unease and also anxious to make amends for a near-gaffe at tea time which she sensed had left her niece puzzled and perhaps anxious.

'Oh, Miss Poole was pleased with me. I got my Grade again.'

'Marvellous. Time for a little piece before dinner, Helen?'

'If you like,' Vicky's mother said. 'The soup isn't ready.'

'Good. How about the little Schumann, Vicky?'

As Vicky moved away to the grand piano, its top as usual covered with objects, for the time being of a seasonal nature, Phyllis murmured to Helen, 'It'll help her over her nerves. First time down for dinner as a grown-up.'

Vicky began to play. She played confidently and well, with intelligence and a sensitive touch. They all listened in respectful silence, until Anne suddenly blurted out, 'I know that! Klaus von Heynig used to play it often. You'll be able to play duets with him, Vicky. He . . . Oh, God!'

Anne's hand flew to her mouth as her face paled. Vicky had stopped playing and turned towards her, hands still poised over the keyboard. She could not fail to interpret the embarrassment of them all this time.

She said numbly, 'Klaus von Heynig? I'm being sent to Munich, aren't I?'

She rose from the piano stool and went to face her mother and father.

'Like Anne. Am I, Mummy? Daddy?'

31

Anne was saying behind her, 'I'm sorry ... It slipped out.'

Arthur said crossly, 'Anne, we did agree ... Vicky, my darling, we were going to tell you after Christmas.'

'You'll love it, Vic,' Anne was insisting desperately. 'Honestly. I did.'

'Oh no, please,' Vicky said softly, looking her mother full in the face.

Helen said with an uncertain smile, 'We didn't know whether to tell you for ... for a Christmas present, or after. Daddy thought we'd wait. But since it's out now, Frau von-Heynig has written to say she can take you on the nineteenth.'

'The nineteenth?'

'Of January. That's ...'

'Only three weeks! Oh, Mummy, oh please no. I don't want to go away when I've only just come home.'

Arthur went to put his arm round her. He said gently, 'Vicky, I suggest we don't discuss it like this, just before dinner and with Granny and Grandpapa here.'

To his surprise she shook herself free, her face flushing with anger as tears came into her eyes.

'I know why you weren't going to tell me,' she blazed. 'You knew it's cruel to pack me off to Germany ...'

'Now Vicky, it's for your good. The nearest we can manage to finishing-school for you.'

'I don't care about finishing-school. You know I'm frightened of people I don't know. I'm not good at making friends, because I'm not pretty like Anne or clever like Liz.'

Helen interjected, 'What on earth do you think you're saying? You're not a child any longer.'

'You just want me out of the way. Sending me away and ruining my Christmas holidays.'

Arthur was becoming angry now. 'You'd better go upstairs again if you can't control yourself.'

Alice Bourne tried to restore the situation through the authority of seniority.

'Vicky, my dear, you know it isn't anything like that,' she

said: but to everyone's horror the girl, too far gone in angry self-pity, rounded on her, too.

'You're all in it, just wanting to get rid of me. You're cruel and brutal, and I *hate* you . . .'

Arthur snapped, 'Go up at once. You can have your supper in your room. You're obviously not fit to dine downstairs.'

'I don't want any . . .' She burst into tears and fled up the stairs, watched by them all with astonishment. Helen said quietly, 'Anne, go and ask Nanny to take her something on a tray. She's tired after a long day.'

'All right. Mummy, I am sorry. It just slipped out.'

'I know, dear. You're not to blame.'

Anne went off to the kitchen region. 'Well!' Lady Bourne exclaimed. She had turned quite pale. 'There's an exhibition of temper for you. Just like her grandfather.'

Charles Ashley, that mildest of men, stared. She shook her head vigorously.

'No, not you, Charles. My Billy. He used to blow up like that quite frequently.'

'It's inexcusable for her to speak like that to you, Mother,' Arthur said.

Aunt Phyllis said, 'She'll be all right in time. Pity it had to come out so soon, that's all.'

Lady Bourne snorted. 'Anyone would think the child was being sent off to the North Pole. Munich'll do her music a world of good, she must know that.'

'Yes, Mother,' Phyllis said dutifully.

To everyone's relief, Nanny appeared to say the soup was ready, if they'd care to sit down.

After dinner, when the adults had settled down to play Bridge, Liz and Anne went up to Anne's room to listen to her portable gramophone and wrap some final presents. They paused outside Vicky's door and listened, but heard nothing. They looked at one another. Liz shook her head and they crept away, and soon the strains of *How Deep is the Ocean* were permeating the upper regions of the house. A little

33

while later there came a tentative tapping at the door and Vicky came in, composed and shamefaced.

'Do you mind if I come in?' she asked Anne, like a junior addressing a prefect.

'Join the party, old thing. Move those parcels and you can sit on the bed.'

'Oh, thanks awfully.'

All three felt instantly at ease again.

'Did you get any supper?' Liz asked.

'Nanny brought me some soup. I didn't want much. Are ... are they very cross with me downstairs?'

'Course not. Just a bit piqued at the time. You were rather rude to Granny.'

'Oh, I know. Only, I'm scared, Anne. I'm scared of going to Germany ...'

'You mustn't be. Must she, Liz?'

'Of course not. You know how kind the von Heynigs were to Anne. Any other girl your age would give her eye teeth to go abroad and get away from home all on their own. I think you're damn lucky.'

'I suppose so,' Vicky had to admit slowly. 'But, this ... this dance, too ...'

'Oh, God! What an infant it is!'

'I'm not!'

'An ungrateful little brat. Isn't she, Anne?'

'Well, Mummy's taken a terrific lot of trouble to arrange all sorts of nice things for you over Christmas. For us all. The least you can do is show your share of gratitude.'

'It's not that. I am grateful, only ... None of the men will look at me. I'll just stand about and nobody will dance with me.'

'Rot!'

'Angela Bailey's told me. She's been to a grown-up dance. She says the boys all congregated at one end of the room and talked to each other.'

'About Soccer, I should think, if Angela was in the offing,' said Liz.

'She's no plainer than me.'

'Oh, well, if that's the way you're determined to feel, there's nothing we can do for you. Is there, Anne?'

'Not a thing, Liz.'

'I mean, I know what I'd do if it were me. I'd stare at them. Glower at them and dare them to risk the experience of dancing with me.'

'That's right. Look at them as if they were a heap of dirt.'

Anne suddenly threw back her head and contorted her face into a grotesque semblance of a sneer. It was so comically exaggerated that Vicky had to laugh. Anne relaxed her features and explained, 'You've got to remember they're just as shy as you, underneath, some of them. Who are they, anyway? It's only that, being young men, they have to look superior and grand.'

'Anyway,' Liz added, 'you can always take a good book and read it in the ladies' lavatory.'

'Liz!'

'I've done it before now. Truly.'

'But, if only I were a *bit* pretty.'

Anne jumped up suddenly and impatiently and to Vicky's alarm seized her by the hair, bunching it up painfully and forcing her off the bed by it and over to the dressing-table stool. She thrust her down on to it.

'Ow!' Vicky squealed. 'You're hurting.'

'I don't care. Look at yourself in the mirror. Now, close your mouth. Purse your lips. Purse your lips!'

Defensively, Vicky did so. Anne seized a lipstick and applied it roughly to her young sister's mouth.

'There,' she said. 'Look, Liz. We could do something with her, if she'd let us, couldn't we?'

Liz, looking over Vicky's shoulder, nodded sagely. 'We could try.'

Gently, she released Anne's grip from Vicky's hair. It tumbled down again and, together with the crudely plastered-on lipstick, gave the poor girl a look of bizarre depravity.

All three girls stared at the reflection in the glass. Anne began to giggle; then Liz joined in. Then even the outraged, pink-faced Vicky gave way, and a few seconds later they were shrieking together so loudly that Helen and Arthur glanced up at one another across the Bridge table and exchanged a secret smile of relief.

Next morning – the morning of Christmas Eve – the transformation was put into rapid effect. Anne contributed a green and yellow evening dress and Liz a pair of high-heeled satin evening shoes. While Liz was assisting Vicky into these garments, Anne sneaked downstairs and made several telephone calls to boys she expected would be at the Pony Club dance. Brashly, she asked each to do her the favour of dancing at least once with her young sister that evening, explaining that it was her first grown-up dance and, without an escort, she would be feeling shy. All readily agreed, and all waived the shilling inducement she ventured to offer. The Bourne girls were universally admired as 'good sports', and pretty into the bargain.

The dress, however, sagged almost everywhere it should have fitted snugly, and when Vicky took some experimental steps in the shoes her feet came right out of them.

'You'll have to find her some of yours,' Liz said to Anne, who had just entered, giving a secret thumbs-up sign. Anne dashed off and came back with her only pair of evening shoes. Vicky forced her right foot into one and grimaced.

'Ow! I'd be crippled.'

'Try the other. You might get used to that one.'

But the result was just as bad.

'They're all right for length, but they're agony across here. Honestly, I couldn't possibly dance in them.'

It was obviously true. Anne removed the shoes, saying, 'You'll have to wear your old ballet shoes, that's all. They won't show in a long dress. Not if you don't kick your feet about too much.'

Vicky indicated the dress itself. 'But I can't wear this. It'd fall off.'

Liz turned her round firmly and began to undo hooks and eyes, declaiming, ' "Courage, my child," said the Ugly Sisters to Cinderella. "You *shall* go to the ball." '

'What are those girls doing?' Alice Bourne asked a few minutes later, as Liz hurried through the hall, carrying an evening dress and calling for Nanny.

'Just amusing themselves, I suppose,' Helen answered. She put another log on the fire and poked the ashes. With most of the preparations completed and Mrs. Gates in command of the kitchen region she was experiencing the onset of that feeling of unreality which surrounds Christmas.

'Are you comfy, dear?'

'Yes, thank you. You're a good girl, Helen.'

'We aim to please.'

'You must find rich husbands for those girls.'

'I'd rather they married suitable ones.'

'Of course. Some of the rich young men today are so dreadfully common. I expect Elizabeth will marry an impoverished but worthy young clergyman. Or a schoolmaster. Don't ask me why.'

Helen sat on a footstool beside her mother-in-law's chair and said seriously, 'I do worry about their futures. But there's not much one can do, except give them a warm and comfortable home, with plenty of love and affection, and hope for the best. If one of them runs off with an engine-driver and the others marry penniless foreigners we must just smile cheerfully and pretend to be pleased. At least they can look forward to years of peace in the world, unlike us.'

Lady Bourne grimaced. 'Peace? How dull.'

There was a silence, then she added, 'There won't be much for any of you from me, you know. When I go.'

Helen pressed her hand.

'Shall we talk about the weather for a change?'

'Seriously. I'm worried about Arthur. I know he's concerned about money.'

'Who isn't, these days?'

'His Navy pension and what his father left him aren't

enough to run this place and bring those girls up, I know. If only he'd gone back to the law instead of staying in the Navy he'd be well off now. Perhaps a K.C., making a fortune like Norman Birkett and the rest of them.'

'We've been into that often enough,' Helen said easily. 'If he had settled into a good career and we'd bought a place in London you know how hard it would have been for us to give it all up and take on Larkfield when Grandpa Bourne died. You wouldn't have wanted him to let Larkfield go, would you?'

The old lady shook her white head.

'Never.'

'Then you mustn't complain because we're short of money. Arthur and I don't. Anyway, perhaps the Stock Exchange will buck up a bit in the New Year.'

'Or you could sell off some land – if the worst comes to the worst.'

They were saved from examining this uncomfortable topic further by the entry, by the front door, of Charles Ashley and Phyllis Bourne, well muffled and pink from the cold air of a fine morning.

'Back mercifully in one piece,' Charles exclaimed. 'My goodness, Phyllis drives that car like Boadicea's chariot. Quite put the wind up me.'

Phyllis laughed. 'Fifty miles an hour. On a good road!'

They all stopped to stare as Anne emerged again from the nether regions, carrying the dress and dashing straight upstairs without a word.

'What on earth *are* they doing up there?' Lady Bourne demanded.

'No doubt we'll find out when we're meant to,' Helen answered, relieved to have found Vicky cheerful and apologetic at breakfast time, even if a little pale and seemingly apprehensive. She went off to arrange for coffee to be brought.

That evening they drank coffee again, after an early dinner. The hall fire was blazing well with the keenness which betokens frost in the air. Arthur and Helen were holding their cups, watching the dance of the flames as they thought their thoughts, which, had they known it, were almost identical and had to do with money. Phyllis was mentally replaying in her mind some insistent numbers from Noel Coward's *Conversation Piece* which had been with her all day and wouldn't go away. Lady Bourne was engaged in some needlework, glancing occasionally with exasperation at Charles Ashley, who had nodded off behind his *Times* and was snoring intermittently.

Phyllis noted her mother's restlessness. 'Shall I wake him up?' she asked, low.

'No, leave him,' Lady Bourne replied, not troubling to keep her voice down. 'I can just about stand it.'

Charles woke up promptly. 'Can't stand what?' he asked.

'The Income Tax. None of us can.'

'Ah, that. They think taxation's the easy answer to everything. Automatic reflex – country's finances in a muddle, simply raise every tax in sight and it'll be all right. They're sowing a whirlwind.'

He looked up as there was movement on the stairs. Liz and Anne were leaning out over the little balustraded gallery at the top.

'Ladies and gentlemen ...' Liz called down to the surprised adults. 'May we present ...'

Ann continued it: '... that glamorous and popular star of the Hollywood silver screen, Miss Victoria Bourne.'

From behind them Vicky came out on to the stairs and began to descend them slowly, somewhat furtively followed by old Nanny Benson, looking as if she were not quite certain of the propriety of being involved.

'Who's that?' Lady Bourne asked, peering towards the slowly descending girl, transformed by the evening dress, the lifted hair and the discreet make-up.

'Good heavens!' Arthur exclaimed. 'Is that Vicky?'

Phyllis, again, was the one to say the right thing to put the obviously embarrassed girl at her ease.

'She looks divine. Doesn't she?'

'Absolutely,' Charles agreed, and added the compliment of getting to his feet. Arthur followed suit.

'I do feel silly,' Vicky said, coming amongst them.

'You look very pretty, dear,' Phyllis reassured her. 'Show yourself to Granny.'

'She's just off to her dance,' Helen explained.

'Ah, yes,' Lady Bourne remembered, inspecting Vicky. 'Turn round. Yes, very pretty indeed.'

A car could be heard approaching the house, its headlights sweeping the curtains. Liz and Anne came down to join the others, carrying between them Vicky's coat, gloves and bag.

'Every stitch she has on is borrowed,' Anne explained. 'You wouldn't think so, would you?'

'I did her hair,' Liz claimed.

'And I did her face.'

'She's a credit to you both,' Arthur agreed, kissing Vicky carefully on the cheek. 'Isn't she, dear?'

'And to herself,' Helen reminded him, kissing her also. 'We'll take you shopping in London after Christmas, for some things of your own.'

'You can come up and stay with me,' Aunt Phyllis offered Vicky. 'We'll do some shows as well.'

The car had halted outside the house, its motor still running. The front door bell rang. Vicky gulped.

'That ... that'll be Marion Bailey and Priscilla. I ... I must be off.'

'Don't be nervous, Vic,' Anne urged.

'I envy you, Vicky,' Aunt Phyllis said, and was rewarded with a grateful smile.

'Stand up straight and stick your chest out,' was Lady Bourne's contribution.

Liz equipped their charge while Anne opened the door and had a brief conversation with the person who had rung. She came back to report, 'Mrs. Bailey won't come in. She says they'll try not to bring her home too late, Mummy, but it all depends on how much Priscilla enjoys herself.'

'That's quite all right,' Helen said. 'Enjoy it, darling. 'Bye!'

There was a chorus of farewells. The door was closed. The car's gear was engaged and it was heard sweeping away on the curve of the drive.

'Enchanting!' Charles Ashley exclaimed, resuming his seat.

'Certainly a change,' Arthur agreed. 'That fire needs another log.'

They all settled down again to their evening pursuits, filling in the time until Christmas.

Christmas Day was already two hours old when Vicky returned. Her mother had determined to be awake for her, but had fallen asleep in bed, reading Agatha Christie's *Murder in Three Acts*. It was Anne who heard the carefully quiet approach of the car, and then the click of the door, and at last the cautious creak of footsteps. She slipped out of her room and drew Vicky into it.

'Well?'

'Oh, Anne, it was wonderful. We stayed until the bitter end. There was bacon and eggs, and I had quite a lot of cider. And lots of dances. There was this band from Hereford and it played all the new tunes.'

'Sssh! You'll wake everyone up.'

'And so many boys wanted to dance with me. It was strange – almost as though they'd been expecting me.'

Anne was relieved to see no suspicion in her sister's eyes. She said, 'Well, your fame must have gone before you. We told you it'd be all right, didn't we?'

'Oh, yes. I'm so grateful, Anne. To you and Liz. It was worth all the trouble you took – really. And Nanny too.'

'You see.'

'And one young man I danced with ... David ... David Willet, or Wilmot, or something – I can find out from Priscilla – he's going to Germany in the New Year, too. He's going there to learn German, because his father wants him

41

to go into the Foreign Office. He was ... very nice. I said, perhaps we might meet sometime and have tea together. Only, that made him laugh. Not nastily, or anything, and he danced with me again. I can't think why he laughed.'

Anne asked, 'Did he say where he's going?'

'Yes. Dresden.'

'And you'd told him you were going to Munich.'

'Yes.'

'No wonder he laughed, you ignoramus.'

'Why?'

'Because Dresden's in Saxony and Munich's in Bavaria. They're hundreds of miles apart. Some hope of meeting up for tea.'

They laughed together. Then Anne said, 'Bavaria's far nicer. Honestly, Vic, you'll enjoy it as much as I did. Munich's such a lovely city. And the von Heynigs will take you skiing – they've got a chalet near Garmisch. And all the concerts ...'

Vicky yawned suddenly. She got up, only just now realizing how desperately tired she was after the school term, the travelling, the homecoming, the dance and the frenzied preparations for it.

She smiled at Anne.

'I'm not afraid of going, any more,' she said. 'It was just everything piling on top of me at once. I think I was more afraid of being a wallflower at the dance. But I wasn't.'

She went away to her room and a few minutes later her light was out. And the last of this new generation of Bournes to have played chase round the cedar tree, and perched up on the little wooden platform, high in its branches, and sat eating sweets in its shade, had put her childhood behind her for good.

CHAPTER THREE

VICKY'S recovered spirits set the seal on a successful Christmas. There was good feasting without over-indulgence; the presents each received were genuinely appreciated; bickering broke out only infrequently, and then mostly over the Bridge table between Lady Bourne and Charles Ashley, as a form of silence-breaker between hands; and the weather held fair and crisp, permitting hearty, digestive walks and rides.

Only Elizabeth suffered, from the cold in her head. It did not spoil her Christmas, but kept her steadily dripping and snuffling, to the jocular contempt of her sisters, who demanded to know what sort of doctor she would ever be if she couldn't cure so little a thing as a common cold.

She threw insults and even objects at them, and sniffed on; but by the morning of Boxing Day she was beaten. Waking with a temperature and a tight chest, she had to stay in bed. Her mother came in to see her.

'It's just a cold,' Liz insisted. 'Nothing worse. The commonest ailment in this land, and the most elusive. Whoever finds the cure for it will be a millionaire overnight.'

'Nanny says . . .'

'Look, don't let Nanny alarm you.'

'No, but she can't forget how ill your father was when he was a schoolboy.'

'That was T.B. This is a *common* cold.'

Three racking sneezes followed. After them, Liz slumped back against her raised pillows, her closed eyes burning. Helen insisted, 'Nanny seems to think you're a bit chesty, too.'

The hot eyes opened.

' "Chesty"? What does that mean? I wish Nanny would get it into her head that I've forgotten – or remembered – more about medicine than she's ever known.'

'I don't think your degree impresses her at all, dear. She's always known better than Dr. Cropper.'

The doctor's name was all that Nanny Benson caught as she opened the door at that moment and came in with a scalding lemon tea for Liz.

'Aye,' she declared, 'it's Dr. Cropper's needed now. No doubt about it, with that chest.'

'Not on Boxing Day,' Helen objected. 'Not just for a cold.'

'Boxing Day or no, I don't like the sound of that cough. Now, you drink this down, my girl, then I'll come and rub your chest with camphorated oil. And if ye're no' better soon, it's the doctor for you.'

Liz and her mother exchanged glances as the sage old soul left the room; but, truthfully, Liz did feel ropey enough to accept a visit from Dr. Cropper.

He came the following morning. Nanny Benson opened the front door to him and was surprised to see that he was accompanied by a neatly dressed, dark young man, perhaps thirty or forty years Dr. Cropper's junior, who had the professional bag in his hand.

' 'Morning, Nanny,' Dr. Cropper greeted with the familiarity of long acquaintance. 'How are you?'

'Very well, thank you, Doctor.'

'Safely over Christmas?'

'Aye, thank you. Come away in.'

'Thank you. This is Dr. Harrington. He'll be taking over my practice later this year. At present we're working together. Nanny Benson – an old friend.'

The young man smiled shyly and pleasantly as he shook hands and stepped over the threshold.

'Pleased to meet you, Miss Benson,' he said respectfully. Nanny was interested to note that his accent was not quite

44

'top drawer'. A touch of the Midlands to it, she noted.

'Family all well?' Dr. Cropper was asking.

'All except Miss Elizabeth, of course. The Commander's out shooting. Mrs. Bourne's gone into Halbury to shop. Lady Bourne's in her room, though, and she'd like to wish you the compliments of the season while you're here, Doctor. But I think you ought to see Miss Elizabeth first. I don't like the sound of that chest of hers.'

Dr. Cropper smiled. 'I think we can safely leave Elizabeth to Dr. Harrington here. He'll be looking after the family from the none too distant future. If you'll just take him along, I'll pop in and see Lady Bourne for a few minutes meanwhile.'

He nodded to his younger colleague and wandered away, completely familiar with Larkfield Manor and the distribution about it of its occupants. After a moment's hesitation Nanny set off up the stairs with the other doctor in tow.

Elizabeth was taken unawares. Her loose hair straggled down the sides of her face and on to her forehead. She wore no make-up and her nose was red against the pale background of her face. Her lips were chapped. She was frowning in concentration upon a medical text book, a damp handkerchief at the ready in one hand.

'Elizabeth,' Nanny said, opening the door, 'this is Dr. Harrington. Dr. *Harrington*.'

Liz looked up, surprised.

'Oh. I thought . . .'

'Dr. Cropper's here, too. He's gone to talk to Lady Bourne. This is his new partner.'

Brian Harrington stepped round Nanny and smiled dutifully at the young woman in the bed. Then, quite together, both his smile and her answering one froze as their gazes interlocked. Though neither knew it at that moment, their mutual non-expression said to one another, 'I have been at large in the world all these years and, without knowing it, waiting to meet you. You are the one.'

Without being aware of doing so, Elizabeth ran her hand through her hair.

'Oh,' she said. 'How do you do. I feel even more of a fraud now.'

He raised his eyebrows. Nanny, busy putting a clean towel on the side of the wash basin, said, 'Don't mind her, Doctor. She's had that weak chest ever since she was a bairn. When she was seven she . . .'

'Oh, do shut up, Nan!' Liz exclaimed with a force which startled the young doctor. 'You don't know what you're talking about.'

'Don't I? When I had you from the first month!'

Dr. Harrington decided it was time to assert some tactful medical authority.

'Perhaps if I could just have a look at you?' he suggested to Liz.

'Quite unnecessary,' he was surprised to hear her reply crisply. 'I can tell you exactly what's wrong with me. I developed a coryza three days ago and decided to ignore it over Christmas. As a result, I had a mild pyrexia yesterday, together with slight congestion of the bronchi and irritation of the sinuses. With the passing of the coryza . . .'

Dr. Harrington, whose expression had first registered mild amusement, was now scowling. His tone betrayed as much irritation with the patient as Nanny's had done, as he said, 'Thank you for your self-diagnosis. I'm most impressed by your knowledge of medical terminology.' He produced a thermometer and forced it into Liz's mouth before she could utter another sound, adding, 'But I'm here to have a look at you, and perhaps that's what I'd better do.'

He seized her wrist and began counting her pulse.

Nanny said, 'She had a temperature of 100 last night, and her cough was . . .'

He frowned her into silence, too. He was slight and dark-haired, not handsome or commanding, but somehow, instinctively to both women, a man of quiet authority, someone whose lack of social veneer left revealed a basic integrity

46

which would probably apply to him as a person as well as a doctor.

He withdrew the thermometer, examined it and shook it.

'Slightly below normal,' he pronounced. 'Only to be expected. Now, Miss Bourne, if you'd kindly sit up and if Miss Benson would lift your nightdress at the back . . .'

He put the thermometer away and got out his stethoscope. It was almost with reluctance that he proceeded to examine her.

'Right,' he said at length, coiling the stethoscope into the bag. 'Just your throat. Open wide, please. Aaah. Good. There's no reason why you shouldn't get up tomorrow, providing your temperature's still down. I took the precaution of bringing you a bottle for the cough. Four times a day, one tablespoon in very hot water. You can start now. Miss Benson, would you fetch the water, please?'

Nanny went out, satisfied that her insistence on the doctor's coming had at least been justified.

'Now,' he said to Elizabeth in a changed tone as she lay back against the pillow again, 'would you mind explaining?'

'Explaining?'

'The self-diagnosis. And this.' He indicated her book on the coverlet, a textbook on pharmacology. 'Unlikely reading for a young lady in bed.'

Liz said simply, 'I took my first M.B. at Oxford this year.'

His astonished expression amused her.

'Well – congratulations,' he said. 'Why didn't you tell me?'

'You didn't give me a chance to – did you?'

The smile they exchanged was warmer than passing politeness required.

Next morning the tightness had gone from her chest. She had slept well, with scarcely any coughing. But she accepted Nanny's demand that she at least have breakfast in bed, and lay there drowsily awaiting it. There was a tap at her door and Vicky came in.

47

'Are you awake, Liz?'

'No. Fast asleep.'

'Silly ass. Pleasant dreams?'

'Actually, yes,' Liz answered, more truthfully than Vicky sensed. 'What do you want?'

'Can I borrow a lipstick? I'm going to buy one, whatever Mummy says.'

'All right. Top little drawer. But don't overdo it, and mind you put it back.'

'Thanks. You look better this morning. Are you?'

Liz hesitated, then said, 'I'll know by the time I've had breakfast.'

'Pity. No more visits from that scrumptious new doctor.'

'Oh, him,' Liz answered as casually as she could. At that moment Nanny returned, with a tray of tea and toast. The thermometer lay there also. Vicky hastily palmed the lipstick and sidled out.

'Now,' Nanny said to Liz, 'just take your temperature first and if it's still down you can get up after breakfast.'

She placed the thermometer in Elizabeth's mouth, leaving the tray on the bedside table.

'I won't be a minute,' she said, going to the door. 'Anne's fussing over her blue jumper. Why she can't remember where she puts things I'll never know.'

Elizabeth's mind had been half made up already. Her seemingly providential being left alone at this precise moment settled the matter completely for her. She removed the thermometer, reached over and raised the teapot lid, and dipped the instrument in. After a few seconds she withdrew it, looked at it, carefully shook the mercury down to a more plausible level, and got the teapot lid back on and the thermometer back in her mouth just in time for Nanny to re-enter.

'That child will lose her own head next,' the old lady grumbled, reaching for the thermometer. Her eyes opened wide when she read it and she peered more closely to verify what she thought she might have been mistaking.

'Gracious heavens!' she said. 'Over 102. Well, I never! Pull up those bedclothes at once, child, and keep yourself covered. I'm going to call the doctor straight away. And no hot tea for you in the meantime, I'm afraid.'

Nanny hurried out, carrying the tray. Liz snuggled back with a smile. She had lost the breakfast to which she had been quite looking forward; but she had gained another encounter with Dr. Brian Harrington.

When Vicky came back later to return the lipstick she was surprised to find that Liz had done her hair carefully and put a little powder on her face. She was wearing a nice bedjacket and looking pretty and perfectly at ease.

'Nanny said you were worse again.'

'I told you I didn't know how I was so soon after waking up. Apparently my temperature's up, though it doesn't feel much.'

She laid the back of a hand to her brow and shook her head. 'If the doctor's cross at a wasted trip it's not my fault. You know what Nanny is.'

Vicky nodded. 'Anyway, guess what.'

'What? You look excited.'

'Robin rang me up. One of the boys I met at the dance. He's asked me to go to the cinema with him tomorrow.'

'Robin who?'

'Downes. They farm just the other side of Halbury.'

'I think I've met his sister. So, your first date. Tell you what – I'll drive you back afterwards if you like, if I can borrow the car. I want to go into Halbury myself tomorrow.'

'How d'you know you'll be up? I must say, you don't look ill.'

'Oh, well, hoping for the best you know,' Liz answered hastily, conscious of having nearly given herself away. 'What's the film?'

'*It happened One Night*. Clark Gable and Claudette Colbert. I was away at school when it came round first time. Priscilla Bailey says it's absolutely smashing.'

'Depends whether you care for Gable. Not my cup of tea.'

'Who is? Honestly, you don't seem to go for any of them. You'll miss out and be sorry some day.'

'Then you can say "I told you so". Listen – there's a car. If that's the doctor he's been quick.'

'Nanny probably told him you're at death's door – or he couldn't wait to see you. I'll go and let him in. Warn him you're not interested.'

Vicky skipped cheerfully from the room. Elizabeth felt her heart thud with anticipation and from the little thrill Vicky's innocent suggestion had given her. She closed her eyes, calming herself while she waited.

A brief murmur of conversation downstairs ceased and she heard the creak of the stairs. Then the door opened, and old Dr. Cropper came in.

'Good morning,' he said heartily. 'My word, I expected to find you at your last gasp.'

The disappointment caused Elizabeth to stammer as she apologized for what might prove to be a wasted errand, caused by Nanny's well known propensity for fussing. The doctor silenced her with the thermometer and sat holding her pulse, saying, 'I was just coming out to Winchley, anyway. Young Mrs. Botley had her baby in the small hours. It wasn't easy and I said I'd look in again this morning. They're fine, I'm glad to say.' He withdrew the thermometer and examined it. 'So is your temperature. Tongue, please. Throat. Aaah. Yes, all healthy enough. I gather Harrington gave your chest a clear bill yesterday.'

'Yes. I'm so sorry, Doctor. Perhaps Nanny misread the thermometer. I didn't think to look myself.'

'No trouble. Better safe than sorry. How did you get on with him, by the way?'

'Who – Dr. Harrington? Oh, he, er, bossed me about a bit.'

The old man chuckled. 'Yes, I hear you told him his business and he struck back. Can't blame him for that, eh?'

'Oh, no, I wasn't doing. I thought he was quite ... pleasant.'

'He's a good doctor and a modern one, which is what's needed in a modern world. You'll all notice the difference when he takes over.'

'We shall miss you when you go.'

'I'll miss myself. The more I think about retiring, the less attractive it seems. Still, I mustn't get in young Harrington's way.'

'Where did you meet him?'

'I didn't. I put an advertisement in the B.M.J. and he answered it – along with a good few others. He seemed the best of the bunch. I believe I chose right.'

Liz said carefully, 'I'm sure you did.'

'Well, if I didn't, you can blame me – all of you, though I'll probably be out of your reach before you find out.'

He got up off the bed. 'I must get on now. Can't sit here chatting with people with nothing wrong with 'em, even if they are pretty girls.'

Liz smiled warmly up at him. 'Will you please tell Nanny I'm all right? She'll never believe it from me, and I should like to get up.'

'I'll tell her I ordered you to. 'Bye, young lady.'

He went. Liz lay back, smiling to herself at the ironic way in which Fate had foiled her. 'Serve you right!' she said aloud. Then she got out of bed, gathered her clothes, and took up occupancy of the bathroom.

Aunt Phyllis returned to London after lunch. One of her pupils was performing at a New Year's charity concert and needed final preparation.

'I do think it's a waste of Aunty Phyl,' Anne remarked, as the family sat about in the hall after dinner that evening. 'She'd make some man a super wife.'

'She would have done, but for the war,' Helen answered. 'He was killed in 1916. But only yesterday she was saying that a spinster's lot is quite a happy one nowadays. Especially in London. She's very happy with her work and she goes to all the concerts and theatres.'

'It seems to me,' Lady Bourne remarked, 'that half the people who get married get divorced anyway.'

'Mind you don't put these girls off,' Charles said, winking at Anne. 'Best life for a woman, I'm sure, looking after a man and bringing up his children.'

'I believe this Dr. Harrington hasn't a wife,' Lady Bourne replied, quite irrelevantly so far as any of the others could judge, apart from Liz, who felt a cold chill sweep up the back of her neck. She pulled closer to her the velvet house-coat Nanny had ordered her to wear, 'just in case'.

'Why should he have, Mother?' asked Arthur, pouring his father-in-law another glass of the dwindling supply of '04 Port his father had laid down during the Russo-Japanese War. The late Admiral would have been appalled, it had occurred to Arthur, to see his port being drunk so 'publicly', with womenfolk sitting around. Port was an accompaniment to the conversation of men, not the prattling of women, in Sir William's view. His widow was equally traditional-minded, in her way.

'Because he should,' she answered. 'A doctor should always be married – especially in the country. It gives his women patients confidence that he knows what's what.'

'Every doctor I ever knew learnt all that at medical school,' Charles said.

'Don't be vulgar in front of the children,' Lady Bourne rebuked him. 'And what about attempting to achieve your revenge at Backgammon – or were you hoping I'd forget?'

'With the greatest pleasure, my dear Alice,' he smiled. 'I warn you, though, I shall be merciless this time.'

'In that case I'm certain to win. Liz, dear, pass my stole, please.'

Elizabeth wished for more conversation about the young new doctor, but dared not start any. She handed over the woollen stole.

'Thank you,' her grandmother said. 'I can't think, Arthur, why you don't use the drawing-room more. I've never liked this idea of sitting in the hall. Your father started it, though

I soon put a stop to it. But, of course, it's nothing to do with me now.'

Arthur glanced at Helen. 'We think it makes a comfortable room. Best fireplace in the house, you know.'

Anne asked, 'Why don't we have central heating put in, Daddy? Nearly everyone's got it now.'

'Yes, dear,' Arthur said heavily. 'Perhaps one of these days.'

'Nonsense!' Helen said quite sharply, annoyed that Anne might have re-awakened her husband's worries about there not being enough money to meet existing commitments. 'It's a very warm house, except in the coldest winters.'

'I suppose so. Vic, how about a game of Racing Demon?'

But Vicky shook her head and wandered over to the piano, to play softly one of the restful pieces she knew they all liked to hear in the background of so family an evening. Anne turned to her other sister, who was gazing intently into the fire again.

'Liz? *Liz?*'

'Mm? Sorry?'

'Racing Demon. How about a few hands?'

'Oh, yes. Why not?'

Anne looked at her curiously, but thought at once that this unaccustomed vagueness must stem from the cold.

'I think you played a five then,' she heard her maternal grandfather say politely to her paternal grandmother.

'I did.'

'You threw a four.'

'Are you accusing me of cheating?'

'We can all of us make mistakes, my dear.'

'I do not make mistakes. It was quite definitely a five. *Your* throw.'

In such ways did this essentially family Christmas period drift by. A time out of context, with usual activities suspended, or performed to a different pattern. Much sitting about, and aimless behaviour, where there was usually bustle and preoccupation. A time when anyone of a philosophical turn of mind might have wondered whether preoccupation and bustle were ever necessary, if they could be dispensed with so easily. Yet, a time at which the demands of everyday life were missed, and their re-imposition looked forward to as a return to what was regarded as 'normality'.

The time passed especially slowly for Vicky, looking forward with pleasurable nervousness to her first visit to a cinema with a boy. Little more than twenty-four hours' waiting, from the receipt of the invitation, was involved, but it seemed the longest twenty-four hours of her life. At last the time had come and Elizabeth, now quite recovered, was fetching the car round to the front door.

'I wish this coat weren't so babyish,' Vicky complained to her grandmother. 'Nothing seems right for me just now.'

The old lady patted her shoulder. 'You must come and stay with me in London before you go off to Germany. We'll do some shopping together. Get your father to give you a cheque and we'll go to Woollands'.'

'That'd be fun, Granny.'

'Here's the car. Have a lovely time, dear.'

'Thanks. *Is* this coat all right?'

'Perfectly. Go on with you.'

When she had dropped Vicky off at the Halbury Cinema and seen her immediately greeted by a pleasant-looking youth whom she now recalled she had met, too, Elizabeth drove her father's five-year-old Wolseley on to the public library. She handed in her books, collected her tickets and went straight to the fiction shelves, hoping against hope that she might find John Buchan's *The Three Fishers*. She was out of luck, so went to look if it was amongst the newly returned books. It wasn't; but Dr. Harrington was there, also searching.

'Hello, Miss Bourne,' he greeted her with a smile. 'Up and about, then.'

'Yes. Croppy . . . Dr. Cropper gave me the order of release yesterday. It was only a mild coryza, after all. Oh, sorry.'

He grinned. 'What are you after in here?'

'John Buchan's latest. I expect I'll have to reserve it. What are you looking for?'

'It's my afternoon off and I just came in here to see if anything struck my fancy. It hasn't done so far. But a cup of tea does, if there's anywhere you recommend.'

'Oh, yes. Quite a nice little place. The Copper Kettle.'

'Now there's an original name. Can I tempt you?'

'Yes,' she said without hesitation. 'We can walk round from here.'

Five minutes later they were seated in a corner of the typically brick and chintz tearoom, with its symbolic array of gleaming copper kettles and moulds, its Rowland Hilder treescape over the mantelpiece, its clean, well-ironed check tablecloths, its bowls of carefully levelled granulated sugar, its chatter of ladies and clatter of cutlery and crockery. The middle-aged proprietress, Miss Pringle, took their order for tea and toast and went away to prepare it herself.

'Very pleasant,' Dr. Harrington said.

'Yes. You can get nice light meals here, too. Everything home made.'

'I'll remember that when I can't be bothered to make myself something. I generally finish up doing without, or getting a pub sandwich.'

'Are you living with Dr. Cropper?'

'I'm . . . in digs. At the moment.'

'Nice?'

He shrugged. 'Bearable.'

'Rather lonely, I should think.'

'A doctor has no time to be lonely. You'll find that out some day.'

'Me?'

'I presume you'll go on to a teaching hospital now and qualify, won't you?'

'I don't know.'

'The old boy tells me you got a very good degree. Somerville?'

'Lady Margaret Hall. Were you up?'

'Not Oxford.'

'London?'

He grinned in his modest way. 'I'm strictly provincial. Birmingham Central. I regret not having done Oxford or Cambridge first, though.'

Liz found herself keenly anxious not to sound at all superior.

'I wouldn't have missed it for anything,' she said. 'It was good of my family to fork out for me. My father's done everything he could for the three of us – 'varsity for me, boarding school and a year in Germany for Anne, that's my second sister, and Vicky – you've met her.'

'No brothers?'

'No. A shame, really, for my father. Anne's the nearest thing to it – riding, fishing, even a bit of shooting.'

'But not you?'

'Oh, no. I'm the "serious" one. My sisters have been known to call me The Governess. I suppose I'm a bit bossy by nature.'

'Eldest children often are, especially if they're the cleverest. But you said you don't know whether you'll go on and qualify.'

'I ... I'm giving it time. The decision. I have to think of the family, too. They were a bit disappointed when I switched to medicine, I know. Afraid I'm going to turn out a career woman.'

'As opposed to what?'

'Oh, the usual things. Marriage ...'

'To a local landowner?'

'That sort of thing.'

'I see. What about your sisters?'

'They take that for granted for themselves. Me, I'm not sure.'

She had poured him a fresh cup of tea. He was stirring it carefully, unnecessarily, concentrating on doing so.

'Is there ... anyone in prospect?' he asked, not looking up.

'No. But if I do plump for medicine I've a feeling that'll be it. I should want to do it really well.'

'Yes, I can imagine that. But you can't be so calculated where ambition's concerned, can you?'

'I know. I've given it a year, give or take a bit. Then I'll make my mind up one way or the other. It won't be any use trying to compromise.'

They sat silently for some moments, the conversation having reached an ending and requiring reviving along new lines. At length, Elizabeth asked conventionally, 'Do you like Halbury, Dr. Harrington?'

'It's very different from the industrial Midlands. Yes, I do like it. Whether it's going to test me enough professionally is another matter. And my name is Brian. I don't suppose I shall be required to go on calling all three of you "Miss Bourne".'

'Brian, then. I'm Liz to most people.'

'Or "The Governess".'

'I'm not all that bossy.'

Again the conversation faltered. This new touch of intimacy had made them both self-conscious. Again it was Liz who resumed it.

'Have you ever thought of specializing?'

He seemed to answer carefully. 'I was tempted. E.N.T. But . . . circumstances didn't permit.'

'I see. I'm rather tempted by occupational diseases, if I go on. I thought I might do it for my thesis.'

The little cautiousness he had momentarily displayed vanished again and he said enthusiastically, 'Good idea! It's a field that hasn't been explored enough and there's a lot of scope. Have you read Hope, Hanna and Stallybrass on it?'

'Not yet. I know of it, of course.'

'As it happens, I've got a copy. I could lend you it. I gathered the other day that you're not forbidding yourself to do medical reading during this . . . this year of decision.'

She shook her head. 'It wouldn't do to drop it altogether for so long, would it?'

'I quite agree. I'll ... be out your way the day after tomorrow. I could bring it then ... if you like.'

'That would be marvellous,' she replied.

They talked on for so long, exploring this avenue and that, though mostly on the levels of the professional and the commonplace, that Miss Pringle had to remind them that she was waiting to close. Liz remembered with horror that she was supposed to be picking Vicky up. The film would have been over nearly fifteen minutes. She took a hasty leave of Brian Harrington and almost ran to the car park. Fortunately, Vicky had enjoyed herself and Robin Downes had been gallant enough to wait with her, so there were no recriminations during the drive home.

'What have you been doing all afternoon?' Vicky inquired idly of her sister, who was driving with what appeared to be silent concentration.

'I? Oh, the library and ... things.'

'Didn't you get any books?'

'There ... wasn't anything I particularly wanted. I spent most of the time in the reference room.'

'Oh.'

Charles Ashley was alone in the hall when they got in. He looked up from his newspaper crossword.

'Hello, my child. Enjoy your cinema?'

'You bet.'

'Your mother's just gone up to change. She said she'd like to see you.'

'I'll go straight up, then.' Vicky bounded energetically up the stairs. Charles found Elizabeth standing beside him, looking at him speculatively. He sensed that she had something to say, and made it easier for her to begin.

'Liz, there's a clue here you might be able to help with. Occupational hazard for workers with hides. Three blanks – H – two blanks ...'

'Anthrax,' Liz answered promptly.

'Clever girl.'

He pretended to write it in: it had been one of the first he himself had got.

'Grandpa . . .' she said.

'Mm?'

'Do you . . . believe in . . . in love at first sight?' She added hastily, 'In principle, I mean. Can it happen?'

He lowered the paper.

'It certainly can, and not only in principle. It happened to me. At a garden party at New College in '86 I saw your late grandmother talking to the Warden. She was wearing a yellow dress. I knew at once that she was the only girl for me. We married two years later and were happy together for over thirty years. You know, you remind me of her sometimes, my dear Liz. I don't know in what way, but you do.'

She kissed him on top of his head.

'Thank you, Grandpa.'

She heard her father's voice and straightened up to see him emerging from his study with Dr. Cropper.

'A glass of sherry before you go, to warm the cockles?' he was saying. The doctor nodded his thanks.

'Hello, young lady,' he greeted Liz. 'Quite all right now?'

'Perfectly, thanks. I'm going up to change, Daddy.'

Her father nodded and she went to the stairs.

'Charles, a glass for you, too?'

'Thank you, yes, although I can't pretend my cockles need warming.'

Arthur went to the decanter to pour. As she began mounting the stairs Liz heard him explaining to her grandfather, 'We've just been talking cottage hospital business. And what Dr. Cropper's going to do when he retires.'

'I'll tell you my recipe,' Charles Ashley said. 'A small, comfortable house, with a housekeeper who can cook. I suppose you'll be selling your place, Doctor?'

'It goes with the practice. Young Harrington will need it when his wife arrives from Wolverhampton.'

59

Half-way up the stairs, Liz almost stopped and turned to look down at them. She hesitated, but forced herself to go on. Her mind felt as if it had been instantly frozen.

'I used to be a brown sherry man,' the doctor was saying.

'I acquired the taste for Fino when I was on shore at Gib.,' Arthur explained.

Charles added, 'And I acquired it in my house at Eton. The boys prefer it.'

The three men laughed. Liz went straight to her room, but did not switch on the light. She closed the door and lay on her bed.

It was five to eight when Anne knocked at the door and entered.

'Liz?'

'Yes?'

Anne switched the light on. She was dressed for dinner. She looked with astonishment at her sister.

'It's five to eight. Mummy sent me to look for you.'

'I'm not coming down,' Liz said in a flat tone which caused Anne's expression to change from surprise to concern. 'Will you say I'm sorry, and I've gone back to bed.'

'What's the matter? Are you ill again?'

Liz shook her head and sat up.

'Shut the door. I want to talk to you. I must talk to someone.'

Anne obeyed, and came back to sit on the bed.

'What is it?'

'First promise . . .' Liz managed a wan smile. 'Like we did when we were children: "See that wet, see that dry . . ." '

' " . . . slit my throat and hope to die." '

Liz said very seriously, 'It's a secret. I really mean a *total* secret, Anne. No one but you.'

'I promise, Liz.'

'I'm . . . I think I'm falling in love.'

Anne's face lit up. 'At last! Someone I know?'

'Brian Harrington.'

'Brian . . .? The new doctor?'

'Yes.'

Anne's young mind grappled urgently with the implications.

'But you hardly know him. And ... you're his patient. Isn't there something about doctors and patients not being allowed to ...'

Liz nodded and said bitterly, 'It doesn't matter, anyway. He's married.'

'Married! Oh, Liz, the first time you fall in love, and ... What rotten luck!'

'Yes, isn't it? Anyway, it's made up my mind for me.'

'What about?'

'Going on with medicine. At least, I think so. The first thing is, I must get away from here for a while. I'll telephone Phyllis. I'm sure she'd put me up in London. I'll do lots of work on my thesis, and see new people, and I might ... I might get over it quickly.'

'Is he ... What does he feel about you?'

'Oh, it hasn't reached that stage. Only, I feel sure there's something. I can't let him risk breaking up his marriage, let alone his career. So, you see, when I tell the family I'm going up to London for a bit, mind you back me up. Promise?'

'Of course, Liz. Oh, it's too awful for you.'

Anne hugged her sister impulsively, her mind still searching the possibilities. They heard Vicky calling, approaching along the landing 'Liz – telephone.' She opened the door and looked in. 'Oliver Horner. Something about going up to the Chelsea Arts Ball on New Year's Eve and wanting you to go – lucky thing!'

Liz sprang up with an energy that surprised Anne. 'Yes!' she exclaimed eagerly. 'Tell him thank you, and say I'll ring him back in the morning, will you?'

As Vicky hurried away, Liz turned to Anne. 'You see how things start sorting themselves out. Just my excuse to go without alarming the family, and once there I might as well stay a while. You go down and tell Mummy I was reading and didn't notice the time. I'll chuck my things on and be down in five minutes.'

Anne nodded and went. Poor Liz! Trust her to get things worked out so soon. But how rotten that it should have to be like this. She hoped it would be plainer sailing for her when her turn came.

Liz positively sparkled at dinner. Everyone was glad that, after her brief illness, she was obviously quite herself again.

CHAPTER FOUR

Liz had gone, with a slight change of plan. For what little there would be left of the night by the time the Arts Ball was over, or she came away from it, she was to stay at Aunt Phyllis's. Later on New Year's day, though, she would take a train to Wales and fulfil a long-standing promise to stay with an Oxford girl friend outside Cardiff. It had occurred to her that totally unfamiliar surroundings might help her even more than London, which she knew well, while her friend's company would disengage her thoughts for her.

At Larkfield it was arranged that the grandparents should stay long enough to see the New Year in, then would be driven to the station next morning for the 11.53 to Paddington. Charles Ashley lived in the Thames Valley, at Datchet, and Lady Bourne at Artillery Mansions in the Victoria district of London. They never saw one another except at Larkfield.

Arthur Bourne spent the morning of New Year's Eve in his study, littering the usually tidy desk with bills, receipts, his cheque book, paying-in-slips and other documents to do with finance. He had woken up with the resolution to clear up as much of this back-log of paper work as possible on the last day of the old year, and begin the new one as methodically as he hoped to go on; but the longer he worked, the grimmer his face became, and more than once he found himself simply staring into space, wondering what he was going to do.

'You're worried,' Helen said, bringing him a mid-morning cup of coffee and some biscuits. 'Is it this man who's coming?'

'No, no.'

'Then it's money.'

'Never you mind.'

'Of course I mind.'

'Well, you know how it is at this time of year. The bills pouring in at their thickest. Christmas shopping accounts. Club subscriptions any moment now. And the overdraft up to the limit. I can't ask for any more, but if that dairy building isn't repaired soon it'll fall down and then it really will cost money.'

'How much would it cost to repair now?'

'At least three hundred.'

Helen put her arm round his shoulders. 'I do wish I could help, darling,' she assured him. 'I do my best to economize, but, honestly, neither the girls nor I have had any new clothes for months. Vicky's things are beginning to look absurdly childish on her.'

'Yes, I thought that.'

'Well, as soon as your mother and my father are out of the way, and we're back to normal, Nanny and I are going to tackle anything Anne can spare Vicky. Thank heaven Anne will at least have finished with the sewing machine after today.'

'What's she doing with it all this time?'

'Making her costume for the Addisons' fancy dress do tonight. A great secret. No one's been allowed to see it.'

Arthur sighed. 'Ah well, the rest of us will just have to get tight and work up a spirit of revelry and optimism.'

'Something will come up. We've always managed. This Commander White who's coming – he wrote about a proposition that might interest you. Perhaps it's business.'

'If he wants me to put up money for something he's coming to the wrong shop.' Arthur indicated the clip of bills. 'I'm hardly in a position to finance anyone else's business if I can't pay my own way.'

'Well, wait and see. Do you know him well?'

'Used to – fairly. He was in Naval Intelligence. Decent, dependable sort.'

64

'That's something, anyway.'

'Oh, don't be afraid I'll let myself in for anything risky. I can't afford to. No, he merely says he's passing this way en route to see the year in in Wales, and he'll drop in at about 11.30 to see if this proposition interests me. In fact, he'll be here any time now.'

'Will he be staying to lunch? He'd be welcome. The girls are going into Halbury and there's plenty of stuff in the house.'

'See what he has to say, eh? I'll invite him if it seems propitious. Listen, there's a car.'

A car swept past the study window and ground to a halt. Helen went to open the front door and greet a sharp-featured, tweed-suited man in his early sixties, with the immaculately groomed appearance of the retired regular Naval officer. He introduced himself as Commander Jack White and after an exchange of pleasantries she showed him into the study, where Arthur had worked swiftly to hide away his bills and return his desk top to a more orderly state.

'Good morning, Arthur,' Commander White said heartily, and Helen closed the door on the two men shaking hands warmly.

'This is a pleasant surprise, Jackie,' Arthur said. 'Ages since I saw you, isn't it?'

'Well over a year. At the Club, I think.'

'Yes, of course. Er, too early for a glass of something?'

'I don't think so. Whisky and a drop of splash, eh?'

They chatted for a while about mutual friends and the recent renunciation by Japan of the Washington Treaties of 1922 and '30, limiting her Navy.

'The thin end of a wedge, in my opinion,' said Commander White. 'I don't like their game in Manchukuo a bit. They're spoiling for an all-out war with the Chinese. I discussed it all in my piece in the *Sphere* the other week. Perhaps you saw it?'

'I did indeed. The whole situation in a nutshell, I thought at the time.'

65

'Thanks. Look here, Arthur, that brings us round to what I called to see you about. I'd have written to you, but I knew I'd be going to my sister's for New Year and I thought it would be more easily discussed face to face. Now, as you know, I do quite a bit for the public prints these days. Supplements the pension handily and keeps me out of mischief. Got a book coming out in the spring.'

'Congratulations.'

'More on the boys' adventure level, though – *Stirring Yarns of the Submarine Service*. Quite a good market for that sort of thing, oddly enough. I'd have thought that, so long after the war ... Well, maybe they like to be reassured that if the old country could rise to the occasion so well last time, it will again next.'

Arthur's eyebrows raised.

'You sound sure there will be a "next".'

'Of course I hope not, but there are too many pointers for my liking. Hitler and Mussolini getting together. Germany laying down rearmament terms. Rearmament for what, I ask? But don't get me going on that one. To get back to why I've come to you, I've been asked by my publisher to do a sequel to my book, dealing with surface actions. Some of the pieces I shall write myself, but others will be done by chaps actually involved – first hand recollection, sort of thing. Now, not to beat about the bush, your *Mansard* action was one of the best destroyer things of the war. It's exactly the sort I want, and I'd like to invite you to write it for me.'

Arthur got up slowly, took his guest's glass and his own and replenished them. Then, instead of returning to his desk, he went to lean on the mantelpiece, over which hung two reproduction paintings of heroic actions of Nelson's ships.

Commander White continued, 'The accent's on daring, courage, excitement – I'm sure you know the kind of thing I mean. Four to five thousand words of good lively stuff, preferably as seen through your own eyes. And, speaking of practicalities, your share of the book rights and almost certain

66

magazine extracts would bring you not less than three hundred pounds. Perhaps more.'

The sum surprised Arthur and his instant thought was that it would pay for the whole of the repairs to the dairy building. But he looked into his whisky glass and replied, 'Sorry, Jackie. I couldn't.'

His visitor laughed shortly. 'Two or three other chaps have given me that answer,' he said. 'I've told 'em they don't know until they try. They have tried, and all except one succeeded. You know, you'd be surprised how many ex-officers R.N. are in the writing game. Something to do with having orderly minds, self-discipline, experience of writing all those long despatches. I don't know quite what it is – but I reckon it would come more easily than you think.'

'Of course,' he added, 'if you're too busy or disinclined, I can write it myself. It would have more authority coming from you, though. More impact. Or I could write it as if by you and publish it under your name – ghosting, they call it. Your share of the booty would be lower, naturally, but I imagine that's neither here nor there.'

Arthur said, 'No, no, no, that's not the point at all. What I couldn't do is show myself off in public for something I chanced to be mixed up in in the war. Merely doing my job.'

'Oh, hardly that, old chap. They gave you the D.S.O. for it.'

'Because I was in command of the ship. Plenty of chaps in the war showed real personal courage and got nothing for it – lost their lives, many of them. If you choose to write about the *Mansard* action I can't stop you – though I'd rather you didn't, quite frankly. But nothing will appear over my name, written by me or anyone else.'

'There's nothing ignoble about inspiring young chaps who might have to go to war themselves some day, Arthur.'

'I agree, and I'm not denigrating your activities, Jackie. Only I myself refuse to make money out of the guts and courage and suffering of my ship's company.'

'I'll arrange for your fees to go to Naval charities, then.'

'No. I'm sorry.'

Commander White drained his glass and put it down. He got up, smiling.

'I'm not going to try to cajole you, Arthur. I respect what you say, but I'd be glad if you'd at least think it over. Tell you what, if I don't hear from you by, say, 10th January, I'll assume you won't do it. But it's going in the book, Arthur, one way or another. I'll play down your personal heroics, if that's what you want, but I think it's only fair to your chaps and the relatives who are proud of them that the incident is included.'

Arthur nodded. 'Yes, that's a fair enough point, and I know I can trust your discretion in the way you put it down. But don't wait until 10th January to hear from me. As it happens, that sort of money would be very welcome just now, what with one commitment and another. But my answer's no, and I've told you why.'

'Ah, well . . .'

'Now, will you lunch with us? We'd be only too delighted.'

Commander White hesitated, then said, 'No, thanks. I've a long way to go and I don't want to go to sleep at the wheel. Besides,' he smiled, 'I might talk you round, given time – or talk your wife into talking you round.'

He held out his hand and again they shook warmly.

Indeed, when Arthur later gave way to Helen's insistence that she be told about his now-departed friend's 'proposition', her reaction showed him that he would have had a sticky time at the luncheon table with the two of them to work on him.

'It's absurd!' she declared. 'For years people have been writing books and articles about what they did in the war. There's no disgrace about it.'

'Well, it's not for me, thanks.'

'It's all right being reticent, darling, but three hundred pounds doesn't drop out of thin air every day.'

'Helen, I've given you my reasons. I've turned it down, and I don't want to discuss it any more.'

'Not discuss it! Look, I do think I've some right ...'

He turned on her with unaccustomed anger, anger that was all the more bitter from being directed really at himself.

'Of course I know we need the money. What do you think I've been doing with those damned accounts all morning?'

'Exactly. I ... just don't understand.'

'A woman wouldn't.'

'That's nothing to do with it at all.'

'Well, if you can't see my point ...'

'I think it's very foolish ...'

'Thanks very much.' He stamped towards the kitchen. 'I'm going to the woodshed to saw some logs. We're getting as short of them as we are of every other damn thing, it seems.'

Arthur Bourne was not the type of man to sulk protractedly. His infrequent angers were explosive, tending to be more violent sometimes than their cause justified, but the quicker over because of it. This time, though, because of nagging suspicion that he might have made the wrong decision too hastily and put his personal scruples before his family's well-being, he remained subdued all day, keeping mostly to himself.

Helen recognized the mood and went about her household duties matter-of-factly. Anne and Vicky returned from Halbury late in the afternoon and Anne promptly shut herself away again with her mystery-surrounded party costume. Charles Ashley read and dozed. Lady Bourne dozed. And so the year 1934 ran down towards its close.

When they had changed for dinner Charles challenged Vicky to a game of *L'Attaque*, by way of light relief from his running contest at Backgammon with Alice Bourne. Although Vicky did not emulate her aunt's unashamed cheating, she soon asserted her superiority, capturing his Commander-in-Chief within minutes by swashbuckling use of her Spy, whom he mistook from its openness of movement for a mere Corporal.

'Attack!' she cried yet again, moving a Sapper across the board.

'Got you!' he rejoined triumphantly. 'A Mine. Boomph!'

'Oh no you haven't, Grandpa,' she was able to point out. 'A Sapper beats a Mine.'

'Hang it!' he moaned to Alice. 'What can I do about this girl?'

'Nothing,' she said without malice. 'The triumph of youth over senility, that's all.'

'I suppose so.'

'Sorry to neglect you,' Helen said, coming in from the kitchen. 'Mrs. Gates wanted a recipe for the sauce. I think it's time we all had some sherry.'

'I'll get it,' Arthur said, coming down the stairs at that moment.

'Well,' said Charles, 'our party's going to be a bit depleted tonight, I gather.'

'I'm afraid so,' Helen said. 'With Liz up in town for the revels and Anne going to her party.'

'Only me and a lot of grown-ups,' Vicky said with a mock pout.

'Never mind,' her grandfather said. 'We shall have our own revels here, in our own way. Ah, and here comes the party queen.'

Anne was making her way downstairs, closely swathed in a coat. Nothing of her costume was visible save a pair of gilded sandals. In the subdued light of the standard lamp and table lamps the extent of her make-up was not fully revealed, but Vicky noted that there was something odd about it and that Anne was tending to stand away from the lights.

'Andrew Shale will be here for me in a minute in his car,' Anne said.

'Then you can give us the benefit of your mysterious costume in the meantime,' Charles Ashley said.

'Oh, I . . . I really haven't time, Grandpapa.'

'What, after all this secrecy and whispering!'

'Sorry, but Andrew will be here any moment . . .'

Helen was looking at her closely. 'What have you got on your face?'

'Just . . . some make-up.'

Charles was persisting, 'We'll all have a guess what you're going as, then you can show who's right. I say Queen Elizabeth.'

'Impossible,' Lady Bourne said. 'There'd be more skirt showing. Nell Gwynn, perhaps.'

'I believe she's a tennis player – or a boy,' Vicky offered. Anne was noticeably edging towards the front door.

'I'm sure I heard the car,' she said.

'It wasn't, darling,' Helen said. 'Come on, now – let's see you, over here in the light.'

Anne positively shrank back. 'Must I?'

Arthur said, rather impatiently, 'We're not going to eat you.'

Slowly, with dragging reluctance, she came forward, paused, then opened her coat and let it slip from her shoulders.

She wore a flimsy slave-girl costume of chiffon, sequins and very little else. The baggy trousers were transparent. Her stomach was bare and a jewel was painted around her navel. The grotesque effect was completed by the exaggerated make-up of rouge, mascara and lipstick, now clearly visible as she stood in the centre of the room.

Vicky giggled in the silence. 'Anne!' she exclaimed. 'Honestly!'

Helen said, aghast, 'You're surely not going like that!'

'I am.' Anne's tone was less than confident. 'I'm a slave from the *Arabian Nights*. Don't I look like one?'

'No!'

The staccato response came from her father. In his most incisive tone of command he ordered, 'Put your coat back on. Then go straight upstairs and take off that dreadful getup.'

Anne goggled at him, frightened and speechless.

'Did you hear what I said?' he demanded.

'Why, Daddy?'

'Isn't that obvious? I'm sure it is to everyone else.'

Anne looked pleadingly round. 'It's *fancy* dress. A

71

slavegirl, that's all. You see them often enough in films – even at Halbury cinema.'

'This is not the films,' Arthur retorted, flushed with anger. 'If you think I'm going to allow my daughter to go to a party half-naked you'd better think again. Now go upstairs and get changed.'

She turned to her mother. 'Must I, Mummy?'

'If your father says so, yes.'

'But you wouldn't have made me.'

'That's not the point, Anne.'

'You see! He's just being stuffy and old fashioned. And very unfair.'

'Go upstairs!' Arthur almost shouted.

'I won't.'

'What!'

'Mummy, please, why won't you back me up? You don't think I look indecent, do you? It's no worse than people will be wearing at the Chelsea Arts Ball and Liz is allowed to go there.'

Retaining what control he could, Arthur answered, 'I've told you this isn't a film, or the Chelsea Arts Ball. You're asked to the house of people we know, and you're not going like that.'

'But I've got nothing else to wear. I've been working on it for days.'

Vicky ventured, 'Couldn't Nanny stitch a piece round the tummy, so it wouldn't be quite so . . . you know?'

'That would spoil the effect completely.'

Helen told her quietly, 'do as your father says, Anne.'

'And wash that stuff off your face while you're about it,' Arthur added. 'You look positively cheap.'

Anne stared. Headlights flashed across the curtains and a car drove swiftly up to the door.

'That does it,' she said. 'I'm going just as I am.'

'You are not!'

'I'm not going to be told what I can or can't wear at a fancy dress party.'

'Anne, I warn you ...'

She tugged her coat back on and moved swiftly to the door.

'I'm sorry, Mummy' – she ignored her father pointedly – 'I hope you all have a nice evening.'

She went out quickly. They heard voices greeting her, the car door slam, and the car drive away.

Arthur had not moved from where he stood. His face was a picture more of distress than anger at having had his authority defied for the first time in a major way by any of his family. Everyone sensed what he was feeling and no one spoke. Helen, whose instinct had been to want to shield her daughter from the violence of his wrath, which she had secretly felt to be unreasonable, went silently to him and took his arm, trying to give him reassurance on a day in which she, too, had quarrelled with him.

He did not respond; merely said, 'I'll pour the sherry now. Perhaps you'd care to join me in a whisky, Charles?' The frozen tableau returned to life, though no reference was made to the painful incident.

Helen said, 'I've asked Nanny to come down later – before midnight – and see the New Year in with us. Is that all right?'

'Of course,' Arthur said without turning round.

'Are we having champagne?' Vicky asked, desperate to do her share towards restoring normality.

'Yes.'

Charles said, 'Still got some of your Clicquot '28, Arthur?'

Arthur brought him his whisky. 'Yes. Not much, though.'

'Pity. A lovely drop.'

'We'll have it tonight.'

He smiled wistfully.

'Might as well live grandly while we can.'

To everyone's relief he raised his own glass in general salutation and said, 'Well, here's to an end of 1934. May next year be ... no worse.'

They echoed his sentiment and drank to one another.

While they were at dinner, which turned out to be more festive than it might have been, Helen was summoned to the telephone by Nanny. She came back soon afterwards and resumed her seat.

'That's a nice surprise for you, Vicky,' she said. 'Aunt Phyllis. She sends her love to everyone, by the way, and wishes she was with us.'

'Why me, though?'

She wondered if, since Liz is going straight on to Wales, you'd like to go to London with Granny and Grandpapa tomorrow and stay with her for a few days. Go to some concerts and theatres. Would you?'

'Oh, yes, Mummy.'

'May she, Arthur?' Helen made a point of asking.

'Of course. Get those clothes and things for going abroad. Phyl's just the one to advise you.'

'Oh, thank you, Daddy, Mummy.'

'I said you'd ring her back yourself after dinner. She'll meet you off the train.'

'Splendid,' Charles said. 'That means the four of us can have tea together in London before we go our separate ways. All right with you, Alice?'

'So long as it isn't the station buffet, that would be nice, thank you, Charles.'

The evening was an even greater success after this. Arthur still felt the hurt of his passage with Anne but fought his feelings down. With the heat of the dispute past he was able to see that if she had gone too far for her part, he had for his. It was her reputation that mattered amongst her friends, not his, except by association. While he could hope that his family would lead precisely the kind of lives he thought best for them, and which best suited him, he could not force them to. The only ship he commanded now was their home and there had just occurred the first mutiny aboard. No doubt there would be others; but he reminded himself that more mutinies had been provoked in navies by tyrannical authority than by calculated dissension.

It would be his duty to take Anne to task in the morning; but at least she was not now shut up in her room, weeping and doubly rebellious, with the dawning of the New Year marred for them all.

Before midnight they listened on the hall wireless to the relay from the Chelsea Arts Ball. Arthur uncorked two bottles of champagne and poured. Nanny came down in her best dress to join them.

'Isn't it funny to think Liz is there?' Vicky said. 'Listen! I could swear I heard her laugh.'

'What a potent imagination,' Charles laughed.

'Or better hearing than yours,' Alice suggested. They exchanged grimaces.

'Come along, Nanny,' Arthur said. 'Some champagne for you.'

'Oh, thank you very much, sir.'

'None for you of course, Vicky.'

'Daddy!'

'Only joking. Sip it slowly, though. Make it last.'

Charles teased, 'Wasted on little girls used to lemon squash. Give it to me, eh?'

'Greedy! You've got your own.'

'Listen!'

The chimes of Big Ben were sounding. They fell silent, holding their glasses expectantly. Lady Bourne, who had remained seated, got up stiffly, aided by Charles.

The first sonorous stroke of the hour seemed ages in coming. And then they were sipping their champagne, exchanging kisses, greetings – and it was 1935.

When it was time for bed both Nanny and Vicky separately asked Helen whether they should wait up for Anne. She had already thought about it and decided that the most tactful course would be to leave her to return and go to bed without encountering anyone, thus perhaps saving a protracted and painful talk and taking away from the enjoyment which she hoped that Anne, like the rest of them, had had.

Next morning, at a little after nine, Anne came downstairs. She wore her customary tweed skirt and jumper. She looked rather washed-out and subdued to Vicky, who encountered her in the hall. Vicky was wearing her best costume and was bustling about with an air of excitement.

'I'm going up to London this morning with Granny and Grandpapa,' she bubbled. 'The Universal Aunt's invited me to go and stay and go to concerts and things, and I'm to get all my new clothes . . .'

' "Universal Aunt"?'

'Auntie Phyl. That's what Daddy called her last night after she'd phoned to invite me. Just fits her, I think.'

'I suppose so. Did he . . . say anything more . . . I mean, about me?'

'No. Nobody did. We had a jolly good time. Champagne. Did you?'

But before Anne had chance to reply Vicky had suddenly remembered something and hurried hastily to the door, saying, 'I must see Gates. Ask him to look after my bantams while I'm away. Back in a jiffy.'

Left alone, Anne looked at herself in the mirror, hesitating to go into the dining-room where breakfast would be laid for fear her father might be there. She was unsure what was in store for her, or how she should behave, and wanted to postpone the meeting as long as possible, or at least until she had been able to see her mother by herself.

Charles Ashley came out of the dining-room, carrying *The Times*. He gave her his usual warm smile.

'Happy New Year, my dear,' he greeted her and gave her a kiss.

'Happy New Year, Grandpapa.'

'Just about to tackle my first crossword of the year,' he said, sitting on the settee. He had perceived her mood at once. 'No, perhaps I'll save it for the train.'

'Is Daddy driving you to the station?'

'No, your mother. Your father was to, only he had a telephone call from Mr. ... What's his name, the farm manager?'

'Chapman? Frank Chapman.'

'That's it. He has some problem or other and it seemed pretty urgent. Your father's asked him to come over this morning.'

He looked at Anne quizzically.

'Rather like running a ship, or a school, I suppose, running an estate. Your people immediately turn to you for advice, and it's your duty to give them it. Even offer it when they don't ask for it and maybe won't be grateful for it.'

Anne smiled back at him.

'All right, Grandpapa, I know. I really am sorry about last night. I felt wretched that it might have spoilt everyone's evening.'

'Good Lord, no! Just went ahead and enjoyed ourselves. But you do see your father's point, don't you?'

'Oh, yes. I did at the time, I suppose. It was just ... well, being bossed about like that ... and being told I looked cheap.'

'Yes, well, I don't think he was too proud of that, either. Between ourselves, I gather he hadn't had too good a day. He has his worries, too, you know.'

'I know. I feel awful.'

'He's in his study.'

'Oh ...'

The implication wasn't lost on her. Visibly, she took a deep breath.

'That's right,' her grandfather said. 'Remember, someone has to be boss. And it's not easy always to be right.'

She stopped to kiss him lightly on the forehead, then went firmly to the study door, knocked, and walked in. Her father was busy with papers at the desk, his head resting on one hand. His posture and the droop of his shoulders conveyed his anxiety. A wave of remorse overcame her. He turned and looked up and a guarded expression came into his eyes, almost as if he had been fearing the meeting more than she had.

'I'm . . . sorry to disturb you,' she stammered.

'That's all right.'

'I hear Vicky's going to London.'

'Yes.'

She felt the onset of tears and stepped forward hastily to put her arms round him.

'I'm sorry, Daddy.'

He buried his face against her. In a muffled voice he said, 'That's my girl.'

'I did so want to wear my silly costume, after all the work I'd put into it.'

'I know. Let's forget it all, shall we?'

'Yes, please.'

He released himself and smiled up at her.

'Anyway, I hope you enjoyed the party.'

She shook her head. 'No, I didn't. It was awful.'

'In what way?'

'None of the young men would dance with me. They just stared at me and whispered to each other. Sonia Shale said they were all too shy because of my costume. So I never got a single dance. Just sat out and talked to Sonia. Next year I'll go as a nun.'

Arthur smiled and reached out for her again.

'You might not get any dances that way, either,' he said.

She heard Vicky returning and speaking to her grandfather. On her way to the study door Anne stopped and turned back.

'I almost forgot . . . Happy New Year, Daddy.'

'The same to you, my dear,' he said. 'A very happy one indeed.'

CHAPTER FIVE

FRANK CHAPMAN arrived promptly at half past eleven that morning. Arthur let him in and took him through to his study. Nanny and Mrs. Gates could be heard working in different parts of the house; otherwise Arthur and Frank were alone.

The farm manager was a stocky, burly native of the neighbourhood in his mid-fifties. He had spent all his working life on the Larkfield Manor estate, first as cowman, when his father was manager. He and his wife occupied the cottage which had once been Frank's now-deceased parents' and in which he himself had been born.

Their only son, Alan, like many other sons of the soil of his generation had made it plain as a schoolboy that he did not intend to perpetuate the family's agricultural tradition. He had shown an aptitude for mechanical work and had got himself a job at Halbury Motors. When it had become clear that he was well suited to it, and that the proprietor, Mr. Monks, was satisfied with him, Alan had given up the motorbike journey from his parents' cottage into Halbury and had moved into lodgings there. He visited his father and mother dutifully most week-ends: a stolid, unimaginative youth, rather slow-moving and slow speaking like his father, though with less of the Herefordshire dialect in his voice.

Frank Chapman was not a man who smiled a great deal, and his countenance expressed little of his feelings at any time. This morning, Arthur Bourne could sense rather than see that the problem Frank had asked to see him about was weighing heavily on him.

'Glorious day, Frank,' he tried, by way of a sighting shot.

'Yes, sir.'

Arthur rubbed his face with one hand as he seated himself a little stiffly in his desk swivel chair and motioned Frank to sit.

'Bit of a late night, seeing the New Year in,' he explained. 'I don't suppose early risers like you go in for that.'

The unhappiness was distinct in Frank's tone as he answered, 'We was up – but we weren't celebrating.'

'Everything . . . all right?'

'At the farm – yes, sir.'

'I see. What is it, then, Frank?'

'I didn't want to bother you, sir, only the missis . . .'

'Fire away.'

With an effort, Frank said, 'It's our Alan. Got a girl into trouble.'

Arthur was not shocked but certainly surprised.

'Oh dear!'

'Usherette at the Tivoli picture house in Halbury. The wife's all cut up about it.'

'I thought your Alan was a pretty steady type.'

'Too steady for his own good, you ask me, sir. Twenty-seven and not wed.'

'Is she his girl friend?'

Frank shrugged. 'They've been walking out for a bit – so far as he's gone steady with any of them. Afraid to let himself in for anything.'

'He seems to have done now. Do you know her?'

'Peggy Short, her name is. Her dad's a plumber with Hodsons'. She lives with him and her sister. The mother died.'

Arthur was thinking how most tactfully to point out that Alan could perhaps do worse than make this the moment to become a husband at last when Frank went on, 'She's only half his age.'

'What! But he's . . .'

'Twenty-seven. She's only seventeen, less than a year out of school.'

'Well, seventeen and twenty-seven's not so bad, Frank. Depends what sort of a girl she is really. Why's she only usheretting if she stayed at school until sixteen?'

'There's not all that much work for a girl in these parts. I dare say they're decent enough folk, only . . .'

Understanding dawned on Arthur at last.

'You're not saying Alan doesn't want to marry her?'

Chapman nodded unhappily. 'It's him all over. He won't take on responsibilities.'

'He's got to, this time.'

'You can't tell your own kids what they've to do, sir. They won't listen.'

'Mine always have,' Arthur retorted automatically, and then winced mentally at the recollection of Anne's defiance of only a few hours before.

'Yours is girls, sir,' Frank was saying. 'Maybe it's different. Anyway, Alan's a man and been living on his own four years. I can't make him do this or that.'

'Well, there's nothing in the law to compel him . . . Has he *said* he won't marry her, though?'

'He wants to go abroad – emigrate – on his own.'

Arthur stared. Frank said heavily, 'Sir – what *am* I to do?'

Arthur got up and moved to the window, to stand in a characteristic posture, legs straddled and hands clasped behind his back, staring out as if from the bridge of his ship. It was a way he often stood, unknowingly, brooding over problems of his own.

'Does anyone else know yet?' he asked at length. 'The girl's father – her sister?'

'I don't reckon so, sir. Our Alan hasn't said much to us. He won't discuss it.'

Arthur turned to face his seated employee. 'Do you want me to have a word with him?'

'I dunno. Better not, maybe. He knows you're on the Bench, and that, and you never know what he might do if he gets scared. Just up and go.'

'Perhaps you're right. Well, I'll have to think it over a bit,

Frank, I'll talk to Mrs. Bourne about it, if you don't mind.'

'Thank you, sir,' said Chapman, getting up. 'The wife thought of coming to Mrs. Bourne herself, but I said it was my place to speak to you. Only for advice, like.'

'I'm not just here to pay you a wage, you know, Frank. Your troubles are our troubles.'

'We've been very grateful for a lot of things, sir. Only . . . well, I don't reckon there's much time to waste.'

Arthur saw him out, then returned to stand at the study window, his own concerns overshadowed by this crisis. When Helen and Anne returned from taking the others to the station he lost no time in telling Helen the situation. He had as yet thought up no solution to it, and she had no pat answer, either.

'He ought to have more thought for his parents,' Arthur said. 'You know how people talk round here.'

'There is one other small consideration,' she reminded him.

'What?'

'The girl.'

'Well, of course.'

'Very much "of course". It's all very well exercising our minds on the Chapmans' behalf. What about that poor girl? Has he even told her he doesn't want to marry her – or just left her wondering?'

'Oh, now! He *is* the son of my farm manager . . .'

'That sounds just a little bit feudal, darling,' she smiled. 'Just because Alan Chapman's the son of good old dependable Frank, you expect him to come out exactly the same mould. He's not everyone's idea of Prince Charming, by a long way. Has anyone asked the girl if she even wants to marry him?'

'The Chapmans haven't even met her. I can't imagine them asking that, if they do.'

'Well, it has to be considered – though if she's going to have a child I suppose she hasn't much choice.'

Helen reached a decision. 'There's too much guesswork

going on, all round. I think you ought to speak to Alan and form your own impression of what he's likely to do.'

She had moved to the telephone and, to his horror, was asking the operator to get her Halbury 230.

'You're not getting him on the telephone – at the garage! I can't talk to him like that!'

She merely smiled and, to his mounting astonishment, embarked upon an incredible conversation with the person who answered her call.

'Hello, Mr. Monks. It's Mrs. Bourne here, Larkfield Manor ... Happy New Year to you, too. Oh, very well, thank you. Mr. Monks, I'm sorry to be a nuisance, but I don't seem able to start my car and I do rather need it this afternoon ... No, I'm afraid everything under the bonnet is a mystery to me, and I'm scared stiff of the starting handle flying back. If I knew when my husband was coming in I wouldn't trouble you, only ... Oh, could he? That would be kind. I don't suppose it's anything that will keep him long ... Thank you *so* much, Mr. Monks. Good-bye.'

Helen replaced the receiver and turned to her almost gaping husband.

'Alan Chapman will be here sometime before lunch.'

'But ... but what ...?'

'You don't have to ask him anything outright, do you? Just get into conversation and find out how things are shaping generally. Then we can discuss it again later.'

Half an hour later Alan Chapman's motorcycle engine was heard. Bracing himself mentally, Arthur went to the door. The young man was wearing his overalls and had old flying goggles dangling round his neck. In one hand he carried a pair of big flying gloves. With the other he was smoothing back his heavily oiled black straight hair.

'Hello, Alan,' Arthur greeted him over-heartily. 'Happy New Year!'

'Same to you, sir,' Alan said. He had smiled easily enough. Arthur was relieved to read no suspicion in his eyes. He launched himself upon his prepared speech.

'Look, Alan, I'm awfully sorry, but I, er, just got back myself a few minutes ago, and ... my wife said there was something wrong with her car. So I, er, took a look, and it was only one of the distributor leads jumped off. There wasn't time to get on the telephone and stop you ...'

To his relief, he saw that the story had been accepted. Alan was putting on one of the gloves.

'Oh, well, that's all right, then, sir,' he was saying. Arthur put the next stage of his plan into action.

'Er, while you're here, though, Alan, I've got a cheque you might take back to Mr. Monks for me.'

He was disconcerted to hear Alan say, 'I'll just give the engine a quick once-over while you're getting it, shall I?'

'No, no. There's really no need. Come in, will you? Cold out here.'

The bait was fully taken at last. Alan came in and followed Arthur to the study, where there began an elaborate charade of searching for the non-existent cheque.

'Always the same,' Arthur grumbled. 'You put something down and it's gone in half a minute. Ah, well, I know the amount. I'll just have to write another.'

He seated himself at the desk, got out his cheque book and uncapped his fountain pen. As he wrote the cheque slowly, not glancing up at all, he conducted his cautious interrogation.

'Keeping well, Alan? We don't see much of you these days.'

'Thanks, sir.'

'Your digs all right still?'

'Can't grumble.'

'How, er, long is it now – you've been at Halbury Motors?'

'Coming up five years.'

'Really! Quite an old hand.'

'Suppose so.'

Arthur ventured, 'You planning to stay?' He was not surprised to hear no response. He ploughed on with difficulty, 'I mean, young men seem to be moving about so much these days. Into the cities ... going abroad ... that sort of thing ...'

There was a distinct wariness about Alan's brief reply.

'Mr. Monks is a good boss.'

Arthur signed the cheque and looked up. He could see that Alan was suspicious now, and dared press him no further. He tore out the cheque and handed it over.

'Ask Mr. Monks to send me a receipt, will you?'

Alan nodded and silently took his leave. When he heard the motorboke start up, rev briefly, then roar away, Arthur seemed to detect a note of anger in the noise. He was standing in the hall. Helen came downstairs to join him.

'Well!' she said, amused. 'And they say something about Naval officers being natural diplomats.'

'You were listening!'

'Of course. "Could do better".'

'Well, if it didn't get us far, I doubt if it did any real harm.'

She surprised him yet again by saying, 'Wouldn't it be ironic if the car didn't start, after all?'

'Eh?'

'I do need it this afternoon.'

'Where are you going?'

'Into Halbury. To the matinee at the Tivoli.'

He shook his head wonderingly, marvelling as always at the devious ways of women.

The Tivoli was a modest establishment for that heyday of the cinema. No Wurlitzer organ, sweetshop, elaborate decoration or deep carpeting. Just a small foyer and ticket box and, at the other side of the curtained doorway, a functionally equipped auditorium.

Helen bought her ticket and passed through the curtain, pausing to adjust her eyes to the darkness and flickering blue light from the screen. From the seat nearest the doorway a figure rose and a torch flashed on her outheld ticket.

'Good afternoon,' the girl said politely. 'Anywhere you like, madam.'

She flashed the torch around. Helen could see that the place was almost deserted.

'This will do,' she said, choosing a seat in the second row from the back. She kept her coat on and settled her handbag and gloves in her lap. She heard the girl sit down again behind her.

For a few moments she watched the screen. The feature film had begun and there was a protracted two-handed scene in progress between the obvious hero-to-be and the heroine, neither of whom at this stage, it was clear, could see that they were upon the brink of being engulfed by something which was Bigger Than Both Of Them.

After a very brief scrutiny of this, Helen turned her head. The girl behind her was sitting inertly, her torch in her lap, her eyes clearly not focused upon the screen.

'Miss Short?' Helen asked softly. 'Peggy?'

The girl came to. She stared and said guardly, 'Yes?'

'I'm Mrs. Bourne, from Larkfield Manor. My husband, Commander Bourne, employs Alan Chapman's father.'

Comprehension came into the girl's eyes. 'Oh, yes. He's mentioned you.'

'Kindly, I hope?'

'Oh, yes.'

Helen moved out of her seat and went up the single step to the back row. She sat down next to Peggy Short, who was watching her warily. The girl was pleasant looking, far from being a beauty, but attractive in a homely, slightly plump way.

'Look, Peggy,' Helen said, anxious to get to the point before any influx of patrons might prevent her, 'Alan's father's told us all about you and Alan. We want to help you.'

Outright suspicion was now manifest in the girl's eyes.

'You don't know me. I'm a stranger.'

'Not to us. Alan's parents have lived and worked on our estate for years. He was born in their cottage.'

'I've never been to their place.'

'Well, what I'm trying to say is that we know what kind of people they are. They're as good and respectable as you'd find anywhere.'

'Until I came along, I suppose.'

'Now please don't be silly.'

'It's what people are going to say, isn't it?'

'Peggy, I want you to tell me something straight away, please. Has Alan asked you to marry him?'

There was the briefest pause, then, 'Not ... yet.'

'How long is it ... since ...?'

'A few weeks.'

'Have you seen a doctor?'

'I didn't need to. I know. I wouldn't pretend. I want to know if he's going to marry me. That's all I want to know.'

The girl was obviously close to tears and relieved to be able to discuss it at last. To Helen's annoyance a young couple came through the curtain at that moment and Peggy Short had to direct them to seats. Helen hoped that the achievement of contact hadn't been wasted. She wondered whether the girl would even return to the seat next to her, but she did.

Helen resumed at once, 'He hasn't said he *won't* marry you?'

'Not exactly. But he hasn't said he will. He isn't going to, is he? You've come to tell me!'

'Sssh. No, Peggy. Just to find out a few things.'

Fully convinced at last, the girl poured out her thoughts with pathetic directness.

'I've got nothing against Alan. It was my fault as much as his. It was ... it was only the once, after a dance. If he doesn't want to marry me I shan't chase after him. You don't want someone to feel they're stuck with you, and hate you.'

She made the effort of pulling herself together.

'I'm sorry, Mrs. Bourne. It's not knowing, you see.'

Helen nodded. 'I want you to tell me one thing, if you will, because it's very important. It's important to you, more

87

than to anyone else. If this .. hadn't happened, would you have wanted to marry Alan?'

'Oh, yes! If he'd ever got round to asking.'

'Wouldn't he have done?'

'I don't know. It's as if he's meaning to say something, and then just can't.'

'Do you love him?'

'It's not for me to tell him that, is it?'

'Not in so many words . . .'

'I mean, I can cook, and make, and housekeep. I look after my Dad and Elsie – she's still at school.'

'They don't know, do they – about this?'

'They'll have to in time. Dad'll have a fit.'

More abruptly, Helen asked, 'Does Alan love you?'

The reply came almost fiercely and with surprising perception.

'Yes! I know he's been with other girls before, but I can tell, as if I can see right inside him. It's like them, on the films. You can always tell when they first see each other how they're going to feel – but one of them can't see it until nearly the end of the picture, and the other just has to go on hoping they will.'

Helen smiled and patted her hand, at the same time gathering her bag and gloves.

'If you see Alan, please don't tell him we've had this talk,' she said. 'Promise?' She started to get up.

'What's going to happen, Mrs. Bourne?' Peggy asked desperately.

'All I can say at present is try not to worry.'

Without conviction Peggy said, 'I'll try. I'm very grateful.'

As Helen got up, she did too.

'Aren't you going to watch the film through?'

Helen smiled again at the ingenuous inquiry.

'As you said, Peggy, we know already how it will turn out for them. Real life needs a little more working on.'

Over tea that afternoon, Helen and Arthur, who had debated briefly whether they should do so or not, and then reminded one another that they must stop looking upon their daughters as children confided in Anne, now rested from the previous night's experience and perhaps a little matured by it. She snorted.

'It sounds to me as if she'd be wasted on him. He's a wet lettuce, Alan Chapman.'

'At least,' her father surprised her by saying, 'he's capable of becoming a father at one go.'

'Arthur!' Helen protested.

Anne giggled. 'I thought that quite good, coming from Daddy.'

Helen said, 'Alan's a bit of an unsteady type, that's all. Once in captivity, they probably make good husbands.'

'I know the type,' Arthur nodded. 'They don't look for promotion. Probably decline it if it's offered. Just happy doing the job they know, and jolly dependable at it.'

Anne couldn't resist trying to cap her father's earlier remark.

'Well, if Alan Chapman's going to go on doing the job *he's* proved so good at ...'

'That's enough, Anne,' her mother reproved sharply, getting to her feet. 'I'm sorry for the poor girl. I'm trying to think what we should do.'

She wandered to the fireplace and sought brief inspiration in the flames. Then her eye caught one of the ornaments on the carved white-painted mantelpiece. It was a small 19th century pottery pastille burner in the form of a country cottage, entwined with roses. She lifted off the detachable red roof and put it back on again thoughtfully.

'The old keeper's cottage across the pasture ...' she said suddenly, surprising both Arthur and Anne. 'For them to live in. Alan and Peggy ...'

'You mean ... *if* he'd marry her?'

'Of course.'

Arthur replied slowly, thoughtfully. 'It's been empty for three years ...'

'But it's perfectly sound and dry, isn't it?'

'What a good idea, Mummy!' Anne enthused. 'He could go on working at the garage. She'll have to give up usheretting, anyway.'

'There remains the matter of getting him to marry her.'

'I think you've hit the nail on the head,' Arthur told Helen. 'What Alan's really afraid of is how they'll manage if they do marry. I don't suppose he's got much money, and Frank won't have any to give him. There isn't much housing to be had cheaply round here.'

'Exactly. He probably sees himself having to give up his job and leave the district, with a wife and baby to be responsible for. It's just the sort of situation he'd tend to run away from.'

Arthur said, 'The cottage isn't a paradise on earth, mind you. I'd have let it ages ago if I'd had the money to do it up.'

'Then charge them the lowest rent we can without making it look too much like charity, and give them a free hand with it. I've a feeling Alan could do wonders.'

Arthur looked at his watch. 'I'll go and speak to Frank straight away,' he said. 'The offer will have to be put through him.'

But it was a gloomy Frank Chapman who turned up at the house to report next morning.

'He wouldn't talk about it, sir. Said he's sent for some leaflets about Canada.'

'Oh, lor'! But did he actually say no to the cottage?'

'Not like that. We weren't on the telephone more than a minute or two. He said he was just going out when I'd got him at his digs.'

Actually, Alan had been going out and had been glad of the excuse to get his father off his landlady's telephone. His appointment was to see Peggy at the Tivoli, where she was on duty. What he did not know was that Helen had paid another swift visit there and told Peggy of the offer of the cottage, which Alan had not been going to mention. He was disconcerted and annoyed when she did, as they sat side by side looking at some cartoon idiocy.

'Mrs. Bourne says it's sound and dry,' Peggy persisted over the quacking of the dialogue. 'It'd be a home.'

He didn't answer.

'You could come into the garage and back on your motor-bike. I'll have to give this up, anyway.'

Without taking his eyes off the screen, Alan said bitterly, 'It's a proper mess. What's the good of an old cottage that's been empty for years? It's rotten through, I'll bet.'

'When did you see in it last?'

'A . . . while back.'

'It'd do, Alan. Honest, I wouldn't mind. You're a clever handyman and I could help. They've offered us a completely free hand with it.'

'Yeh. And who gets houses for next to nothing these days? There'll be a catch to it. Next thing, they'll want me working on the farm.'

'There was nothing said about that.'

'Not now, maybe.'

He had lit upon an excuse to convince himself, and could therefore use it confidently on her.

'Just you wait till after. They'll not get me working on any farm for twopence-halfpenny a day. I've watched my dad all these years, and a long way it's got him. Come to that, Halbury Motors isn't all there is in the world.'

'I know, love. There must be bigger places.'

'Yeh. Brummaghen! No thanks. More like Canada.'

'Canada!'

'I've heard they want mechanics. Skilled men. There's opportunities in Canada.'

She answered tentatively, hopefully, 'Well, I . . . I wouldn't mind . . . as long as . . .'

But he didn't turn his eyes to her. She searched his profile and knew that he had not meant it the way she had hoped.

Frank Chapman had scarcely finished speaking to Arthur and gone back to the farm when there came a ring at the front door. It was close to lunchtime. Helen and Mrs. Gates were busy in the kitchen and Anne was just back from a ride. She went to the door and came back with a tall man in early middle age, wearing an overcoat and carrying his hat.

'Daddy,' Anne said, 'this is Mr. Wickham to see you.'

'Headmaster of Halbury School,' the man explained in a marked northern accent. He did not smile and made no gesture to shake hands.

'Oh, yes,' Arthur smiled. 'We haven't met, have we? I was just going to have a glass of sherry before lunch. Would you . . .?'

'I don't, thank you. Mr. Bourne, I don't want to take up your time. If I could have a word . . . in private, please.'

'I see,' Arthur answered, sensing that the word did not promise to be an agreeable one. 'My study's through here.'

In the study, with the door closed, Mr. Wickham remained standing. He had not looked about him since entering the house. He was clearly a man with a purpose.

'I've been talking to one Alan Chapman,' he said. 'I think you know who I mean.'

'I do indeed.' Arthur was very surprised. 'When?'

'About an hour ago. I took a bus straight out here. No doubt you can guess it's about this business of Peggy Short. She happens to be a former pupil at my school.'

'Oh, yes. Unfortunate business.'

'Yes. But I gather you condone the relationship.'

Arthur shook his head. 'It's not my business to condone or otherwise, Mr. Wickham. Alan's father is a long-standing employee of mine. Not unnaturally, he came to me for advice about his son. I . . . my wife and I are trying to help.'

Wickham's eyebrows had risen during this. Arthur judged him to be a man with a very low flashpoint of anger.

'Are you telling me that you, a Justice of the Peace, can say you don't condemn it?'

'Oh, come now!' Arthur tried to turn the anger aside with a smile. 'These things happen. They haven't committed a crime.'

'That's a matter of opinion.'

'Mr. Wickham, were you ever in the Services?'

'I fail to see what that's got ... Yes, as a matter of fact, I was in the Army.'

'And you can still be shocked by a situation like this?'

Wickham nearly, but not quite, shook a forefinger.

'Don't misinterpret me, Mr. Bourne. I deplore what these two have done. And the fact that the man is ten years older than Peggy tastes pretty nasty to me. But that's not the point. What does shock me is the action you've seen fit to take.'

'Oh, you mean by offering them a cottage to live in?' Arthur could not restrain the sarcasm. 'Is that what you object to?'

'Everything it implies, yes. It smacks to me of paternalism and patronage. There was a time when a country gentleman could order the lives of his tenants how he chose. Well, those days are over, Mr. Bourne.'

Arthur swallowed hard, before answering. 'I'm usually addressed as Commander, if it's all the same to you.'

'Oh, my apologies, *Commander*.'

'No, no. It's not self-aggrandizement. It's a custom of my old Service, the Royal Navy, whose traditions I happen to cherish and try to uphold. You see, when I first entered the Navy I learnt that it is an officer's duty to be concerned for the private lives of the men under his command.'

'Ah! You did say *under* his command?'

'I meant the men for whom he is responsible.'

'Well, I didn't come here for a lecture on Naval tradition. I came ...'

'I'm not giving you one. I'm attempting to explain my own attitude towards Alan Chapman and Peggy Short.'

'Oh! And where's the connection with sailors on a battle-ship?'

'If you'll let me explain ... A sailor with a problem on his mind is an unhappy and inefficient fellow. He goes to his Petty Officer. If his advice can't help, he goes to the Officer of his Watch. If that doesn't resolve it, he takes the problem all

93

the way up to his Captain: the father of his ship. Paternalism, as you'd call it, yes, at every stage. And believe me, it gets results.'

Wickham almost sneered. 'Thanks very much for enlightening me. I've heard it said you're an easy touch on the Bench, and now I know why.'

'I try to help people when it's help they need, not punishment. If that's what you mean by an easy touch, then yes, I am.'

'And, of course, you're the best judge of which it should be.'

'Not at all. I happen to have seen the results of just and unjust punishment often enough . . .'

It was as though something had snapped in the schoolmaster's mind. He shouted, 'You're supposed to be a Justice of the Peace. An officer of the Law, not the damn Navy!'

'Kindly watch your language in this house.'

Ignoring the rebuke, Wickham continued, 'Since you seem uncertain of your duty in the matter, I'd better tell you it. Instead of trying to use your local influence and wealth to buy young Chapman's consent to marry the girl, it seems to me you should be explaining to him the meaning of a Paternity Order. As it happens, I've saved you the trouble . . .'

Arthur was horrified. 'You've *what*!'

'Luckily, after some sort of unsatisfactory conversation with young Chapman last night, the girl came to my wife. My wife reported the matter to me and I decided to speak to him myself this morning.'

'Of all the idiotic . . . ! Don't you realize that . . .'

'I realize that the Law Society, or whoever else controls J.Ps., might have something to say about a gentleman magistrate covering up a case like this until his employee's erring son can wriggle off the hook and leave the girl in the lurch. Or was it a nice chance to get a free maidservant by way of payment in kind? Of course, the wretched girl wouldn't suspect anything like that, would she? Just be oh so grateful to the kindly squire and his lady.'

94

At that moment, Arthur came very close to hitting him. Clenching his hands at his side he said, 'You will please not refer to my wife in that tone. In my opinion, you're in no state to discuss this rationally, nor are you likely to understand my actions and motives.'

'Aren't I?'

'And, incidentally, an Affiliation Order, as it's called, can't be applied for until a child is born. In the meantime, there is no law to compel a marriage between the two parties in dispute.'

Arthur strode to the study door and jerked it open, saying, 'If you want to question my conduct as a J.P. I suggest you go to the Lord Lieutenant of the County. Or you could try the Lord Chancellor. You'll find him in London – sitting on a sack of wool.'

Helen, coming down the stairs, had paused at the bend of them, listening surprised to Arthur's raised voice. She saw the recipient of his anger leave the study and cross the hall to the front door, saying at the evident height of anger, 'I'm not entirely ignorant, even if I wasn't an officer in the Royal Navy. You're not getting away with this, I can tell you that.'

The front door opened and slammed. Helen came down to find Arthur making angrily for the whisky bottle for the second time inside a week.

For once he found it hard to shake off the feeling of upset which inevitably followed. It soured his luncheon, so that indigestion nagged at him. Apart from reporting to Helen and Anne what had passed, he chose to keep off the subject of Alan Chapman, heartily wishing the boy hadn't made a mess of things in the first place.

He was extra annoyed because he had to attend the cricket club's annual dinner that evening, to which he had been looking forward. Despite Helen's soothing re-assurances, he was still in morose mood when he set off. She and Anne were almost glad to have him out of the house. They sat in front of the hall fire, Anne reading *Horse and Hound*, her mother taking up a skirt hem for her. Nanny had reclaimed the machine after the affair of the party dress and Anne lacked the patience to sew by hand.

'There!' Helen said at length. 'That's done.'

'Oh, thanks.' Anne had not raised her eyes from the magazine.

'Well, try it.'

'I'm sure it's fine, Mummy.'

'Honestly, you are the end! Jolly well do your own altering in future.'

Anne smiled up. 'Sorry, Mummy. I wonder how Daddy's getting on?'

'I hope he's had one or two stiff drinks. All that cricket talk should take his mind off things, poor dear.'

Anne said, 'If Alan would take the cottage, Peggy could always come and help here, once she's had to stop work. It would take a lot off Nanny.'

'For heaven's sake don't say that,' Helen groaned. 'That schoolmaster accused your father of wanting to get himself a free domestic servant.'

'Well, perhaps that's the way Alan Chapman's looking at it, too.'

'You might be right. More from his own point of view than Peggy's, though. Yes, he probably sees himself becoming some sort of appendage to us, in a tied cottage.'

'Gosh, if I were Peggy Short I'd sooner dust and sweep someone's nice house than be an usherette in some flea-pit of a cinema.'

'I agree, dear. I'd rather be a waitress than sit there in the dark.'

'Any day. By the way, did I tell you Susan Riley's thinking of applying for that job at the Copper Kettle for a few weeks until she goes abroad?'

'What job?'

'Waitress. The last one was hopeless, apparently. Miss Pringle's got a notice in the window.'

Helen became thoughtful.

'D'you know,' she said, 'it's ages since I went in there. Is it still the same?'

'Oh, yes. The same old ladies whispering at corner tables.'

'The perfect place, in fact, for a confidential chat with someone.'

'Mummy, you're cooking something up! Peggy Short again?'

'Not this time. Someone else.'

Elizabeth, away in Wales, would have felt her stomach sink rapidly if she could have seen her mother entering the Copper Kettle so soon after her own long afternoon there with Dr. Brian Harrington. Perhaps fortunately for her, Miss Pringle was far too busy to linger for any conversation with her mother. The morning coffee trade was at its height and she was still without a waitress.

'I'm waiting for someone,' Helen explained, taking a corner table for two, keeping on her coat and hat. 'Oh, perhaps . . .'

She had seen another lady enter and stand uncertainly, as though looking for someone.

'That's Mrs. Wickham,' Miss Pringle explained. 'Is she . . .?'

'Yes.'

Miss Pringle brought the newcomer across. After they had shaken hands, Helen said, 'I'm going to have coffee and biscuits, please. What about you, Mrs. Wickham?'

'I'll . . . have the same, please.'

From her guest's manner and tone, Helen could read her guardedness at this encounter, which was in response to a telephone call she had made to Mrs. Wickham that morning, at a time when she had judged her husband would already have left for school. The headmaster's wife appeared older than he, with more lines to her face and a harassed look about the eyes.

She did not attempt to open a conversation.

'It's bitter, isn't it?' Helen said with an expressive little shiver. 'I'm sure we shall get snow by tonight.'

'I shouldn't be surprised.'

'I like to see snow on the countryside, but it gets so messy on the pavements.'

'Yes.'

'Telling people to wipe their feet all the time. Have you a family, Mrs. Wickham?'

'A son. Yes.'

'Does he live with you here?'

'No. He married and stayed in Birmingham.'

'Oh. That was where you came from to Halbury?'

'That's right.'

'Quite a change,' Helen said. She could feel herself beginning to run out of commonplaces and knew that Mrs. Wickham was only waiting for her to come to the point of the invitation. She was reprieved by Miss Pringle's return with the tray of coffee things. When they had been set out and Miss Pringle had gone, Helen poured for them both, saying, 'This is a nice little place, isn't it. I used to . . .'

'Mrs. Bourne . . .' Mrs. Wickham took over the initiative for the first time. 'Why did you invite me?'

Helen knew she must be careful how she replied.

'I thought it would be a good idea. You know our husbands have met?'

Mrs. Wickham nodded, unhappily, Helen thought. She smiled at the headmaster's wife, and said, 'It seems they didn't find much common ground. So I wondered if . . . if we could.'

Mrs. Wickham's reply came with the suddenness of relief and even the hint of a smile.

'Yes, I wondered if that was it. Well, I agree, Mrs. Bourne. I think if you hadn't telephoned me I would have rung you. I *think* I would . . . if only to apologize for my husband.'

'Oh, no . . .'

'He gets emotional very easily. He was shell-shocked in the war. It wasn't bad enough for him to be discharged. They moved him into the Educational Corps. He was a Sergeant. He has these terrible moods – tempers – just like that.'

'I do understand,' Helen replied sincerely. 'My husband served in the war, too. He does appreciate your husband's concern for one of his former pupils. I don't imagine all schoolmasters think twice about their pupils, once they've left school.'

'I'm afraid that's true.'

Helen said earnestly, 'Alan Chapman's very much to blame for what's happened. But, you see, we know his character quite well. He's basically as decent and honest as his parents. He just has this touch of weakness – inability to face responsibility. It's quite a common failing, isn't it?'

'I'm sure it is.'

'Peggy wants to marry him. His parents want him to. Insofar as it's any of our business, *we* think it would work very well. But the move has to be made by Alan himself.'

'*If* he makes it.'

'If nothing happens to make him panic in the meantime. And that's why, if you'll forgive my saying so, your husband could do more harm than good if he tries to force him. Talk of Affiliation Orders and things like that.'

Mrs. Wickham nodded, her countenance gloomy again. 'If he should get worked up about it again – one of his moods . . .'

Once more, Helen chose her words carefully. 'Why – I mean, apart from this emotional difficulty, which I'm very sorry about – why does your husband feel so resentful at our trying to help?'

She reached over and poured Mrs. Wickham more coffee, giving her the chance to consider a reply which was clearly difficult to make.

'You see,' Mrs. Wickham said at length, 'you have to understand that he had to leave school early and do a man's work. Everything he's achieved has been by his own efforts. No one helped him at any stage. And yet he's spent all his career helping others. *Trying* to help them, I should say, in spite of themselves and their families. He taught for years in Birmingham, in the Ladywood area, one of the worst.'

'I've heard about it.'

'You see everything there – utter poverty, despair, crime, violence, promiscuity. It's a very different world from ... well, around here.'

Her gesture signified not only the pretty town of Halbury and its surroundings, but rurality in general.

'The fact that you just happen to have an empty cottage to offer – *happen* to have, when most people we're used to living amongst lived several families to a house – to a room, even ... In my husband's mind that's the squire being able to take people under his wing, or turn them off again without a penny, just as and when he pleases.'

'Yes, I see,' Helen nodded. 'Is that how you see us, too, Mrs. Wickham?'

She could detect a struggle between frankness and civility.

'I ... It's hard to say. You do live in a manor house and have a lot of land. Your husband's a Commander and a J.P. All that sort of thing.'

'The squire and his lady, lording it up at the manor? Well, I can assure you we're not in the least bit grand. We live very simply. My husband inherited a lot of responsibilities and expense with the estate, you know.'

Mrs. Wickham didn't appear altogether convinced, though. Helen tried again.

'Your husband has been to our house. Didn't he tell you it isn't particularly luxurious?'

Mrs. Wickham smiled wistfully. 'Of course, I asked him, out of sheer curiosity. He couldn't tell me. I don't think he'd noticed his surroundings at all.'

Helen put down her coffee cup suddenly. 'Why don't you both come to tea with us?'

'Oh, I ...!'

'Please do. I promise you there's no acrimony on my husband's part. And since we're all concerned about this problem, and there isn't all the time in the world to spare, perhaps we'd better thrash it out over a friendly cup of tea.'

Mrs. Wickham hesitated still. Once again Miss Pringle

took the edge off the tension by returning to ask, 'Would you like some more coffee, ladies?'

It was at Helen that Mrs. Wickham smiled as she answered, 'Why not?'

An appointment was fixed for half-past four the following afternoon, although Mrs. Wickham added the proviso that she would have to telephone and cancel it if her husband refused to come. She was fairly confident that he would agree, having already expressed to her his remorse for the rude behaviour he had been unable to suppress. No telephone call was received and Helen mustered Anne's assistance in preparing the tea things.

'I can't think what you hope to achieve,' Anne said. 'In fact, I'm getting rather bored with the whole business. What with that rude man barging in here insulting Daddy, all over a bit of a girl we don't even know, and that soft, greasy-haired Alan Chapman.'

'Please, Anne, that'll do. Just be polite to them, and . . .'

The doorbell rang. They stared at one another.

'Oh, no!' Helen exclaimed, instinctively touching her hair. 'Not already!'

Anne took a quick glance from the window. 'I think it is. It's only just gone four.'

'Go and let them in,' Helen ordered, tugging off her apron and pushing it under a cushion, pausing in front of the mirror to pat her hair straight. 'Arthur!'

Arthur came inquiringly out of the study just as Anne came back from the front door saying, 'Mummy, Mr. and Mrs. Wickham.'

'I'm so sorry, Mrs. Bourne,' Mrs. Wickham was saying, 'There wouldn't have been another bus for an hour, so we risked coming early rather than late.'

'That's quite all right. How do you do, Mr. Wickham?'

The headmaster, who had been standing a pace or so behind his wife, came forward almost eagerly to shake hands. He was smiling shyly.

When the greetings and introductions were over Helen returned to the kitchen with Anne, leaving Arthur to remove from the settee and chairs the magazines and sewing things which they had been leaving until last. The homely clutter, though not intended for the visitors' sight, was not lost on Mr. Wickham as his eyes roved the room: the worn carpet contrasting with much-polished antique furniture; thin patches in the upholstery of the chair arms; Staffordshire flatback figures on the mantelpiece, flanking a cottage-shaped ornament and a box of matches; a grand piano, liberally bestrewn with music, magazines and the morning's newspaper; and the contents of the chairs, which Arthur Bourne was tutting over to Mrs. Wickham.

'Pins and needles are a constant hazard here,' he was apologizing. 'I do hate muddle, but it's a losing battle.'

'That's the Navy, I suppose,' Mrs. Wickham offered. 'All that polished brass and coiled ropes. Everything ... ship-shape.'

'Fortunately,' Arthur answered unthinking, 'the Navy isn't run by women who sew. Oh, I do beg your pardon, Mrs. Wickham.'

He was relieved to hear her husband chuckle, 'I agree all the way.'

When enough of the jumble had been cleared, Arthur indicated a chair for Mrs. Wickham and the settee for her husband. The headmaster sat down, winced and grimaced, then half-stood again, feeling the seat of his trousers.

'I think one of them's got me,' he said.

Anne, at the kitchen doorway, couldn't suppress a giggle.

'Anne! Really!' her mother said at her elbow; but Mr. Wickham was grinning.

'Here I've been,' he declared, 'all these years, talking about people being sharp as a needle – and I've only just found out what it means.'

They all joined in his laughter.

The Sunday morning church bells were pealing. Arthur

Bourne, in his dark suit, looked at his watch, wondering just how much longer everyone was likely to be. Helen and Anne were upstairs, getting ready for church. Frank Chapman stood with him in the hall. He was frowning.

'I dunno what it's all about, sir. What's the headmaster of Halbury School got to do with our Alan's affairs?'

Arthur was in airy mood, more relaxed than he had been since New Year's Eve.

'Didn't Alan tell you?'

'Nothing.'

'Then it doesn't matter, does it?'

The countryman regarded him suspiciously. 'You ask me, sir, there's been some conniving going on that I don't know about.'

'Oh, I wouldn't say conniving, exactly.'

Frank sighed. 'Well, it's not for me to ask too many questions. All I know is that our Alan and Peggy are looking at your cottage this minute.'

'Yes. And I hope they won't be too long.'

The doorbell went.

'Ah! Come on, Frank. And fingers crossed.'

Chapman did cross two thick fingers of his left hand as they went to the door together. Arthur opened it and admitted Alan and Peggy. There was a moment's anxious searching of the young couple's expressions before Frank asked, 'Is . . . is it all right?'

His son grinned. 'Just the place, Dad.'

Arthur saw Frank's shoulders positively heave with his breath of relief.

'Oh, it's lovely!' Peggy Short was saying. 'All those beams – and that big fireplace!'

'Well,' Arthur said, as relieved as Frank Chapman, you certainly won't find time on your hands. There's a lot to do to it.'

Peggy turned to him. 'Alan says he can do anything in that line, sir. Can he, Mr. Chapman?' she asked Frank.

'He can't wash up or help keep a place tidy – I'll warn you of that.'

They laughed happily.

'So,' Arthur asked, 'it'll really suit you both?'

'Down to the ground, sir, thanks very much,' Alan replied.

'Of course, you couldn't live there straight away. It'll take a few weeks even to make it habitable.'

Alan glanced at Peggy's figure, as yet showing no sign of the baby. 'I reckon we can afford to wait a while, sir,' he said.

Frank said tentatively, 'Would you . . . both . . . come and live with me and your mum, meantime?'

'We couldn't do that, Dad,' Alan answered, startled. 'I mean, it wouldn't be . . .'

Peggy tugged at his arm. 'Of course we could, Alan.'

'Good for you, girl!' Frank chuckled. 'You start as you mean to go on with him.'

'You heard your dad, Alan. You know we couldn't live in your digs, and it'd be hopeless at my dad's. Yes, thanks very much, Mr. Chapman. If we're wanted, we'll be very much obliged – and we won't outstay our welcome.'

Frank impulsively stepped forward and gave her a warm hug and a kiss. Arthur shook Alan by the hand, saying, 'Congratulations. Everyone will be delighted. Er, when er . . .?'

Alan glanced towards Peggy and caught her eye. There was no mistaking the resolution in it. He replied, 'I reckon pretty soon, sir. Before her dad hears and gets his shotgun out.'

Frank turned to look him in the eyes. Arthur, who had known him since long before Alan had been born, was surprised to hear him say, 'Don't you mock at shotgun weddings, boy. Your mother and me had one twenty-eight years ago next month. I don't reckon it's lasted too bad. Now, come along, the pair of you, and talk to your mum. The Commander's waiting to go to church.'

They went, talking eagerly. Arthur put on his coat, looked at his watch again, and was just going to the foot of the stairs to call up when Helen and Anne came down in their hats and coats.

'Was I *seeing* things just now, from the window?' Helen asked.

'Alan's accepted the cottage,' Arthur answered matter-of-factly. 'We'll be late.'

'But . . . what made up his mind for him?'

'Well, don't fall down in a faint, or anything, but it was Wickham. It seems he went back to Alan and persuaded him what a chance it was for them to start married life in a cottage of their own. Said he'd known hundreds of young couples who'd have given their right arms for the chance. Now do let's get a move on . . .'

The single bell was tolling now. They moved towards the door.

'It was making friends with her and having them here to tea,' Helen said, smug with herself.

'Yes,' Anne agreed. 'Showing them we weren't horrible rich nasty people.'

'I expect so,' Arthur was content to answer. 'Come *on*, now.'

He almost pushed them through the front door, the head of the family ushering his charges to church one cold, sunny morning in England in 1935.

CHAPTER SIX

CROCUSES – yellow, purple and white – stabbed gently through the grass around the cedar tree, and, approved by the sun, ventured boldly forth to form miniature thickets of bright colour.

A few weeks had passed since Christmas. Vicky had gone off to the von Heynigs at Munich, well equipped with new clothes and new confidence in herself. Her letters displayed increasing enthusiasm: where she had once been resentful about going, she was now grateful for having been sent.

Liz returned from Wales, though not to Larkfield Manor. She stayed in London, part of the time with her Aunt Phyllis, and worked hard in medical libraries on her thesis. She thought often of Brian Harrington, but more in a speculative way than as a yearning. She was surprised, and rather annoyed, to have proved so vulnerable, to have fallen so suddenly and so intensely for him that she had virtually had to run away from his presence to prevent being overwhelmed and doing something rash. She, who at Oxford had been so much one of the anti-romantic love brigade, and had often saddened her mother by her scornful rejection of the notion of marriage.

So far as Helen and Arthur knew, these were still her feelings. Anne had kept her secret faithfully, refraining from so much as a hint that Liz might be more susceptible than she had always made out. Anne knew how much this would have pleased her mother. If Liz's brief encounter had been with anyone else, she might have alluded to it off-handedly; but the fact that it had been with the family doctor made the risk of interrogation too great for Anne to take.

Dr. Cropper had still not left the district and Dr. Harrington's wife had not yet come to it. Having had no need for medical services since Liz's cold, the Bournes had had no contact with either of them. The fact of Dr. Harrington's wife's not having joined him yet reached the ears of none of the household.

But Fate, having been thwarted once by Liz's decisive action, was now ready for another foray. Nanny Benson awoke one morning feeling unwell and drained of energy, and could not leave her bed. The surgery was telephoned and Dr. Harrington said he would come out. While Helen was waiting for him, the telephone rang. It was Liz, to say she was coming home at last.

Helen told him this when he arrived and made his polite routine inquiry as to the wellbeing of the various family members. Anne was with her. She watched him interestedly and was almost disappointed that there was no dramatic reaction to the news; in fact, no visible reaction at all. He went on to ask how old Nanny Benson was – about sixty-eight, Helen calculated, though she looked older and would never tell anyone when she was born – and then he went upstairs, bag in hand, escorted by Helen.

The following afternoon Anne was in the tack room warm with the scent of her pony Tallulah, surrounded by her Pony Club rosettes, when Liz hailed her across the half-door.

'Well, well!' Liz exclaimed. 'Fancy you doing some work for once!'

'I've always cleaned my own tack, you know. I asked Gates to do it last week, but Daddy was not amused. Liz, it's lovely to see you!'

Liz came in and they embraced.

'I've got a car,' Liz said. 'Did they tell you?'

'Yes. A Wolseley Hornet, isn't it? Daddy said he wished you'd waited to buy it from Halbury Motors. They need the business.'

'It isn't a new one. A friend of a friend was selling it off quickly, so I grabbed it. I only just had enough in the bank.'

'Well, lucky you, all the same. I wish I'd a car of my own.'

'You spend all your money on that horse of yours.'

'I wouldn't swop Tallulah for a Rolls-Royce, would I, Tallulah darling?'

'Ugh!'

'Anyway, how was London? What've you been doing?'

'I wrote my thesis – only a short one. Some extra-mural lectures at University College Hospital. I went out quite a lot with Phyllis. She really is angelic. She was always introducing me to interesting men. I think ... she knew I was running away from a love affaire.'

'Any good – any of them?'

'Not really.'

'So the escape from your doctor heartthrob didn't work?'

'I wouldn't say that.'

'You mean, you *have* got over him?'

'I think so. I'm nearly sure.'

'Funny, he was here yesterday. For the first time since ...'

'Yes, Mummy told me. Anyway, what about you, Anne?'

'Oh, everything much the same. I've got a new young man, though.'

'Who?'

'He's called Michael Sherwood. He's twenty-six. Been to Ampleforth and Cambridge. I met him at that ghastly fancy dress dance. He was about the only one who dared to talk to me. I suppose because he was dressed as Mephistopheles.'

'What's he do?'

'The City, poor dear. A commodity broker in his uncle's firm. But he's taken up flying with the Auxiliary Air Force. They fly Hawkers – they're fighter planes – at Hendon at week-ends.'

'I'm duly impressed.'

'He's coming to stay this week-end. But Daddy may not approve.'

'Why not?'

'Well, Michael's a Roman Catholic.'

'Oh. Bad luck.'

It wasn't that their father was renowned for religious bigotry or prejudice; just that his family had always been Anglicans and that he had been known to declare, from time to time, that no child of his would marry out of their church. So far, there had been no occasion for the strength of this resolution to be tested. But it was a ready-made obstacle for the first one who might chance to come to it.

'Ah, well!' Anne sighed philosophically. 'Anyway, did you see anything of Oliver Manson in town?'

Oliver Manson was a county young gentleman who had been a friend of the family since childhood and a contemporary of Liz. He was a well-off bachelor farmer. Helen was well known to have hopes that he and Elizabeth would one day make the first match of the Bourne girls, and it was with Oliver especially in mind that she had been so disappointed by Liz's refusal to take any interest in getting married.

'Yes,' she told Anne. 'Once or twice. He drove me through the City in the Hornet when I got her. I wasn't a bit nervous, but I think he was.'

'How is Oliver?'

'Quite fun to be with, as usual.'

'Do you . . . like him any better?'

'I'll never be in love with him, if that's what you mean.'

'Pity. Well, I've finished. We'd better go in. Soon be time for tea.'

They went in and met their mother just coming downstairs.

'There you are,' she said. 'I was going to look for you. Nanny would like to see you for a bit, Liz.'

'Yes, I'll go up. Is there time before tea?'

'Yes. Dr. Harrington said she's just over-tired. If you'll take the new tonic up she can start with it now.'

'Tonic?' Liz asked. She heard Anne groan beside her. 'Oh, lor', I forgot!'

Dr. Harrington had left a small supply, though only

enough for twenty-four hours. Anne had been into Halbury on an errand and had been asked to pick up a bigger bottle from the surgery.

'I'm terribly sorry, Mummy,' she said. 'Is it urgent?'

'Fortunately not. It's only a tonic and there's a bit left. But really, you might have given poor old Nanny a thought.'

'I know. She's always said I'll forget my head one day.'

Liz said, 'I can drive in, if you like.'

'No, no. Tomorrow will do. Are you going in then?'

'I can.'

'Thanks, then. At least you're not likely to forget.'

In the late Victorian house beside whose doorway were fixed two gleaming brass plates, one well-worn, one newly inscribed, bearing the respective names 'Dr. A. J. Cropper' and 'Dr. B. Harrington', the latter was concluding late morning surgery. The secretary-receptionist ushered an infirm old countryman from the room, then returned.

'It's a quarter to one,' he told her. 'You go to lunch. Just leave the waiting-room door and I'll see to it.'

She went, thinking how unusually strained he looked today, as though he were on edge about something. Well, who wouldn't feel some strain, with a doctor's life? She would never marry one, even if one offered. And she switched her mind to the more important matter of what she needed at the grocer's on the way home to lunch.

Brian Harrington was, indeed, on edge. He looked at his watch yet again, tidied his desk a second time, riffled through a card index, seeking nothing, then looked at his watch once more. He heard the waiting-room door at last and went to open the door connecting the surgery with it. The woman he had been expecting was crossing the room.

She was petite and slim, with a good figure, and fair good looks made firm by determined eyes. She was well dressed, in a tailor-made green suit, a fox fur and a 'saucer' hat coquettishly tilted over one eye. She was about his own age. She was his wife.

'Kaye,' he greeted her without either warmth or coldness. 'Come in.'

He hesitated whether to kiss her, but she moved quickly past him into the surgery, glancing round with an air of disapproval.

'Why did we have to meet here?' she asked. 'I hate surgeries. They make me think of illness and death.' Her voice was sharp with nervousness.

'I thought it would be easier to talk privately for a bit. I've booked a table at the White Hart for after, but I didn't want everyone to hear . . .'

'Why can't we go and talk in your digs?'

'You know my landlady doesn't know I'm married. It was your idea I should keep it quiet until we'd . . .'

'All right. Don't rub it in.'

There was an edge to everything she said, not so much aggressive as defensive. Her voice bore the same traces of regional accent as his.

'Besides,' he explained, 'I want you to see over the house while Dr. Cropper's out. He said I could. See if you like it.'

'I can tell you now. You know I hate old-fashioned houses. Especially this sort. I knew from the outside what it'd be like.'

'It's really rather nice.'

She drew a cigarette case-cum-lighter from her handbag, took one out and lit it, without offering one to him. Then she wandered over to the scales and stood on them, measuring her weight.

His placatory manner left him. 'Do stop fidgeting, Kaye. You agreed to come here so we could talk, as you seem incapable of answering my letters.'

'I hate writing letters.'

'Look, you don't seem to realize what a difficult position I'm in. I'm a married man, but not seen to be one. They expect it of you in the country, but we agreed I'd keep it as quiet as possible while you made up your mind. I can't go on waiting, Kaye.'

She sighed and stubbed out her partially smoked cigarette.

'I know, Brian. Why pretend any longer? You don't love me, do you?'

'I . . . did once. I believe I could again.'

She said more softly, 'It isn't enough, is it? And I'm just not cut out to be a doctor's wife, am I?'

She got up and wandered across the room, saying, with her back to him, 'Besides, I've . . . got someone now. Someone I'm cosy with – who likes the same things I do.'

He had not expected that things had gone this far.

'Anyone I know?' he asked stiffly.

'Yes, actually. It's Norman.'

'Norman!'

They had both known him since their courting days.

'You should have married him in the first place,' he said.

'I know.'

There was no acrimony in the exchange. It was true, and they both knew it.

'Cheer up, Brian,' she was moved to say. 'You wanted this talk, so I decided we'd better get it over with, once and for all. Norman drove me over. He's waiting for me in the car. We're going on to Portmeirion for a few days. Don't bother about the lunch. Pity things didn't work out. I . . .'

She was about to add something else, but her defensive hardness had deserted her and she hurried out of the surgery and the house.

Brian Harrington stood where he was in the surgery, looking at nothing in particular, feeling drained of emotion as he went through the processes of accepting that their marriage was over at last. He had known for long enough that it was on the brink, and that it was more likely to go over it than to retreat to secure ground. They were too unsuited to one another, that was all. He felt no bitterness against his wife. It wasn't her fault.

The outer door opened again. The thought flashed into his mind that she might have come back to ask for a little more grace before deciding finally. He saw a woman enter; but not his wife. It was Liz Bourne.

'Excuse me!' she called from the waiting-room, evidently not having seen him standing still. 'Is anyone there?'

'Come in!' he called and went to meet her at the surgery door.

Face to face once again, they each felt the shock of that little electric force arcing between them. The weeks had changed nothing for either.

Liz stammered, 'I ... I just came to pick up a bottle of tonic ... for Nanny Benson ...'

'Oh, yes. It's here. It was to be called for yesterday.'

'I know. Anne forgot. I'm sorry.'

'How is Nanny?'

'Oh, quite well, really.' Liz laughed nervously. 'Resentful at having to rest. I gave her a lecture and said you were quite right.'

'Thanks. And you? How are you?'

'I'm very well, thank you. I just got back from town.'

'Yes, your parents told me you were coming. You've got yourself a car, I hear?'

'Yes.'

'That'll be nice for you.'

'Yes.'

'Why ... did you go away ... so suddenly?'

Liz dropped her gaze. 'A sudden impulse. I ... I mustn't keep you. You'll miss your lunch.'

He asked, 'Have you had yours?'

'I'm just going back for it.'

'Would you ... have lunch with me? I was due to go with someone to the White Hart, but there's been a change of plan. I haven't cancelled the table.'

'Well ...'

'Please.'

Liz smiled. 'I'd like that. May I ring home and tell them I won't be back?'

His heart leaped and he reached the telephone across from

his side of his desk. The operator connected her with her home and he gathered that Anne had answered. He didn't miss the quick and almost furtive glance Liz threw in his direction as she told her sister that she would be staying in Halbury to lunch with a friend she'd just run into. She did not volunteer that friend's name.

Over the meal he told her all – almost all. She had expected to hear that his wife was living with him now in Dr. Cropper's house, and was surprised to learn that he was still alone and in digs. Then he had taken the plunge and told her the situation which had led up to his sitting there with her at a table for two in the dining-room of the White Hart, instead of with his wife.

They had reached the coffee. 'I'm sorry,' he said, 'I seem to have been talking about myself and my troubles.'

'Not at all.'

'Lucky for me to have an ear so soon. Prevent me getting too broody.'

Liz said, 'Can I ask you a question? Rather an impertinent one?'

'Of course.'

'If you and your wife had so little in common, why did you get married?'

'It was very much our parents' doing. Her father and mine were joint owners of a biggish grocer's shop in Wolverhampton. They'd been at school together. They were lifelong friends.'

'A dynastic marriage,' Liz smiled.

He smiled back. 'Hardly that, but naturally when they saw that Kaye and I were attracted to one another they made the most of it. She and I had known each other all our lives, too. As a small boy I liked her. As an older boy I despised her simply for being a girl. As an adolescent I was . . . well, knocked sideways by her. She's very attractive.'

'Was she knocked sideways, too?'

'I think she was. For a few months we were wildly in love. You know how it is at eighteen or so.'

'Well, I can imagine.'

He was plainly astonished. 'You mean you . . . don't *know*? You weren't ever . . .?'

She shook her head. 'Afraid not. It . . . sort of . . missed me . . .'

There was a long pause. He would have liked to have said, 'And you're so beautiful,' but he held himself back. He returned instead to the subject of himself.

'Our families were delighted. There was an engagement, though, of course, it had to be a long one. I'd only just started at medical school, and there was no question of marriage till I'd qualified.'

'Was she interested in your career?'

Liz was asking about those early years, but realized that her question covered the immediate past, too.

'No,' he said flatly. 'That was half the trouble. She always said she'd make a hopeless wife for a doctor. I didn't believe her at first. I was studying, but she was always wanting me to take her out . . . It was the same after we married, I'm afraid. You must know what's involved in being a doctor's wife. I'm afraid poor Kaye could never accept it.'

'And so, eventually, she couldn't take any more?'

'Neither of us could, the way things were going on. I applied for this post, as much to get away from the old surroundings as anything else. Perhaps I thought a change of scene would work the trick.'

'Only, it didn't.'

'Far from it. It made things worse. Kaye's a city type, through and through. Every time I suggested she come over here and see the lie of the land she found some excuse. In the end I had to say yes or no to Dr. Cropper. We . . . agreed that I'd accept and Kaye would think things over.'

He shrugged.

'And she's thought, and that's it.'

'This other man . . .'

'Oh, Norman's just the type for the occasion. Extrovert, well-off . . . I think it's pretty final.'

Liz did not know what to answer. She had no practical counsel to offer; she was in no position to offer more than formal comfort. The silence between them hung longer this time, potentially dangerous to the breaker of it. It was Liz who took the chance.

'What will you do now? I mean, about the house. What will you tell Croppy?'

He shook his head. 'I don't know yet. For the moment I won't tell him anything, I think. I don't want anyone to know, please. Not a word ... promise?'

Her hand was on the tablecloth. He placed his over it.

'I promise,' she said in a voice new to herself. 'I ... I did write to explain ... why I was running away. But I tore the letter up.'

'I think I know why,' he said. 'I'd have torn up letters around that time, too.'

The old waiter approached. They withdrew their hands guiltily and Brian Harrington looked at his wristwatch.

'Good heavens, I'm late!' he exclaimed. 'I'm sorry. I must get back.'

The waiter had placed the bill on its plate on the table and turned away a few paces. Liz said, more urgently than she would have wished to do, 'If it helps you to talk, we could meet one evening. Now that I've got my car.'

He nodded gratefully. 'In Hereford, perhaps? Liz, you do realize ... well, I've treated you for one slight cold. I daren't be your doctor any more.'

She nodded, fully understanding; and this mutual recognition of the code of practice between doctor and patient affirmed to each of them what the other was now feeling more than any careful words could have conveyed. They went further than that: they got up and shook hands formally for the waiter to see, before Liz wandered off to the Ladies while he hurried from the hotel, straight back to the surgery. Their conspiracy was joined.

Liz arrived back at Larkfield Manor soon after four o'clock. She found Anne in the hall, practising a new dance

116

step to a record on the portable gramophone. Anne moved easily, with the relaxation of a good-looking young woman with no especial cares in the world. Elizabeth watched her for some moments with almost envious sensations.

When the record had clicked to a stop she said, 'That's new, isn't it?' Anne said, lifting the disc with her finger tips, 'Oh, hello. Yes, but I think I've got it now. I don't want to make a fool of myself.'

'When?'

'Next week. Michael's giving me a lift to London for a week of parties and things. The Universal Aunt says it's my turn.'

She slid the record back into its sleeve, then looked hard at her sister.

'You're jolly late.'

'I rang up. I told you.'

'Hm!'

'What's that supposed to mean?'

Anne glanced round and lowered her voice. 'You've been lunching with *him* – haven't you?'

'Who?'

'Oh, of course, if you don't want to tell me ... If you don't trust me ...' It was said in the most melodramatic of ways, but Liz tried to hold her ground.

'I trust you, silly.'

'Then, why *didn't* you come back for lunch?'

Liz had her story ready.

'You remember Lydia Fairlie? In my form at school. We were prefects together.'

'Oh, yes.'

'Yes. Well, I ran into her outside Halbury Motors. We decided to lunch together. I always rather liked her, you know.'

'You rather carefully didn't mention her when you 'phoned.'

'Carefully? Oh, well, you know how Mummy always hated her mother? Lydia's. So I ... I didn't make a point of telling you who it was I was lunching with.'

'Oh, I see.'

'Yes.'

Elizabeth was uncomfortable under Anne's steady, ironical gaze.

'And I thought we were such pals,' Anne was saying.

'We *are*. How d'you mean?'

'Did she say where they're living now?'

'Who?'

'Lydia Fairlie, of course.'

'Well ... er ...'

'They moved while you were away. Her father was transferred to Warwick. Oh, Liz, you really are in love, aren't you?' Anne giggled, but kept her tone tactfully low.

Liz, who had coloured heavily at the simple uncovering of her deception, had to smile back. Anne tut-tutted, with mock severity, 'And him a married man!'

Liz glanced stairwards, kitchenwards and studywards. Anne shook her head reassuringly. Liz told her, low, 'This is utterly secret. As secret as before – understand?'

'Yes.'

'Swear.'

'Not all that rigmarole again. I swear.'

'She ... she's left him ... for good.'

'Oh, Liz!'

'And she's got someone else'

'So – you'll marry him?'

'Silly ass! I've only talked to him this once – really talked, I mean.'

'But all this secrecy ... Why, if you don't feel ...'

'Of course I feel ... Oh, Anne, we haven't discussed anything properly, yet. We scarcely know each other. And he is the family doctor, remember.'

'Oh, yes. That. But you do feel something, don't you? I could tell that first time.'

'I ...'

'Oh, Liz, I'd be so happy for you if it came to something. I've always hoped ... Everyone has, except ...'

'Except me? Well, we'll see. But deadly hush, promise! His wife only told him today. There's a long way to go yet, and it may not go anywhere at all.'

Liz deliberately changed this risky subject.

'Anyway, what about your Michael Sherwood. When do we get a look at him?'

'Oh, tomorrow. He 'phoned while you were out. He's flying all day at Hendon and coming down afterwards. And on Sunday he'll drive me to town after tea.'

'What you might call a "flying visit".'

'Ha, ha! Joke, joke!'

The conversation between Elizabeth, Anne, their parents and the visiting Michael Sherwood after dinner the following evening was inconsequential and exclusive of foreign and domestic politics, the disturbing rise in Germany's rate of rearmament, the welcome fall in Britain's unemployment figures, now dipping, for the first time in five years, to below the two-million mark. Such topics were not ones for filling an agreeably leisured evening.

Although Michael, a pleasantly unremarkable boy, was training enthusiastically as a spare-time fighter-pilot, he was doing so in the spirit with which others of his age and class spent their week-ends motor-racing or rugger-playing – keeping themselves vigorously occupied in the convivial company of kindred spirited males. The aircraft he flew was designed as a weapon of war; but it was less with war in mind than for the elation of flying a fast and excitingly man-oeuvrable machine that Michael spent his week-ends thus. He had not dedicated himself to the killing trade.

More than once he was seen to stifle a yawn.

'I'm so sorry,' he apologized to Helen, seeing that she had noticed this. 'I was flying at dawn. Practising for the Hendon Show. I hope Anne will come and watch – and any of you who are able, of course.' He yawned again. 'Dear me!'

Helen got up. 'It's time we were all going to bed, anyway.

We breakfast at half-past nine on Sundays. We usually leave for church at about quarter to eleven.'

Michael said, 'Oh, but I'll be driving into Halbury to Mass. I gather there's a church there.'

Arthur stared, taken by surprise. Anne said, 'Yes, and I'm going with him. I've never been to a Catholic service.'

Michael Sherwood was too preoccupied with getting to bed to notice the effect he had unwittingly made. He bade them all good night and went off up to his room.

'Well!' Arthur said. 'I didn't know the young man was a Catholic. Anne, I don't want to come the heavy father, but I'd prefer you not to go to Mass with him.'

'Why not? It's the same God, isn't it?'

Helen reminded her, 'The rector's coming to lunch, remember.'

'I'm sorry, Mummy, Daddy, but Michael's my guest and I'm not letting him go to church on his own. If I were visiting I wouldn't like my host to do it to me.'

She went decisively up the stairs, leaving her father to sigh and shrug helplessly.

The rector of Winchley, the Reverend the Honourable Maurice Fuller had been the youngest son of an impoverished peer. Having spent many years out of England he had taken orders in middle age and come to Winchley in his fifties. Now in his seventies, he proposed to remain where he was, even after death, upon which event his remains were to be laid in the pretty churchyard. Wise, benign and comfortable, he was a liberal churchman and a willing guest at the tables of many of the larger houses of the district. The Bournes regarded him as a family friend, on first-name terms with Arthur and Helen.

'Nanny was so disappointed to have to miss the service,' Helen was telling him as they came into the house after church that next morning. 'She wanted to come, but I'm insisting she obeys doctor's orders and stays in bed for a few days yet.'

'Very wise,' the rector agreed. 'I missed her in her place.

One can't help noticing when such a regular attender's not there. I didn't see Anne today.'

Arthur handed him a glass of sherry, explaining a shade apprehensively, 'She's gone to the R.C. church in Halbury with a young man we have staying. She didn't want him to have to go alone.'

'Quite right, too,' the rector said firmly. 'Politeness to her visitor. In any case, I think it does everyone good to have a look at the different ways we all have of going about the same thing. The Roman rite has many charms – the vestments, the incense, the old Latin form of service.'

'And that horrid little tin church,' Liz chimed in, cheerful to see that the rector's hearty acceptance of the reason for Anne's absence had eased her parents' minds. 'Don't you feel guilty sometimes, Mr. Fuller, when you look at our beautiful church. After all, it was built by Catholics. We stole it at the Reformation.'

'Liz!' Arthur exclaimed, shocked, but the rector laughed.

'No, no, there's truth in that. You know, I've often wished we could make our church available to them to worship in from time to time. I won't live to see it myself, but it's possible the oecumenical movement will grow to the point where we shall all worship the same God in the same church – though we'll doubtless go on differing on points of dogma.'

Arthur shook his head. 'I'm afraid I can't second that, Maurice.'

The rector's eyes twinkled as he sipped his sherry. 'I didn't think you would,' he replied.

'Here are the others,' Helen said as Michael Sherwood's car drew up outside. A few moments later they came in, Anne glancing with some anxiety at her parents and then the rector, and much relieved to hear the latter say, 'Hello, Anne. So you've been to hear my old friend Father Leonard. I hope I didn't suffer too much by comparison?'

Anne smiled gratefully and introduced Michael.

'Such a funny little church, though,' she said. 'But it was

packed. All the O'Connells were there, Mummy. They sent their love.'

'Thank you, dear. It's ages since we've seen them. Anyone else there we know?'

'We don't know any R.Cs. other than the O'Connells, do we?' Arthur asked.

Michael said to Anne, as he accepted the proffered sherry glass, 'Wasn't that someone you know in the pew behind us?'

'Not . . . really,' Anne said quickly. The evasiveness in her tone, and the way she glanced away, intrigued Helen.

'Oh? Who was it, dear?' she asked.

'No one. Honestly.' But the desperation in Anne's voice was obvious to them all except Michael.

Liz demanded teasingly, 'Come on.' She addressed him. 'A young man, I'll bet.'

He wrinkled his brow and looked questioningly at Anne.

'Doctor . . . something, wasn't he? I heard the priest speak to him.'

'Harrington?' Helen asked.

Anne dared not look at Liz, but she could sense the effect of her reply as she was forced to say, as matter-of-factly as she could, 'Yes. I didn't think to count him.'

Arthur said, 'I didn't know Harrington was an R.C.'

Anne heard the cold, level voice of Liz answer him.

'How should we? After all, he's not a close friend – just the new doctor.'

CHAPTER SEVEN

WHEN she had had time to think about it for a while, Elizabeth came to decide that she did not feel bitterness about Brian Harrington's undisclosed 'secret'. After testing the matter one way and another, she came to the conclusion that it wasn't a deception at all; that the question of his religion simply hadn't arisen in their conversation. That he was attracted by her was obvious, and must be obvious to him. It must be equally plain that the feeling was mutual. Yet it had been only the second conversation they had ever had together; and it had been only a matter of minutes before it began that his wife had told him their marriage was over.

It would have been absurdly early, and presumptuous, of him to have made some such declaration as: 'There's something I think you ought to know, though. I'm a Roman Catholic. My marriage may be in ruins, but don't start entertaining hopes about me yourself, because there's nothing I can do about it.'

That sort of consideration would have to come much later; when, and if, the question of marriage should ever arise. Liz realized this, and didn't hold it against him that he hadn't mentioned the matter at that point. All the same, she felt her spirits lowered by the spectacle of another, and a major, obstacle which had suddenly reared itself up between them.

She saw nothing of Brian in the week following that day of disclosures, and heard nothing from him. Once or twice she was tempted to telephone, or find some excuse to go to the surgery. As if perversely, though, Nanny Benson made a rapid recovery from her fatigue and soon left her bed with little more than half of the bottle of tonic finished. Liz was left in that unhappy state of limbo and doubt which uncertainty makes all the more desolate.

Two nights of strong wind, which threshed the cedar tree and kept waking her with its moaning in the eaves, did nothing for her spirits. But the handwriting of a letter her mother held out for her when she came down to breakfast on the second morning afterwards made her heart beat quicker.

'Oh, just ... the hospital library,' she said in answer to Helen's casual inquiry. 'About a book, I expect. I'll read it later.'

Helen watched her a little anxiously as she walked away into the dining-room, where the remains of breakfast awaited her. Liz had seemed quite down in the mouth these last few days. Helen knew her better than to pester her with solicitudes, though. She had put it down to a renewed bout of the old uncertainty over whether to resume the medical career or finish with it for good. Helen could sympathize with that. Much as she would prefer Liz to marry Oliver Manson or someone else of his sort, she still remembered vividly Arthur's struggle with his desire to stay on in the Navy and his feeling that he should give it all up for the sake of domestic continuity. Poor Liz was probably in the grip of a similar dilemma. When she wanted counsel, she would ask for it.

Anyway, Helen's thoughts that morning were principally on another of her daughters, Vicky. The post had also brought a letter from Munich, which Helen read out to Arthur as soon as she could engage his attention for a few minutes.

'Darling Mummy and Daddy' (Vicky wrote) 'How is everything at home? I'm having a lovely time. We all went to the opera last week to see *Lohengrin*. Julius Patzak was singing. He's the tenor here who all the people adore. He has a withered hand, poor man. Hans Knappertsbusch is the conductor and is very good.

'Elli von Heynig goes twice a week to a thing called

B.D.M., which stands for Bund Deutscher Mädel, or League of German Girls, which is exactly like our Girl Guides, and Klaus belongs to the same as our Boy Scouts, which they call the Hitler Jugend, or Hitler Youth. Next year he will be called up for his Arbeitsdienst. That means labour service. They all go to camp, apparently, to dig ditches and work on the land, etc. Very healthy, Klaus says.

'Unfortunately, we can't ski any more now, as the snow is melting in the Alps, but we went over from the chalet to see a wonderful fairy castle built for King Ludwig of Bavaria, who was mad. It's enormous, and all turrets and things. Are my bantams all right? The new hens ought to start laying soon. Please thank Gates for feeding them . . .'

And so on, in similarly erratic vein, for several pages.

'Well,' Arthur said at the end of the reading, 'she sounds all right. When you think how she resented being made to go . . . Anything else in the post?'

'Just a library thing for Liz.'

'No more bills, at any rate? Oh, by the way, Parish Council meeting's been fixed for tomorrow afternoon.'

'But it's Anne's point-to-point. You know it is.'

'Oh, damn. I had it at the back of my mind there was something. Where is it again?'

'Over at High Barrow. She's there now, walking the course with Marjorie Shepherd.'

'That's twenty miles the other side of Hereford,' he groaned.

'Well, we did promise we'd be there to see her ride. She'll be terribly disappointed.'

Arthur nodded. 'I know. Anyway, it won't hurt if I turn up at the meeting late. Could we leave after the Ladies' Race, though?'

'Yes, we could. I'm sorry, darling, only I do think we ought to encourage the girls when they go in for things – even when they're nearly grown up. It's like going down to St. Mary's for their sports and lacrosse. They do like one to be there.'

'Oh, I quite agree.'

'Besides, you never know, she might win.'

Arthur shook his head firmly at that. 'Oh, I doubt it. I really do.' And he went back to his study.

'Do you think you'll win?' Liz asked Anne later that day. They were communing in Anne's room, as she dressed for dinner. She pursed her lips and shrugged.

'Some of the jumps looked pretty formidable from ground level – especially the open ditch. And it's very uphill in places. Poor old Tallulah won't like that.'

Anne eyed her sister's reflection in the dressing-table mirror.

'Still, you didn't really come slinking in here to ask me about the point-to-point, did you?'

She saw Liz smile a little guiltily, though more happily than she had seen her look lately.

'No. I just ... wanted to tell you that I had a long and ... and rather wonderful letter this morning – from Brian.'

Anne turned to look at her apprehensively. She, too, had been having her thoughts about the relationship which seemed too fraught with difficulties, and her conclusion so far had been that Liz was heading for trouble.

Liz went on eagerly, 'I really believe he's as ... fond of me as I am of him. Only he's too, well, you know, aware of ... everything to risk upsetting me by putting it into words.'

'Is that what he says?'

'No, not exactly. But reading between the lines ... Anyway, he's asked me to meet him tomorrow afternoon outside Halbury library and go for a long drive.'

'That's risky, isn't it?'

'Not really. We'll probably go right away from Halbury – miles out into the open country. It just means ... oh, dear me ... !'

Anne spared her. 'Missing my race? Never mind that, silly! Much more fun to go driving with a man than watch me make a fool of myself in front of half the county. You go.'

'Thanks, darling – for not minding.'

'Well, I do mind a bit. Not you missing the point-to-point – I mean I mind you getting mixed up in a hopeless love affaire. Surely, whatever the situation is with his wife, they can't ever be divorced. So isn't it all rather ... a waste of time?'

Liz replied firmly, almost sharply, as she had answered herself mentally time and again in those last few days. 'No, it's not a waste of time. We can still be together ... whenever possible. Nobody can stop that. As long as we can go on meeting, I don't care.' She went on in a duller, less certain tone, 'It's just his having a wife, and this wretched religion of his.'

'Poor old Liz,' Anne said, genuinely sympathetic. 'But what will you say to the parents about tomorrow? You'll need an excuse for them.'

'I know. I had this letter from Brian this morning. I said it was from the hospital library about a book. I'm going to say I can only see the book tomorrow, because someone has it on permanent loan but can just let me get at it for a few hours.'

'Oh, Liz!'

'Well, it's the best I can think of. So long as you back me up and say you don't mind me not coming to see you ride, I'll be able to see Brian and spend the afternoon with him.'

Anne turned back to the mirror with a sigh.

'O.K. I still think you're a fool ... but I wouldn't let you down.'

Liz leaned forward to kiss her on the back of the neck.

'You're a good sister, old thing. You deserve to win your race for that.'

'Anything to oblige, old bean. But somehow I think the odds are much too long – for both of us. I don't think either of us'll win.'

The excuse was duly made over dinner. After a mild protest from Arthur that since he was sacrificing some public duty for a personal one he didn't see why Liz shouldn't follow his example, it was accepted, largely due to the urging of Anne that she quite understood why Liz couldn't be at the race.

'I'd be even more nervous,' she said, 'with those critical eyes boring into me.'

'Oh, well,' her father shrugged. 'I suppose there'll be just the two of us, then – unless Nanny's coming?'

'No, she won't come,' Helen said. 'Too cold for her, so soon after being ill.'

Anne said, 'I keep saying, I don't want a great family audience. All I want is to beat that horrible Mrs. Appleton. I don't care if I'm last but one, as long as I can finish in front of her.'

'Who on earth is Mrs. Appleton?' her father asked.

'Oh, a terrible, rather shrill woman, with dyed hair and several expensive horses. A real show-off.'

'Ah, I know the one. You pointed her out to us at the Meet. She was shouting at everyone, including the Master.'

'That's her. They came from the Beaufort country to near Leominster, so naturally, "mah deer gel", she thinks she's slumming amongst us. Yes, I've simply got to beat Brenda Appleton. I just hope the going stays firm.'

Arthur glanced towards the window. 'It should. There's no sign of rain, and the wind must have dried out the ground a lot.'

'I've ordered the horsebox from Sutton's, by the way, Daddy. Is that all right?'

Arthur gave a resigned shrug and a little smile of acceptance. Just one more bill to pay.

Anne went on, 'Gates and I'll go over there early with Tallulah, so she can have a canter round.'

'Don't exhaust her before the race,' her father warned mischievously.

'Daddy! Are you saying she isn't up to it?'

'I doubt if you'll even get her round the course once. Or yourself, come to that – all the gadding about you've been doing lately.'

'Gates exercises her when I'm away.'

'Oh, yes. A gentle trot round the paddock. What that mare needs is a damned good five-mile gallop every day.'

'Arthur!' Helen intervened. 'Don't tease the child.'

He and Anne exchanged smiles. She said, in a Mae West accent, 'I can take it, baby.'

'Perhaps,' Arthur said, 'we should all have a bet on you. At least we'd get long odds. Once the bookies spot that broken-down, gone-in-the-wind mare, they'll offer 200-1 against and find no takers.'

'Wait till they spot the rider,' Liz said. Anne made a gesture of mock threat towards her; but she was pleased to see her sister in lively mood again, for the first time in days.

Liz and Nanny saw Arthur and Helen off next morning, furnished with a hamper of cold chicken, hard boiled eggs, tomatoes, lettuce, a thermos of coffee, and, Arthur's personal treat to himself, some Gentleman's Relish sandwiches, expensive but a great favourite of his.

'What about you, dear?' Nanny asked Liz when the car had gone. 'Mrs. Gates can make you an omelette or something.'

'No, thanks, Nanny. I'll get something in Halbury. I'm off in a few minutes. Let Mrs. Gates have a quiet afternoon, for once. And you, too.'

Half an hour later Nanny and Mrs. Gates sat together over cups of tea at the kitchen table. Mrs. Gates was middle-aged, dark and quite handsome. Unlike Scottish Nanny Benson, she was locally-born and had rarely been away from the neighbourhood.

'I don't know what time Fred'll be back,' she mused. 'Depends on the traffic, I should imagine, getting away from the race course.'

'What time did Mrs. Bourne order their dinner for?' Nanny asked.

'Eight-fifteen. And all my vegetables done already. You know, Nan, I think I'll go back to the lodge and have a lie down, while Fred's out.'

'I should, if I were you.'

'Why don't you have a nice rest yourself?'

'Oh, I shall. I've got a nice fire in the schoolroom. And a bit of darning to get on with, and my wireless . . .'

She broke off to listen to a prolonged strong gust of wind.

'Hark at that wind!' Nanny exclaimed. 'It's getting up again. It always makes me afraid the old cedar tree might blow down and fall on the house.'

'It'll take more than a bit of March wind to blow that down,' Mrs. Gates reassured her. 'They say it's hundreds of years old, with roots right down deep in the earth.'

Nanny yawned.

'Well, I'll go up. Perhaps I won't get all my darning done, after all.'

She didn't. Under the influence of the fire glowing brightly in the little grate, she felt her eyes soon becoming heavy and her yawns came more frequently. After a while she gave up the effort to resist, laid her work aside, switched off the radio concert, and settled back in her chair, her hands in her lap.

One of the last things her eyes rested on before she dozed off was the old rocking-horse in the corner, a relic of Arthur's own infancy. All his daughters had delighted in it in their turn. Now it waited, metaphorically put out to pasture, until one of the girls should at last marry and some day bring an infant over to ride the old horse into new life.

Nanny slept long and heavily; and towards the end of her sleep she had a dream. She saw the rocking-horse begin to move, slowly at first, then 'cantering', and then into an almost frenzied 'gallop'. And the sound of the wind, buffeting the roof and penetrating her ears, became transformed into the thunder of hooves on turf, the urgent cries of riders, the creak of leather and crack of whips, the roar of a crowd. These sounds increased, and there materialized, on the back of the wildly rocking wooden horse, the figure of a child, holding tightly on to the reins, leaning forward concentratedly as if urging the horse to even greater efforts. Nanny, in her dream, delightedly recognized this little girl as one of the children-to-be whom perhaps she would sadly not live to see in the flesh. But then, although still asleep, it was as if she leaned forward for a closer look, and realized that the rider was Anne, as a little girl.

Nanny woke up suddenly. Her first glance was at the rocking-horse. It was motionless in its corner. The wind was still blowing strongly. It was almost dark in the unlit room, with the gloom of late afternoon. And the telephone was ringing downstairs.

With difficulty, Nanny hurried down, wondering why Eileen Gates didn't trouble to answer the 'phone, then remembering that she had gone back to her lodge for the afternoon. Nanny herself had slept much longer than she had intended, she realized with annoyance.

The operator was clearly determined to get some answer and was still persisting by the time Nanny, panting heavily, reached the instrument in the hall. She answered it with difficulty in getting her breath to speak; but what she heard from the other end took her breath away in a different fashion. Nanny's face turned ashen and her hands trembled. Just as she had put the telephone down again Mrs. Gates came in. She stared to see the distress on Nanny's countenance.

'Eileen!' the old lady cried. 'Oh, thank heavens you're back!'

Mrs. Gates hurried to her. 'What is it, Nanny? What's happened?'

'That was Mrs. Bourne. Anne's had a very bad fall. They've taken her off to Hereford in the ambulance unconscious. She was speaking from the infirmary.'

'Oh, there now! Sit down, Nanny,' Mrs. Gates urged, paling too.

Nanny shook her head. 'I've to ring Dr. Cropper at once and tell him. They're going to ring here again later – when there's some news.'

'Did she . . . say what . . .?'

'No. They're waiting the result of the examination. Oh

dear, that child! Always was a dare-devil on a horse. It's not the first time she's come off, either.'

As Nanny turned back to the telephone, to ask for the surgery, she remembered her dream. She could have sworn that she had heard distinctly, just before waking, a crash and a cry, as if a horse had fallen, and someone call out anxiously, 'One come down!'

She was all the more startled, an hour later, to hear Gates saying, 'She was falling back a bit – dropped back from second to about fourth – then I saw her disappear through a jump and all at once someone shouted, "Coo, there's one come down!".'

He had come back alone, bringing Tallulah in the horse box. The mare had been examined by a vet at the scene and pronounced only slightly injured.

'She'd been going well, too,' Gates continued, addressing his wife, Nanny and Elizabeth, who had come home a few minutes after his return. 'She hit two fences running, but she was keeping up second. She was riding the mare for all she was worth, was Miss Anne, but I reckoned Tallulah was tiring.'

'Oh, I do hope there'll be some news soon,' Nanny despaired. It was seven o'clock now, but the telephone had not rung. Nanny had been told by the doctors' receptionist that both were out. The agony of waiting without information was beginning to tell on the old lady. Liz insisted she sit down. She consented, but on the chair nearest to the telephone.

Gates told his wife, 'I'll get back to the lodge, Eileen, and get out of me leggings. Then if I'm needed . . .'

He paused, listening to a car drive up.

'Is it them?' Nanny asked.

'But they said they'd telephone,' Mrs. Gates reminded her.

Gates left by the back door, as Liz went to the front one and opened it. Brian Harrington stood there. He wore a very different expression from the one Liz had left him with only half an hour earlier.

'I've come about your sister,' he said. 'There was a message waiting at the surgery, after . . .'

Liz quickly and silently motioned him not to complete what he had been going to say. She said formally, 'It's very kind of you to come, Dr. Harrington. Do come in, please.'

He nodded to Nanny and Mrs. Gates, giving the older woman an anxious glance. She saw it.

'I'm all right now, Doctor,' she said. 'It was just the shock. Oh, but this waiting . . .!'

'How badly injured is she?' he asked.

'That's what we don't know. She was unconscious, they said.'

'Concussion, I expect?' Liz suggested to Brian. He nodded. 'I imagine so. It can cause a longish period of unconsciousness, so they may not have been able to do all the tests yet. Of course, they'll have to X-ray and' – he glanced meaningfully at Liz, who realized the implications the other women wouldn't understand – 'do an Encephalograph.'

Nanny asked, 'Doctor, could you telephone the infirmary and ask? I mean, as the family doctor.'

He answered, 'Unfortunately, Nanny, I can't really intervene at this stage, while she's under the doctors there. Naturally, I'll . . .'

The sharp *ping*! as the telephone began to ring startled them all. Liz forestalled Nanny to answer it. She heard her father's voice, strained and tired. He told her: 'She's still unconscious, Liz. She's badly concussed. The Ambulance men said she's probably broken her left arm and possibly a rib or two. It's hard to get anyone here to say anything definite. They'll be carrying out various tests over the next few hours . . . Oh, Liz, it's all my fault. Entirely my fault.'

'Why, Daddy?' she protested. 'That's ridiculous. How can you possibly blame yourself for someone else's accident?'

'I knew the mare was unfit – and Anne, too. Instead of making idiotic jokes about it, I should have forbidden her to

133

ride a race under those conditions. I ought to have put my foot down.'

'Please, it's no time for recriminations. Try to . . .'

'You see . . . she was also kicked on her head. It's . . . a . . . a question of possible damage to her brain . . .'

Liz swallowed and glanced towards Nanny. Fortunately, she was standing too far away and was too hard of hearing, to have caught any of this.

'I understand, Daddy,' Liz said. 'We must just wait and see. But you're not to blame yourself. Please.'

There was an uncertain silence at the other end. She resumed, 'Dr. Harrington's here. He came out when he got Nanny's message at the surgery. Would you like to speak to him?'

Her father said, 'No, no. Thank him for coming out, but there's really nothing he can do. Your mother and I will come back later. We must wait a while, in case there's more news. I'll telephone when we're setting off.'

The conversation ended. Liz delivered a carefully phrased version of it to Nanny and Mrs. Gates, and a detailed one to Brian, whom she took into her father's study for a whisky and soda.

'I think, on reflection,' he told her, 'I could telephone the hospital, as your G.P.'

'As Anne's,' she couldn't resist correcting him.

'I meant, as your family's,' he said; but each knew the meaning implicit in the little exchange.

They decided to leave the matter as it stood, and after declining a further drink he drove away. Liz went off to sit with Nanny and Mrs. Gates, until the telephone rang again and her father told her they were leaving for home, but wouldn't be wanting dinner. Anne was still unconscious and was expected to be for some time. They had been told there was no point in their remaining at the hospital.

It had been Saturday when Anne had fallen. It was not until Monday afternoon that she regained consciousness, to ask immediately about Tallulah. The Encephalograph tests and X-rays had proved satisfactory. Apart from the concussion, a dislocated shoulder, some cuts in her head deep enough to require stitching, and a good deal of heavy bruising, she was quite sound. At Brian Harrington's strong request, prompted by the family, the hospital authorities allowed her to be brought home by ambulance on the Tuesday, bandaged about the head, and on the strict understanding that she be put straight to bed and kept there until her doctor allowed her up.

'Sorry, Daddy,' she told Arthur, as he sat beside her own bed, Helen and Nanny having just left them alone.

'Sorry? What have you got to be sorry about, darling?'

'Coming off. You said I'd make a fool of myself, and I did.'

'No, no. It was my fault for letting you ride. I should have stopped you.'

'At least poor old Tallulah's all right, except for a stiff knee,' she mused. 'It certainly wasn't *her* fault. She galloped beautifully and she was jumping well – most of the way. I can't quite remember, but I think I . . . got very puffed the second time round. I just vaguely remember not being able to help her . . . had no strength left . . . and we sort of . . . went right into it . . . right through it, instead of over. And I saw stars, and something hit me on the head, and it all went black.'

'All right, Anne,' he comforted her. 'It's all over now, thank God.' There was a knock at the door. 'Come in.'

Brian Harrington entered, carrying his bag.

'Good morning, sir,' he said. 'Mrs. Bourne said I was to come up.'

'Yes, yes, come in Harrington, please. Thanks again for all your help.'

'Not at all. How is she now?'

'Much more herself, I'd say. I'll leave you to decide.'

Arthur gave Anne a little wave and went out. Brian approached the bed, smiling. 'Well, now,' he said. 'Let's have that bandage off and have a look, shall we?'

Despite her enfeebled state, Anne felt a little thrill of interest in this first close encounter with her sister's secret admirer, that fellow skater-on-thin-ice in more ways than one. She almost wanted to tell him she sympathized, but didn't dare. She didn't know whether Liz had told him that their secret had been shared with her. Instead, the interview proceeded along formal though friendly lines.

'Well, that's quite satisfactory,' he said, finishing replacing the head bandage. 'Now, what about that shoulder? How painful is it?'

'Pretty foul,' she admitted truthfully. 'Sharp twinges every so often.'

'Hard to lie comfortably?'

'Almost impossible.'

'Mm. Well, I want you to get plenty of sleep, and you won't be able to while that keeps up. I think you should have a little pain-killing injection, don't you?'

'So long as it doesn't send me off for another three days.'

'It won't do that. Just make you nice and drowsy and comfortable. Can you just unbutton . . .?'

He was preparing the syringe. Anne couldn't help thinking wryly of Liz as she unbuttoned her bed jacket and let him slip down one of the shoulders of her nightie.

The little ordeal was quickly over. He helped her back into the bed jacket and settled her against her raised pillow. Liz came in as he was doing so. She hesitated.

'I'm so sorry . . . Dr. Harrington. I didn't know you were here.'

Anne watched them closely. Liz could feel as much, without looking at her.

'Oh . . . good afternoon,' Anne heard him say. 'We've finished. Just a touch of morphine to ease the shoulder-pain.'

'How soon will she be able to get about, Dr. Harrington?' Liz asked.

He was stowing away his things in his bag.

'That depends on the shoulder . . . and that head, of course. We should be able to cut the stitches out in a week, but it's very important after severe concussion to keep absolutely quiet for several days.' He turned to Anne. 'So I'm afraid you're in for quite a spell in bed.'

'Oh, dear, I'll get so bored,' she complained; but already a new sort of tiredness was beginning to be felt – one which she had no wish to resist.

'I'll come up and read to you,' Liz was promising. 'Later on, you can have your gramophone.'

Brian Harrington snapped his bag to and got up.

'Well, ladies, I shall leave you now. Plenty of sleep,' he reminded Anne, 'and not too much talking yet.'

'I'll ... come and see you out,' Liz said quickly. Instead of saying he could easily manage for himself, he said, 'Thank you.'

They went out, Liz closing the door. Through the increasing drowsiness, Anne could hear nothing for a good few moments. Then she heard the doctor say, quite loudly, 'if you'd just tell Mrs. Bourne I'll look in again at this time tomorrow?' and Liz answer, 'Yes I will. Thank you so much for coming, Dr. Harrington.'

There was more silence, then the door opened and Liz came in again.

'I was just seeing the doctor off,' she explained.

Almost asleep, Anne managed a smile and the question, 'Did you kiss outside the door?'

The last thing she was aware of was Liz smiling back at her.

CHAPTER EIGHT

THROUGH a combination of the strength of youth, natural resilience of character and an impatience to be out and about again, Anne's recovery proceeded apace. To her it seemed to drag out for ages. To her family and their staff, deeply relieved that the injuries had not been more serious, it seemed almost miraculously short. In fact, it was her father, who had been so quick to blame himself for her disaster, who gave her permission to ride gently again, under Gates's close supervision, on the theory that the best way to regain confidence after an accident at riding, playing, driving, or almost anything else, is to return to the activity as soon as possible.

Helen was not so sure.

'I really don't like her riding again so soon,' she said, not for the first time, as they stood at the window and watched. 'Especially with her arm still in a sling.'

'She'll be all right,' Arthur said. 'She's being very careful and I've told Gates he can be as strict as he likes. Anyway, she's had enough now. She's packing it in.'

It was the Thursday afternoon before Easter. Arthur's sister Phyllis had just arrived for the ritual get-together at this time of year. The respective grandparents were due the following day. An even more welcome addition to the household at present was Vicky, back from Munich for a break. The one absentee was Elizabeth, who had been pressed to go back to her friend in Wales whose parents were abroad and who wanted company.

Anne, in her favourite garb of jersey and jodhpurs, came in to join them. She went straight over to kiss her aunt.

'I saw you racing up the drive in your car,' she told Phyllis. 'I couldn't wave, because of this.' She signified her slung arm.

'And I saw you racing round the paddock.'

'I wasn't racing!'

'Well, neither was I.' Phyllis turned to Arthur. 'Though to hear Mother's opinion of my driving, you'd think I was a maniac behind the wheel. I asked her if she'd like to come down with me. She said, "Certainly not. I'll take the train." '

'Have you heard all the gory details about my accident?' Anne asked her. 'They thought they'd have to shoot me.'

'Well, to be honest, I heard they had.'

They all laughed again. Phyllis's extrovert nature was of the sort which made others eager to respond to her ebullience.

'Anyway,' she asked Anne, 'who's this new flame of yours who's coming for Easter? I must say, you don't believe in letting moss grow.'

'He's not a new flame. I met him at Bunny Bickerton's, at a party. Michael – Michael Sherwood, you know – couldn't come, so I asked Gerald. Anyway, you ought to get on all right with him. He's an actor.'

'Yes,' her father snorted. 'I must say, Anne does collect some extraordinary people.'

Anne told her aunt, 'Daddy thinks actors are a cross between African witch doctors and dancing bears.'

'Yes, I know,' Phyllis agreed. 'But I hate to think what *his* father would have had to say if I'd ever invited an actor here. Anyway, Gerald Who?'

'Hope-Langley.'

Phyllis wrinkled her brow in thought.

'I don't think I've heard of him. What's he in at the moment?'

'Well . . . nothing, actually – just at the moment. But he's going to Nottingham soon to play Algernon in *The Importance of Being Earnest*. At least, he hopes he is.'

'Mm. Might I have seen him in the West End?'

'He . . . hasn't acted in London yet. But he will, probably quite soon. He's very handsome.'

Arthur said drily, 'As long as he doesn't come down to breakfast with greasepaint on his face.'

'Stop it, Arthur,' his sister ordered. 'You're not really such a bigot as you make out. I seem to remember you spending the entire evening at one of my supper parties in town talking to Cecile Joubert.'

'That's different,' he riposted. 'She's not a man.'

And so the friendly banter continued until Vicky returned from the village, where she had taken Anne's bicycle for some small repairs, and they sat down to tea.

Gerald Hope-Langley, the object by now of everyone's curiosity, arrived the following day, soon after Lady Bourne and Charles Ashley. He proved to be young, dark and tall, somewhat too suave for Arthur's taste, but self-confident and studiedly polite. Helen secretly thought him romantic-looking. Vicky envied her sister. But it was Phyllis who was soon in the closest communion with him, exchanging impressions of plays and musical comedies, current and past, and trying to hit upon mutual acquaintances in the acting profession. Although Phyllis's own sphere was music, it took her much into acting circles. She had the fellow-artist's fondness for actors and actresses, with their ready humour, love of gossip and anecdote, and that easygoing attitude towards the conventions of life which is as much a defence for their own vulnerability and insecurity as an inability to throw away the set of masks and live out a single identity. She and Gerald hit it off together instantly, not entirely to Anne's pleasure.

'I know who you remind me of,' Phyllis was saying, next morning, looking up at Gerald who was leaning, elegantly arranged, against the grand piano, on which she was strumming a number from the show *That's A Good Girl.* 'Jack Buchanan.'

'I do?' he said delightedly. He was, in fact, not unaware

already of the resemblance, to which he proceeded to add by skipping a few dance steps.

'Graceful,' Phyllis praised him. 'No, not grace – style. That's it. Jack has such style. A movement here, an inflection there. Can you imagine Marlene Dietrich as Shanghai Lil without style?' She turned to Anne, who was feeling out of the conversation. 'Did you ever see it, Anne?'

'What?'

'*Shanghai Express.* The film. Marlene Dietrich.'

'No.'

Gerald enthused, 'Oh, but you must! It's marvellous.' He readdressed himself to Phyllis. 'When I was in *Charley's Aunt* at Aberdeen there was . . .'

It was some minutes before either of them noticed that Anne had drifted away.

'Honestly,' she complained to Vicky, whom she found searching in volume after volume in a bookcase whose glass doors were seldom opened, 'all these plays and films and actors I've never heard of! They might as well be talking Japanese.'

'Well, it's not their fault we never go to the theatre, is it?' said Vicky, who had been quite impressed by much of the theatrical talk she had heard. 'It is his job. And Aunt Phyllis knows so many stage people. I think Gerald's the most handsome man I've ever seen.'

There was a touch of resentment in Anne's response. 'I thought you were all gone on Klaus von Heynig.'

'Oh, not in the same way. Klaus is handsome, but more . . . more solid. You know, without being anything like beautiful. I mean, I can't imagine Gerald spending his Easter marching off with a spade on his shoulder to dig ditches. That's what Klaus is doing. He really enjoys his Labour Corps service.'

'That doesn't surprise me.' The hint of sarcasm surprised Vicky. 'Anyway,' Anne was asking, 'what *are* you looking for?'

Vicky closed and replaced yet another book.

'It just came back to me this afternoon that I pressed some flowers in a book to commemorate my birthday. I suppose it'll turn out to be the very last one I look in.'

In the kitchen, Helen and her mother-in-law were arranging flowers in vases. They talked of commonplace things – of other relatives and friends, of a few national events of feminine interest, of comings-and-goings in Winchley and Halbury. Then, hearing yet another tune begun on the piano out in the hall, Helen said suddenly, 'I do wish Phyllis wouldn't monopolize Gerald. They've been together almost since he arrived.'

'I rather thought it was he monopolizing Phyllis,' Lady Bourne said.

'Whichever way it is, Gerald is Anne's guest. It isn't like Phyllis to be so unthoughtful.'

'Helen, dear, do remember that etiquette isn't everything. Anne's a sweet girl, but she's a country girl, essentially. She knows almost nothing of art or the theatre. It's natural that this young man should find Phyllis interesting.'

'Come to that,' she added, 'I don't think it will do Anne any harm to learn what it is to be jealous. I've seen beautiful women reach forty and suddenly find they've been left behind, because they've never troubled to cultivate their personality beyond fluttering their eyelashes.'

Helen was not much convinced by this. A few minutes later, when she went out into the hall, the piano was still tinkling, though clearly without Phyllis's expert touch. Gerald was at the keyboard, trying to tap out 'Tea for Two', under the instruction of Phyllis who, bent over him, was directing his fingers without actually touching them.

They looked up and smiled at Helen as she passed through. Her smile in return was anything but a warm one. She had noted Anne's absence.

When they had finished playing about with the piano, Gerald sat back on the stool and said, 'You are lucky, Phyllis, living permanently in London and seeing all the plays. I mean, if there's anything I frantically want to see in town I find I'm starring in something depressing by Chekhov in Leeds. By the time I do see the play, the original cast has scattered. I hardly ever seem to go to a first night, except my own.'

Phyllis had moved away a little, to perch on a chair arm. She was regarding his profile. It really was strikingly chis-elled. Her mind suddenly sprang to two slips of paper re-posing in her handbag. She found herself saying, almost unintentionally, 'Well, as it happens I have two tickets for a first night next week . . . and the person I was going with has let me down. Such a shame, because Ivor sent me them specially, and the house will be packed. I can't leave a seat vacant . . .'

'Ivor? Not . . .?'

'Ivor Novello. Of course. And I'm to go to his party afterwards, but I simply couldn't if I hadn't watched the show.'

Gerald almost stammered, 'But . . . but you *must* go. I mean, God, there must be queues of people who'd want to go with you to an Ivor first night.'

Phyllis shrugged. 'Everyone seems . . . a little busy at the moment.' She turned to him with an innocent expression. 'Unless . . . *you* wouldn't like to come, would you? That is, if you're free.'

'I'd give my right arm to. I mean, I'd be proud and honoured to escort you.'

'You're not playing at Leeds, or anywhere?'

'No. I'm resting for the moment.'

'Then, please come.'

'I'll be delighted.'

'And you'll come back to the party, too? Ivor gives the most marvellous parties. I've never met a man who so enjoys seeing other people happy.'

Gerald gripped the piano stool.

'I can't believe it!' he exclaimed. 'I thought you meant just the show. That would have been enough, but . . . Oh, how wonderful! We'll have the most marvellous evening. I shall buy you masses of orchids . . .'

Anne, who had been about to re-enter the hall, lingered in the doorway just long enough to hear Phyllis list some of the people who were bound to be there – Isabel Jeans, Gladys Cooper, Constance Collier, Lily Elsie, Lilian Braithwaite . . . She turned away unseen and went back to rejoin Vicky, whose search through the books was continuing fruitlessly.

'What's the matter?' Vicky asked, glancing up to see her sister's expression and the flush on her cheeks.

'She's asked him to go to a party with her at Ivor Novello's after a show in London and meet all sorts of famous people.'

'No!'

'It's a bit thick, isn't it? I might just as well not exist.'

'Well, they are both . . .'

'Don't say they're both connected with the theatre, and all that, or I'll clonk you one. I think she's after him. She's years older than he is. It's disgusting!'

'Anne!'

'I think she's making a fool of herself. She's been throwing herself at him ever since he walked into this house.'

'Hang on,' Vicky stopped her, struck by an idea. 'What if it's him, using her?'

'Why should he? What for?'

'I think he's shallow and vain. And I don't believe half he says about the things he's done. He knows she's got connections he hasn't, and he's playing up to her to get in on them.'

'She isn't exactly turning the cold shoulder.'

'No. Because she's flattered. That's the point. I bet you, if she had a glass eye and a wooden leg he'd still flatter her to get taken to a party at Ivor Novello's.'

Even the enraged Anne had to laugh at the idea of their personable aunt flaunting such disabilities before an attendant young man. Vicky was relieved to see as much.

'And he says he's going to buy her masses of orchids,'

Anne told her. 'I expect that'll mean another loan from poor old Bunny.'

'Bunny? Bunny Bickerton?'

'Yes. He told me Gerald's always borrowing things from him when he's in town. If ever he's going anywhere at all smart he even borrows poor old Bunny's evening things.'

'I'd have thought Aunt Phyllis would have seen through someone like that,' Vicky said thoughtfully. 'But then, if you know him for what he's worth, what are you doing, being so jealous?'

Anne flushed again. 'I did invite him. I admit he wasn't first choice, by a long way. But I resent being squeezed out like this, especially by her. I've always thought of her as our best friend.'

'Perhaps she's ... fallen for him. Properly, I mean.'

'Then it's even more disgusting. Oh, my God! That's it!'

Vicky looked at her in alarm. Anne was staring out of the window. Book in hand, her sister went to stand alongside her and look out into the garden. She saw Phyllis and Gerald strolling away from the house, still talking animatedly. But now they were hand in hand.

Helen saw them, too, and mentioned it to Arthur when he came in later.

'I just hope Anne didn't see them,' she added.

'Or mother,' he grunted, not entirely displeased to find his opinion of actors' behaviour so soon confirmed.

'I don't know,' Helen said. 'I had a few words yesterday with her about him and Anne, and she wasn't all that sympathetic. She seemed to me to be taking the view that Phyllis has every right to come here and take over Anne's young man without a qualm. She said some competition might do Anne good.'

'That sounds a pretty enlightened attitude for mother.'

'What do you mean "enlightened"? D'you mean she'd be ready to set off her daughter against her granddaughter?'

He had spoken unseriously, without any thought, and hadn't expected to be asked to explain meanings. He floundered for some seconds, then managed to produce a more considered opinion: 'I think mother may feel that Anne's too young to get hurt. I hope Phyl isn't too old not to.'

Like most actors, Gerald Hope-Langley was a ready talker; and like most people outside his profession, the Bourne family were intrigued after dinner by his stories of the eccentric and outrageous goings-on of other stage folk, especially in relation to that singular breed of ladies who regularly let digs to 'theatricals' touring in the provinces. Even Anne had to laugh at some of his stories, though it did seem to her remarkable that he could have had so many uproarious encounters in so short a career as she knew his to be. She suspected that he was passing on the embroidered experiences of others, modified to the first person singular.

Less acceptable were the accounts of his prowess.

'... and Marie Tempest walked straight down centre stage, looked directly at me, and said, "I want *him*!" So they had to give me the part there and then. In all modesty, I believe I had given a better audition than the others. But when it came down to it, it needed her greatness to see that perhaps I had that extra special bit to offer as well.'

Anne glanced at her Aunt Phyllis and felt something like nausea at seeing her admiring gaze on Gerald.

'I didn't know you'd been in a play with Marie Tempest,' Anne said sharply.

'Oh, yes, yes. And then there was the time when ...'

'When was it, Gerald?' Vicky chimed in. 'The Marie Tempest play?'

'Oh, er, a couple of years ago. One's in so many things you know ...'

'Where? Where was it?'

'Let's see, it would be ... Dash it, I should remember.'

Yes, Anne thought, you should.

Her mother, too, had noted the unsatisfactory answers and could see Arthur frowning a little. Both Charles and Alice were half-dozing. Helen took the opportunity to say, getting up, 'I think it's time we all made a move in the direction of our nicely warmed beds. Come along, girls. I want everyone bright-eyed for church in the morning.'

Alice and Charles got up stiffly and went to the stairs. Gerald gave Helen a little bow and went, too, with some alacrity, it seemed to Arthur, watching him. Above all things, Arthur Bourne detested a fake or a liar. The sailor in him had long since subjugated the lawyer, and his sense of values had become a relatively simple one. Sophisticated people could impress him now more easily than once they might have been able to; but when he saw into them, he tended to see all.

'Phyl,' he said to his sister quietly, as she moved last towards the staircase. 'Come and sit down with me for a few minutes, will you?'

She looked surprised. He added, 'I feel like another brandy, and I don't seem to have had a moment to talk to you since you came.'

She smiled and went back to her chair. He crossed to the decanter.

'And I've never known you refuse a small nightcap,' he said, pouring for them both.

'No,' she agreed, 'we haven't had much time, have we? All this paper-work for the estate seems to keep you awfully busy, Arthur.'

'I'm afraid it does. I keep trying to catch up, but ... Cheers!'

'Cheers!'

'Phyl ...' he started again, but hesitated.

She sighed. 'Yes, Arthur, I know. I noticed Helen had turned rather cool, and I'm sorry. I'm sorry about Anne, I mean.'

'It's not just Anne, you see,' he said. 'That's only a case of battered pride. She's plenty of young men and young Hope-Langley would be well down her list at the best of times, I'm sure. No, dear, don't worry about Anne. She'll forget him half an hour after he leaves.'

'But it was so rude of me. I did try to include her in the

147

conversation at first, but we found ourselves continually talking theatre and she isn't interested. I did try to change the subject now and again, but Gerald . . .'

'Look, Phyl, it doesn't matter about Anne and I don't want to interfere, but what I'm trying to say to you now is what I would be trying to say to Anne, if you hadn't even been here and she'd become besotted with him.'

His sister stared. 'What do you mean?'

'I don't want you to get hurt.'

She goggled for a moment, then laughed. 'Hurt? Me? Darling, I'm no longer your baby sister.'

'Yes. And Hope-Langley's twenty-five.' He hastened to add, 'Oh, not that that matters. You're attractive and amusing, and I admit he's got a certain charm. But he's empty, Phyl. You must realize that.'

'I . . .' she began an automatic and sharp retort, but checked herself and sat silently for some moments, thinking. At length she said flatly, 'Oh, hell! I've been making a fool of myself, haven't I?'

'No, no, my dear. My goodness, if I were a young actor and I met an attractive woman who knew half the famous people in the theatre, I'd probably think all my birthdays had come at once. He liked you from the start, I'm sure, but he'll use you if you let him, for just as long as it suits him. He'll fly in attached to your coat tails and they'll take him on trust because they like you. But for my money he's a sham, and when they find it out they'll remember who brought him into their circle – and I'd hate them to think up their own spiteful reasons why.'

Phyllis sighed. 'You don't miss a trick, Arthur, do you? You stay as solid and calm as a grandfather clock, but you don't miss a damned trick.'

'I'm sorry, I didn't mean to hurt you, but . . .'

'You haven't hurt me, darling, even if I do feel like crying just a little bit . . .'

'Sip that bit of brandy and have another little one. You can cry while my back's turned.'

148

She obeyed. When he brought her glass back she was putting her handkerchief away. She smiled.

'You know,' she told him, 'I think you're not noticing something, but when it comes to it you've always got it worked out just that bit clearer than anyone else. The only other man I've ever known who could do it was Father. He'd have told me exactly the same thing as you have, wouldn't he? Only he'd have made more noise about it.'

'Perhaps so. You know you've always been the only woman in the world – well, apart from Helen – I could talk to as a *friend*. You won't change, will you?'

She shook her head, then drained the small brandy at a gulp.

'I'll try and make things up to Anne in the morning,' she said.

'Oh, don't worry about Anne. She's a tough little thing, really. Anyway, youth has to learn to grow its own shell.'

They both got up. She went over and kissed him gently.

'Good night, Arthur,' she said. 'And thanks. And I won't change ... even if I could.'

For the walk to church next morning, Phyllis took care to pair herself, arm-in-arm, with Lady Bourne. Helen accompanied her father and Vicky her father. Anne was perforce left to walk with Gerald Hope-Langley. Theirs was the most perfunctory conversation of anyone's, both there and back.

When they had all returned, Gerald looked hopefully round for Phyllis, but failed to see her. He accepted a glass of sherry from Arthur and was forced into conversation with him and Charles Ashley. Nothing that was said gave him any cue to talk about the theatre.

Anne was absent, too. She was in her room, putting away her hat and coat and gloves. Phyllis had followed her in.

'When can you get that thing off?' she asked brightly, indicating Anne's sling.

'Couple of weeks.' The answer was studiedly terse, as Phyllis had expected. She didn't let that deter her.

149

'I expect you'll be glad. I cracked my wrist when I was twelve. My hand still shakes a little if I've been carrying anything heavy. You'll find your shoulder and arm rather weak for a while.'

'Uhu.'

'When . . . does Michael Sherwood get back? Next week?'

'Yes.'

'Oh. Well, d'you suppose he'd mind too much if you went to that first night . . . with Gerald?'

Anne turned from the wardrobe to stare at her.

Phyllis went on, 'That's if you'd like to. You see, I've remembered I've something to do instead. I can't disappoint him from going at all, so if you don't want to he'll just have to take the tickets and find someone else.'

'But . . . it's you he's looking forward to going with, isn't it? And to that party at Ivor Novello's.'

'Oh, that. Oh, I'll probably go to that, anyway. I mean, any woman can go by herself to one of Ivor's parties with impunity. In fact, it's more fun. One can circulate more freely without an escort.'

She went over to Anne and put a hand on her arm.

'Darling,' she said, 'I've been very selfish, keeping him away from you so much. I'm afraid that talking theatre's an awfully anti-social habit. I should have made myself stop.'

Anne said glumly, 'I don't suppose he'd have found me much company, anyway. I can't talk about that sort of thing. Honestly, I don't mind.'

'Yes you do. I upset you, and I didn't mean to, and I'm sorry. Truly.'

To her profound relief, Anne accepted her kiss.

'Anyway,' Phyllis added, 'You haven't missed anything. He can't talk about anything but theatre and himself, and more than half of it's second-hand or made up – on both subjects, I suspect. Ivor and his friends wouldn't thank me for inflicting him on them.'

'But . . . I thought . . . I mean, you seemed . . .'

'Well, it was quite a good performance at first. Perhaps I

was a bit too impressed. But when I think about it, I've seen the role played too often, and heard the lines before.'

She flipped open her handbag and drew out the two pale green tickets. She held them out to Anne.

'So – do you want them?'

Anne shook her head.

Her aunt nodded. 'Luckily I always have the excuse of pupils needing my moral support at recitals. I sometimes think I could have made quite an actress myself, the times I've played that part to get out of things.'

She flourished the tickets.

'Come on and watch me perform. I sense an appreciative audience down there.'

They went downstairs happily, arm-in-arm.

CHAPTER NINE

ARTHUR had said that Anne seemed to collect some extraordinary people: it was perhaps as well for everyone that he
was away when Rex Burton-Smith strutted on to the scene at
Larkfield Manor. Arther had gone to Kent, to Chatham, to
attend the funeral of a retired Captain of the Dockyard
who had been a close colleague of his during his post-war
service. Chatham is a long way from Halbury, so he had
decided to make the most of the chance to stay for a few
days in the Officers' Quarters and renew old acquaintances
at a Mess dinner for King George V's Silver Jubilee.

It was a hot May afternoon, and Vicky, luxuriating in the
long stay at home, had climbed up into the cedar tree, to a
place of cool comfort which had served her for years as a
retreat for reading and contemplation. Above the clash of
swordplay in *The Prisoner of Zenda* the more conscious part
of her mind registered the plop-plop of tennis balls being
driven to and fro, and male and female cries and laughter.
One male voice, louder than the rest, irritated her.

Glancing down, she saw her mother waving at her from the
hall window and pointing to the tall lemonade jug she held
in her other hand. It was worth descending for, Vicky
thought, and got easily down to the springy turf, stooping
almost double to pass under the lower branches. In the hall
she found her mother putting out plates of sandwiches and
cakes.

'Who's making all that noise with Liz and Anne?' Vicky
asked. 'Besides Giles and Rosemary.'

'Rex . . . something or other. He *is* rather noisy, isn't he?'

'I can hardly hear myself read. Where on earth's she found him?'

'He lives out on the Hereford road, I gather. A place called West Norton. His parents built themselves a new luxury house out there.'

Vicky made a face. 'You mean one of those modern things?'

'Yes. White stucco, and green tiles on the roof.'

'How ghastly.'

'Everyone to his taste, dear. The father's a retired businessman from Birmingham. And very rich, according to Anne. The boy's got a 3-litre Bentley. Don't drink all the lemonade.'

The voices were louder now and approaching. Vicky's sisters came in, wearing tennis things, pink-cheeked and wild-haired. With them Liz's friends, Giles and Rosemary Hamilton, a brother and sister. The other member of the little group was the stranger.

Vicky looked him over quickly, taking in the impression that he was good-looking in an Errol Flynn-like way, and immaculately dressed in tennis uniform. Almost over-well dressed, she thought. He would be about twenty-two.

And that voice! He was talking as they entered, recounting some incident at a tennis tournament he had watched. His voice was abrasive and too loud for good manners. He spoke in almost a parody of an Oxford accent, with a good leavening of Americanisms and screen slang.

'You've met my mother,' Liz interrupted him.

'Howdy, Mrs. Bourne!' was his response to that and across the hall he gave her a familiar wave.

'Good afternoon,' Helen replied formally. 'You're all just in time. Lemonade or tea, and do help yourselves to sandwiches and things.'

'This is my youngest sister, Vicky,' Anne told the newcomer. 'Rex Burton-Smith.'

He bounded over to Vicky and seized her hand. 'Am I

glad to meet *you,* Vicky!' he declared. Then he turned away and, ignoring the sandwiches, helped himself to a cake. He ate it by stuffing a large portion into his mouth for the first bite and polishing off the rest with a second. He immediately picked up another. Without waiting to empty his mouth, he mumbled, 'Jolly good cakes, these. Home made, I bet.' He reached right across the table for the lemonade, poured himself a glass and washed down the rest of the cake with a great gulp of it.

'I say!' he exclaimed, breaking into a conversation between the girls about finishing school. 'Who plays the old joanna?'

Anne answered him. 'Vicky does. Well ... all of us at times, but Vicky's the expert.'

He grinned, put down his glass, and to Vicky's horror, sat down on the piano stool. He raised the piano lid and plunged into a cacophonous attempt at 'Chopsticks'. Vicky reddened, furious at this sticky-fingered mauling of her beloved piano. Helen winced at the noise. She murmured something about fetching more lemonade and hurried away into the haven of the kitchen.

'Hey, Anne!' Rex was shouting. 'What was that Fred Astaire song ... when they were in the old bandstand in the rain?' He sang untunefully, 'Isn't it a ... something ... day to be ...'

'... caught in the rain,' Anne concluded for him. 'You can't play that!'

It was clear that he was going to try, though. Liz intervened, 'We've got the sheet music for it – on the piano. Anne, you play it.'

'I can't. Too many sharps and flats for me.' Anne turned to Vicky. 'Go on – you play it for us.'

Vicky hesitated. Giles Hamilton encouraged her politely, 'Yes, please, Vicky. You show us.'

'Perhaps we could dance to it,' Rosemary suggested eagerly, to Liz's annoyance.

'I can't syncopate,' Vicky said, but thought to herself,

anything to get him away from my piano. She found the music and took Rex's place at the keyboard.

She was a fluent sight-reader, but her training and interest were entirely classical. She played the tune 'correctly', but with no rhythmic zest.

'It's a bit slow,' Rosemary said, trying not to sound critical. 'I mean, to dance to.'

Anne said, 'Can't you jazz it up a bit? You know, like Carroll Gibbons.'

Rex's loud voice cut in. 'Watch me, kid. I'll show you the rhythm and you just follow.'

He moved into a clear patch of floor and began to jig about in a crude travesty of Fred Astaire's relaxed style, snapping his fingers as he chanted the words. Reluctantly, Vicky tried to accompany him, but his interpretation of the rhythm was as flawed as his singing. No one else moved to dance. They stood in varying degrees of embarrassment as he plunged about, once or twice knocking into pieces of furniture. He seemed to Helen, who had come to the kitchen door with a fresh jug of lemonade, to move almost unnaturally in a way she couldn't have analysed. Certainly, his clumsiness contrasted noticeably with his good looks and faultless dress.

He caught sight of her and approached her, still jigging and clicking his fingers.

'Our dance, I think, Mrs. Bourne,' he cried, and seized her free hand, jerking her so that she nearly spilt the lemonade. She pulled away.

'I'm afraid my dancing days are over,' she said icily. 'Please excuse me.' She placed the jug on the table and went back into the kitchen.

Vicky had perceived her mother's anger. Even Rex had taken the hint at last and was standing still. Vicky lifted her hands from the keys in mid-bar and closed the piano with significant firmness.

Anne glanced at Liz and said brightly, 'Well, come on, if we're to get in another set.'

'Yes, come on,' Rosemary said. 'It's you and me versus Giles and Liz. Your turn to sit out, Rex.'

'Suits me, old thing,' he grinned. 'My feet are killing me.'

To Vicky's dismay he threw himself into an armchair. Anne smiled wickedly at her younger sister.

'You can have him for a bit,' she said, and ran out of the house, followed by the other three players. Vicky remained seated at the closed piano. Rex regarded her in a way which made her feel uncomfortable.

'Don't you play tennis?' he asked at length.

She shook her head. 'Not really. I was never much good at games.'

'What are you good at, then?'

She restrained the temptation to walk out of the room and leave him. She replied, 'I suppose, music.'

'So I gather. Play some more.'

If he had not, after a fractional pause, added 'please', she certainly would have walked out. She decided to play something, instinctively hoping that it would bore him and send him off to watch the tennis. Her book of Chopin Nocturnes lay near to the top of the pile of her current practice pieces. She extracted it. It came open at the soulful, brooding work she liked the best of those she had learnt. Vicky propped the music up on its stand and began to play.

Despite her awareness of the boorish audience of one, and the almost peremptory order to her to play, she gave the lovely music of her best. In the space of a few bars her listener had been forgotten. She was playing for herself, and she played with understanding and real feeling.

When the last chords had finished their long dying Vicky suddenly remembered that she was not alone, though when she looked across towards the armchair she half expected to see it empty. Rex was still there. He had neither stirred nor made a sound throughout the few minutes of the recital. Vicky saw with surprise, though, that his expression was completely altered. The eyes which had glittered with mischief and arrogance were soft and mournful. There was no grin or smirk now, but a look of wistful longing, almost of regret.

He said quietly, 'That was nice.'

The transformation was hard to believe. Vicky said, 'Thank you. I ... wouldn't have thought you'd care for Chopin.'

A hint of mockery returned to his expression.

'Why not?'

'You're not really a ... quiet person, are you?'

'Quiet?'

She gave a little shy laugh. 'Well, when I was reading my book, up in the cedar tree this afternoon, I heard your voice all the time and louder than any of the others'. I thought to myself, "What a very *noisy* young man." '

The expected bantering retort did not come. His eyes remained on hers. She saw the smile leave the corners of his lips and the intense expression return. Both sat very still for a few moments, neither breaking the gaze.

Then, abruptly, Rex almost propelled himself to his feet, the broad grin back on his face.

'Think I *will* go and see how the tennis is getting on,' he said. 'If you'll excusez-moi.'

He went quickly out, singing untunefully, 'Isn't it a lovely day to be caught in the rain?'

That evening he took Anne for a river bathe to be followed by dinner somewhere. Vicky went to bed early, before they had returned. She settled back comfortably to read, but somehow *The Prisoner of Zenda* had become less interesting, a made-up character going through the motions of made-up exploits. She put the book aside, smoothed her pillows down and switched off the bedside light. She lay staring into the darkness, her mind unable to rid itself of that film tune, which insisted on replaying itself over and over again.

She heard a car drive up unusually quickly and come to a halt with a little skid. Rex's loud voice grated on the air, and Anne's quieter one, calling a cheerful good night. Car doors slammed and the vehicle drove off fast, with a voluntary of toots on the horn.

'Well!' she heard Liz greet Anne next morning, when they met at breakfast. 'I heard you and that ghastly, loud-mouthed Romeo of yours getting home last night.'

'I should think the whole neighbourhood did,' Vicky agreed.

'Darling,' their mother said to Anne, 'do remember what I said when you came in last night. Ask him to be a bit more considerate, if there's another time.'

Anne giggled. 'He is a bit hearty, isn't he?'

'Hearty!' Liz echoed. 'He's like a man permanently talk-ing through a megaphone.'

The telephone was ringing. Liz started to get up to go to it, but Helen motioned her to stay.

'I'll go,' she said. 'I think it will be Daddy.'

She went out into the hall. Liz said to Anne, 'Anyway, did you have a good time?'

'Rather! We had our swim, then dinner at a hotel in Glou-cester.'

'Gloucester!'

'I know. That car really covers some ground – not like your poor old rattle-trap. Anyway, when we got back to Halbury Rex noticed some sort of hop going on at the White Hart, and we went to investigate. It turned out to be the Hereford Young Farmers' Association, celebrating the Silver Jubilee. You needed tickets, but Rex talked our way in some-how.'

'I can just imagine. Was it any good?'

'Not much. We danced a bit, but Rex got bored. He said it needed jazzing up, and . . .'

'Anne,' her mother's voice came from the doorway. Its sharpness startled all three of them. Helen came back to the table, her face grim.

'What's the matter, Mummy?' Vicky asked. 'Was it Daddy?'

'No, it was not Daddy. It was Mr. Mason, from the White Hart.'

Helen turned upon Anne, who had blanched.

'He was complaining strongly about your behaviour last night – yours and that uncouth young man's. Anne, you're a stupid, thoughtless, irresponsible girl, and you can thank heaven Daddy isn't here. How dare you and that creature gatecrash a private party, and then try to take over the band – the drums, and things – and make a perfect nuisance of yourselves? In Halbury, what's worse, where nearly everyone knows you. How *dare* you?'

Anne faltered, 'We . . . only tried to brighten things up a bit. Nobody seemed to mind – at least, not everyone . . .'

'Well the Young Farmers' secretary seems to have done so enough to complain to Mr. Mason about your having been allowed in. And Mr. Mason minds, and *I* mind. You'll go straight to the writing desk and write a letter of apology to both of them – I've written the secretary's name and address on the telephone pad. And as for that young man, you will not invite him into this house again. Do you understand? In fact, I'd prefer it if you didn't see him any more.'

'Oh, mummy, he isn't as bad as all that,' Anne protested. 'He's just a bit noisy and spoilt . . .'

'Anyone can see that. His parents obviously pamper him with far too much money. But that's no excuse for loutish behaviour, and it's certainly no excuse for you.'

'I'm sorry, Mummy. Truly. Are you . . . going to tell Daddy?'

'I don't know. If I don't, he'll probably still hear about it from someone else.'

'Oh, lor'!'

'Yes, exactly. All right, I won't tell him.'

'Oh, thank you, Mummy.'

'More for his benefit than yours, though. He has enough worries without your behaviour. But remember, that young man does not come here again.'

'Yes, Mummy.'

'Now, finish your breakfast and go and get those letters written.'

'Yes, Mummy.'

'And then you can telephone your "friend" and tell him not to show his face here.'

'Yes, Mummy.'

'Will you see him again?' Vicky asked Anne later that day, well out of their mother's earshot.

'If I choose to – yes. I'm furious, being ticked off like that, as if I were a child.'

'You didn't put up much of a fight.'

'That'd make her sure to tell Daddy. That's the one thing I don't want.'

'Well, you daren't risk him coming here.'

'I know that, silly. There's nothing to stop me meeting him somewhere, is there? And there's still the telephone – or the post.'

And Anne did meet Rex Burton-Smith again, the following morning. She went for one of her rides, and just 'chanced' to find him sitting in his big car in a lane. The thrill of the clandestine meeting soon evaporated, however, and they talked commonplaces. In an attempt to restore her spirits, as much as to enjoy carrying out a secret act of defiance of her mother's wishes, Anne told him of a party being given two evenings later by some young friends. She said she had been going to go alone, but was sure he would be welcome if he would take her. He hesitated uncharacteristically before agreeing, but she didn't notice it. She rode home pleased with herself again.

She was not to know that her reference to the telephone and the post had had an unknowing irony to it. She had used the telephone to arrange the morning's 'chance' meeting; but it was to Vicky that the postman had brought a letter with a local postmark. Fortunately, her mother did not see it arrive and question her. Liz did, though, and got as big a surprise as Vicky had had when she opened it and saw who it was from.

'Rex! Writing to you!'

In a voice which trembled a little, Vicky read it out.

'Dear Vicky,

I hear from Anne that I'm "persona non grata" at Larkfield Manor. Pity I can't come and hear you play the piano any more. I'd love to see you again, though, and as I'm not allowed to DARKEN YOUR DOORSTEP perhaps we could meet somewhere else. Would you like to have tea with me in Halbury, at The Copper Kettle or somewhere? Suggest Tuesday afternoon, if it will suit. Will you give me a ring?

Rex.'

'Of all the nerve!' Liz exclaimed. But Vicky didn't respond in the way she expected.

'I don't know,' she said slowly, folding the letter away into its envelope. 'I'd quite like to.'

'You're mad.'

'No, I'm not, and you've no right to say so. You're not Mummy.'

'Oh, don't fly off at me so fast! I'm just saying you can't possibly go.'

'Well, for that, I'm saying I can and jolly well shall.'

'He's Anne's friend.'

'Not specially. They're not serious or anything.'

'Catch Anne being serious about anyone, him especially! What on earth can you see in him, anyway?'

Vicky paused a moment before answering. 'I'm not sure,' she admitted. 'There is something, though – behind all that noise and showing-off. I think he's a different sort of person, really.'

'He certainly conceals it thoroughly, then.'

'Oh, sucks to you!'

Vicky made for the telephone. Her sister shrugged.

'Well, it'll be on your own head if Mummy finds out.'

'You wouldn't tell her!'

'What do you take me for? But for heaven's sake get him

to make it somewhere else than The Copper Kettle, or the cat'll be out of the bag in no time.'

Vicky paused at the telephone table. Then she smiled.

'Thanks, old sport. I hadn't thought of that. We'll make it one of the other places.'

The place they agreed upon was not 'olde worlde' like The Copper Kettle, but modern, with furniture veneered in light wood, bright flame-coloured curtains, travel posters on the walls, and a selection of sauce-bottles on every table. It was the counterpart to the staid Copper Kettle, with a much younger clientele. Its cakes were of the mass-produced variety and it dispensed more soft drinks than tea.

Vicky actually preferred it to the older-established place. Rex was obviously a regular habitué. He exchanged some raillery with the good-humoured proprietress, accusing her of serving stale cakes and dog-biscuits, to which she replied spiritedly.

When they were alone with their tea and perfectly fresh cakes, Rex reverted to his quieter manner and smiled across at Vicky.

'Thanks for coming,' he said. 'How are you?'

'Very well, thank you.'

'Been practising any good tunes lately?'

'I have to practise every day.'

'You really are going to make a career of it?' He sounded genuinely impressed.

'That's the general idea – if I'm good enough. What about you?'

The innocent question seemed to take him aback rather. He actually stammered slightly in saying, 'M-me? Oh, some sort of business.' He went on quickly to say, 'I suppose your mother doesn't know we're meeting – after that fiasco over Anne?'

'No fear!'

'Pity about the other night,' he said airily. 'Anyhow, I'm quite used to being banned from people's houses.'

'Are you?'

'Oh, yes. Daily occurrence.'

She smiled. 'Do you always do awful things?'

'Yes. Always. Have a stale cake.'

Vicky took a wrapped chocolate swiss roll.

'I like these better than home-made,' she admitted. 'They're far less stodgy.'

Rex had taken a small bottle from his pocket. He shook out a white pill and put it in his mouth, washing it down with a sip of tea.

'Have you a cold?' Vicky asked.

'No, no. Just something I take from time to time. Peps me up.'

'I shouldn't think you need pepping up.'

'Don't we all at times? Anyway, what else do you do, apart from playing the piano?'

'Lots of things. I ride a bit – not as much as Anne, though. I like walking. I read a lot. Do you read?'

'I used to,' he answered, and she was surprised to see again in his eyes that withdrawn look he had worn after hearing her play the piano.

'Why not now?'

'Oh, because ... there never seems to be enough time.' He smiled again, but there was no brashness in his saying, 'Besides, I'm lazy. I like being entertained – listening to people like you playing the piano, for instance.'

'What's your favourite music?'

'I don't remember titles much, or composers. I know – *Clair de Lune*. Who's that by?'

'Debussy. Yes, I love it. It always makes me think of the sunrise.'

'Sunrise? Doesn't it mean moonlight?'

'Yes, really. But you see, I like to go out sometimes and watch the sun coming up. And the light and the colours always makes me think of that piece.'

The intensity of sadness in his look made her keep talking.

'I sometimes go on my bicycle to Hayden Barrow, the

other side of Layford, you know? It's a great deep ravine, with trees and hills the other side, and a river with a waterfall. It's the perfect place to watch the sun come up over the hill. Only, you have to be there while it's still dark, so's to be in time. I take a thermos and sandwiches. Liz and Anne think I'm crazy.'

She broke off, and asked, 'Do you know where I mean?'

He shook his head. 'I've heard of it, but I've never bothered to go. Let's go. Us. Tonight.'

Vicky stared across at him.

'In my car,' he was saying. 'Please say yes.'

'But ... I mean, you're not to come to our house any more.'

'I don't need to. We could meet outside the gates.'

'They'd ... they'd hear you at the lodge – the car.'

'What, an hour or so before dawn! They'll be snoring their heads off. Anyway, I'll cruise up quietly.'

Vicky was now finding herself torn between an attractive notion and its attendant risks. Trying to reassure herself, she said, 'But I'd have to sneak out in the early hours.'

'Well, you say you've done it several times before. Tell them you're going again – only I'll be waiting for you.'

'I ... suppose I could.'

'Of course. No one else will insist on coming, will they?'

'I told you – they think I'm crazy.'

'I don't. Is it settled, then?'

She nodded her head firmly at last. 'I'll bring the thermos and sandwiches just as usual. Then no one will be suspicious.'

The prospect had become all the more exciting because of the conspiracy it entailed. They agreed upon a time – half-past three in the morning – and a place round the corner of the lane from the lodge.

'You won't forget to wake up, or anything?' she asked anxiously, as they prepared to separate.

'I've got an infallible alarm. And once I'm awake I'm really awake. Anyway, I wouldn't let you down.'

'I'm sure.'

'But don't tell anyone – none of them – that you're meeting me.'

'I wouldn't dare.'

They met as arranged. The car was already there, looming big in the moonlight, when Vicky reached the appointed spot. She hid her bicycle behind the hedge. Apart from her sisters' usual jeers, and her mother's admonitions to be careful, she had aroused no curiosity. Her mother had packed the sandwiches and filled the thermos herself.

'Lucky I thought to sneak an extra cup out in my pocket,' Vicky remarked to Rex half an hour later. They sat side by side in his car, drinking the coffee, parked on a track high up at one end of the ravine. With a window open they could hear the distant rumble of the waterfall and the stirring of the river. Drowsy birds were beginning to sing small waking songs.

'It's weird,' Rex said. 'Why haven't I been here before? Why didn't I meet you sooner?'

She glanced at him. 'Are you glad you came?'

He took her hand. 'Yes.'

She pointed ahead of them. 'Look at the colour! You'll be surprised how fast it spreads. One minute it's dark, and the next it's . . . Look! Look at the mountain over there!'

He gasped with admiration. The transformation scene was, indeed, incredible for its speed and the lavishness of its effects. Pinks and golds appeared and brightened and spread, until at last the sun itself came peeping round, illuminating first one side of the ravine, then the whole deep cleft. They watched it all in almost unbroken silence, still hand in hand.

'Marvellous!' he exclaimed at last. 'Like a postcard. D'you know, it's the first time I've watched a dawn properly.'

'There! That's it. Now it's day.'

'Listen to those damned birds. Sounds like a cocktail party.'

'They're happy.'

165

'Are you, Vicky?'

She turned to look at him. 'Yes, Rex. Thanks.'

'You're sweet,' he said, and leaned over to her. She closed her eyes and held up her mouth, but was disappointed to feel only a light kiss on her cheek. He sat back again and said, 'You're quite a special person.'

'Am I?'

'Yes.' But he disappointed her again by saying, 'I think we ought to be getting back, don't you?'

'But . . . it's far too soon. I'm never back as early as this.'

'Ah! I'd forgotten.' He looked at his watch. She sensed some sort of impatience to get away, now that the spectacle was over. But he brightened suddenly. 'Tell you what – let's have a nice dawn drive all over the district. Then I'll stand you breakfast at some pub. I'm famished.'

He looked so eager that she didn't wish to disappoint him, and agreed. She would much rather have stayed there, with her hand in his, though preferably with his arm round her. But he pleased her later by asking her to go to the seaside with him the following afternoon, if she could get away. She thought quickly and decided to tell her mother she had been invited by Giles and Rosemary Hamilton. She would confide in Liz, whose friends they were, to cover up for her if the need arose.

Vicky had to be out a lot that day and it was early evening before she got home again. Liz was out, too, and so was her mother. Mrs. Gates gave her a meal and then went home. There was no sign of Anne, whose whereabouts Mrs. Gates hadn't known. Vicky wandered about the house, feeling alone and deflated, wishing the telephone would ring and that she would hear Rex's voice. It was unlikely to happen. She wondered whether to ring him, but thought she had better not. She sat in the hall with her book, but the Prisoner's appeal had quite vanished by now.

Liz came in when darkness had fallen. She carried a medical book. 'Hello, dear child,' she greeted Vicky. 'All on your own.'

'Yes. And bored. I bet you've been with Brian Harrington.'

Liz put a finger to her lips and smiled enigmatically, holding up the book as proof of something or other.

'It's all right,' Vicky said. 'There's not another soul here. Mummy's at her W.I. supper. Heaven knows where Anne is.'

'Oh, I do,' Liz said. 'Gone to a party with your mutual friend.'

Vicky stared. 'Who? Not Rex!'

'Yes. I thought you'd have known.'

'I haven't seen Anne. But he never said anything to me about . . . When was this fixed?'

'This morning. He rang up.'

'Did you speak to him?'

'No. Anne took it. Lucky it wasn't Mummy.'

'There wasn't . . . any message for me?'

'Not that I know of. You're not upset, are you?'

Vicky said flatly, 'Of course not.'

'Look, darling, I did tell you what he's like.'

'It doesn't matter. How did he fetch her?'

'They had to meet secretly. Not too near, so his car wouldn't be seen, and not too far for her to walk in a long dress and high heels.'

Vicky felt the cut of this. There had been such a sense of exclusivity about her own secret rendezvous with him. Now the experience was shared. She felt let down. It showed in her face. Liz regarded her closely.

'You *are* upset, aren't you?'

' 'Course not. It's just . . . rather annoying. I might as well go to bed, I think.'

But at that moment they heard a key in the front door. It opened and Anne came in. She marched angrily into the hall and flung her handbag into a chair.

'Whatever's the matter with you?' Liz asked.

'I'm furious.' She looked it.

'What for?'

'We had a flaming row – that's what for.'

'You and Rex?'

'Who else? Stupid idiot. I don't care if I never see him again as long as I live.'

Vicky, who had been on the point of resuming her move towards bed, heard this with interest. She said nothing, but stayed to listen.

'I made him drive me home,' Anne was raging. 'But, of course, because of Mummy and her stupid ban I had to be dropped outside in the road and trudge all the way here in my best shoes. Oh God, what a waste of an evening!'

'That was it about – the row?'

'I don't even know that. Nothing seemed right, from the start. He seemed a bit on edge – strange, somehow.' She turned on Vicky. 'He kept asking me about you.'

'Me?' Surely Rex hadn't told Anne about their dawn meeting. But it appeared not.

'What sort of person you are, and so forth. I told him it was the height of bad manners to be with one person and talk about someone else. Then he told me not to be silly. He was really cross about it. *He* was the one being silly. I tried to snap him out of it, but he was in a sulk by then. If there's one thing I can't stand it's a moody man. In the end, he had the cheek to say would I stop talking, as I was getting on his nerves. Coming from him! Anyway, that was enough, and I said I wished I'd stayed at home playing Ludo with you two, and I made him bring me.'

The telephone rang. Liz said, 'There you are. What's the betting he's ringing to apologize?'

'Apologize? Rex!'

'Are you going to answer it?'

'No fear,' Anne said. 'I'm going to play hard to get.'

Vicky was tempted to go to the telephone herself, but something warned her that it might just be him calling her. She didn't wish to speak to him in front of the enraged Anne.

Liz lifted the receiver herself and gave the number.

'No, this is Elizabeth,' she told the caller. 'Oh, hello, Rex ... Yes ... Just a moment, please ...'

168

Anne was shaking her head emphatically; but it was to Vicky that Liz turned, holding out the instrument.

'He wants you,' she said. Then, as an afterthought, 'Rex Burton-Smith.'

'What the hell for?' Anne demanded explosively. Liz put her hand over the mouthpiece, while Vicky hesitated.

'Ssh! He'll hear you.'

'Let him. I suppose he's trying to make me jealous.'

Liz said amusedly, 'He seems to be succeeding.'

'He is *not* succeeding,' Anne raged. She swung round on Vicky. 'He's all yours!' she stormed, and, gathering her long skirt in a gesture of finality, ran off upstairs.

When Anne had turned the corner of the landing Vicky went to take the phone. Liz made a wry face at her as she handed it over.

'I'll leave you,' she whispered.

Vicky smiled her thanks and took the telephone. In contrast to Anne, Rex sounded calm and untroubled. He had rung, he said, to confirm the time of their meeting for the trip to the sea the following afternoon. She noted that he didn't inquire after Anne, or send any apology.

The time until the trip seemed endless to Vicky. Next morning seemed to last at least twelve hours and the unwanted lunch was a torment. Anne, the disliker of moody men, was moody and silent herself, and it was only through Liz's efforts that Helen was kept from sensing an atmosphere and asking questions.

At long last the time came for Vicky to leave for her purported outing with the Hamiltons. Anne had asked where she was going and merely grunted unsuspiciously when she told her. Her mother had offered to drive Vicky over to her friends', but she told her they had said they would pick her up in the lane at half-past two, to save driving up to the house.

'Good luck, Vic,' Liz whispered as she closed the door behind her. Vicky gave her a happy wink.

Two hours later she returned, drooping and close to tears.

'What's happened?' Anne asked her, genuinely concerned.

'Where's Mummy?' Vicky replied.

'Over at the cottage talking to Peggy Chapman.'

'Thank God for that!'

Alan Chapman and Peggy Short had duly married and had moved into the cottage only a few weeks ago. From time to time Helen went over unannounced to help Peggy with her home-making, or just to chat.

'Why "thank God",' Anne was persisting. Liz, who had heard the voices, came out from her father's study, where she had been reading at the desk.

'It's no use, Anne,' Vicky said despondently. 'You might as well know I really went to meet Rex.'

The tantrum she had expected did not eventuate. Anne shrugged and said, 'More fool you. More fool any girl who does.'

'What happened?' Liz asked. Vicky had the presence of mind to conceal her eldest sister's involvement.

'I . . . When he telephoned . . . last night . . . it was to ask if I'd like to go for a drive with him. I didn't tell either of you, because Anne was so cross.'

'Huh!' Anne snorted. 'One of his famous secret rendezvous? I had enough of that last night, thank you.'

'I'm sorry, Anne,' Vicky said. 'I didn't think there'd be any harm in accepting. I didn't want to do you down.'

'As I said last night, old sport, he's all yours. Good riddance.'

'But what's happened . . . to make you so miserable?' Liz asked Vicky.

'Only that he never turned up.'

'Oh, no!'

'He hasn't telephoned, has he?'

'No. I've been in all afternoon. Do you mean to say you've been waiting in the lane all this time?'

'There was nothing else I could do. I couldn't come back here, because I thought Mummy would be in and she'd know I'd been lying when I said the Hamiltons were picking me up. She'd have phoned them and found there was no arrangement. I wanted to come back and telephone him, but I didn't dare.'

'There's the box at the crossroads.'

'I know. Only, it's so far that I was afraid he would come while I was walking to it, and think I'd given up waiting, and just drive off again. In any case,' she added pitifully, 'he did promise. If he was coming, he'd have come.'

'That pig!' Anne burst out. 'If I know him, he's gone out with someone else instead, and never even bothered to phone.'

'He wouldn't!'

'Oh, yes he would!'

It had occurred to Vicky during her long wait that he had been playing a careful double game with her and Anne, ensuring that his meetings with each didn't clash with the other, and that Anne did not even know he was seeing Vicky at all. His date with Anne which had ended disastrously still rankled with Vicky, evidently more than it did with Anne.

'Perhaps . . . his car's broken down,' she tried lamely.

'Not it. If it had, he'd have phoned.'

Liz said gently, 'Vic, hadn't you better be realistic about it?'

'Better still,' Anne said firmly, 'I'm going to ring him. I've got a few choice words to say to him on my own account, so I'll add some for you.'

But before she could reach the telephone they heard the kitchen door and their mother's voice calling. Liz urgently motioned Anne back. Their chance was gone.

'Darling!' Helen exclaimed, when she came into the hall and saw Vicky standing with her sisters. 'What are you doing back?'

Vicky tried desperately, 'The . . . car broke down. Giles and Rosemary's. They telephoned here, and . . . and Liz came down to the lane and fetched me.'

'Hard luck. But why keep your hat on in the house? It does look formal.'

'Oh ... they're coming when they can ... So I didn't bother to change.'

'Darling, it's five o'clock. It's far too late to go anywhere now.'

A car was, in fact, coming up the drive. Vicky's heart, already thumping with the effort of lying, started to pound. Surely he wouldn't dare ...!

'How's Peggy?' Liz asked her mother, deliberately trying to draw her off the subject.

'Very well. You see, Alan turned up trumps after all. She thinks the world of him and apparently he loves the cottage far more than he's been able to make us realize. We had quite a heart to heart.'

The car had stopped at the door. Vicky was almost holding her breath. Her mother said, 'Well – aren't you going to open the door for them?'

Vicky dreaded the moment so much that she found herself quite unable to move. Liz walked past her as the doorbell sounded and opened the door only slightly, hoping to be able to give Rex some sort of warning to go away at once. Then she opened it wide. The man who stood there was elderly, a stranger.

'Is this Commander Bourne's house?' he asked. His voice carried the accent of Birmingham. When Liz nodded he said, 'Are ... are you Vicky, by any chance?'

'No. I'm her sister,' she said. 'But she's here. Will you come in?'

He said, with an air of desperation, 'Look is the Commander in, please? Or Mrs. Bourne?'

'My mother's here,' Liz replied, and stood aside for him to enter. He came forward to the expectant group and went up to Helen.

'Mrs. Bourne,' he said heavily, I'm ... er ... Norman Burton-Smith. You ... know my son, Rex.'

'Yes, we have met him,' Helen said, shaking hands civilly. She was about to introduce the girls, but he said, speaking quickly. 'I believe my boy was expected here this afternoon to fetch your daughter, Vicky, for a drive to the seaside.'

From the corner of her eye Vicky saw her mother turn to stare at her. But the visitor was continuing.

'I thought I'd better come myself, rather than telephone, to bring some . . . news. I'm sorry to tell you our son died . . . just before three o'clock this afternoon.'

There was complete silence for a moment. Then he added, 'He was getting changed, ready to come out. He was . . . very happy . . . looking forward to it. He collapsed in his room, and died an hour later. He . . . he never regained consciousness. He can't have known anything about it.'

A sound between a sigh and a moan made all the others turn to Vicky, to see her crumpling to the floor. The diversion had at least the effect of sending them all into action, dispelling the numbness of shock and incredulousness. Liz attended expertly to Vicky and within less than a minute had her conscious again. Then she and Anne supported her up the stairs to her bedroom, leaving Helen with the stricken man.

'Please sit down, Mr. Burton-Smith,' she said. He obeyed.

'It's hit us all,' he said dully, 'even though we've known for years it would happen. We've lived with . . . like . . . a shadow over us, the wife and I, for four years . . . since the doctors told us about our boy's heart. There was nothing could be done for him, except he had pills to take to help him a bit.'

'I'm terribly, deeply sorry,' Helen said. 'Did . . . Rex know how ill he was?'

'Yes. It couldn't be kept from him. It was the cause of quite a bit of trouble. Knowing he hadn't long . . . made him behave badly sometimes. He'd show off and get up to silly tricks. He annoyed a lot of people. I hope he didn't you.'

Helen shook her head. He looked relieved. He went on. 'I suppose it could be said we spoilt him, letting him have an expensive car, too much money – but it seemed all we *could* give him. Do you know what I mean?'

'I do exactly. I wish *I* could do more than offer you and your wife our deepest sympathy – from all of us.'

He nodded thanks and got up.

'I'm sure we appreciate it, and that you kept inviting our boy here and being so kind to him. We're having the funeral at four o'clock on Monday – St. Michael's in Halbury.'

'Of course we shall come,' Helen promised, accompanying him to the door. He paused to shake hands again.

'I hope your ... Vicky won't take it too hard,' he said finally, and went to his car.

'I still can't believe it,' Vicky told her mother later. She was in bed, her eyes dry at last, her body limp, drained even of the energy to cry.

'I know, darling,' Helen said yet again. 'Sudden death is the hardest to accept. Even in the war one never got used to it.'

Vicky was not taking in her mother's words, though. She was remembering aloud: 'Seeing him only yesterday. Watching the sun come up at Hayden Barrow ...'

This information surprised Helen, but she did not allude to it, letting Vicky go on.

'... He said he'd never watched a dawn before ... and now he never will again. He was so happy, so full of life ...'

She broke off, realizing what she had said.

'Oh, Mummy, I lied to you about going to the Barrow alone. I'm so sorry.'

Helen held her hand. She said, 'If I'd been a little more understanding about Rex you wouldn't have had to lie. But then, who was to know that behind all that ... Well, at least his poor father believes he was always welcome here. I'm sorry, too, darling.'

Vicky said slowly, 'It makes me feel ... almost a cheat, to be living and he's dead – just like that.'

'Vicky,' Helen said, in a firmer tone, 'listen to me. We all have to die sooner or later. You know what they say – "Whom the gods love ..." – but most of us never stop to think that we might be the chosen ones. Rex knew he couldn't live long. He didn't sit down and feel sorry for himself about it. He faced death, and you're facing life. So just remember him as a rather brave and special young man you helped to make happy to the last. Will you do that?'

'I'll try, Mummy. Do you . . . think he will know?'

Helen nodded.

'I'm sure he will. *Sure* he will.'

CHAPTER TEN

PEGGY Chapman gave birth to her baby in July. It was a boy. There was some discussion between the young couple about what he should be named. Peggy was for calling him Frank, after Alan's father. Alan – surprisingly to the Bournes, when they heard of it – wanted Arthur, after their benefactor. They settled, by some obscure route, upon George.

Perhaps not quite so obscure, however, for it was the king's name, and the echoes of the Silver Jubilee of his reign had not yet died away. The Chapmans and the Shorts, the two families now acquainted with one another and on good terms, were staunch nationalists and patriots. So were the Bournes and the Ashleys.

'I'm not so sure. Not so sure at all,' Charles Ashley said, shaking his head gravely at Lady Bourne, who sat facing him on the other side of the empty fireplace in the hall of Larkfield Manor. It was the coolest place on a very hot afternoon, and neither felt inclined to do anything but glance at periodicals and chat desultorily. The subject Charles was expressing doubt about was Stanley Baldwin's return to the Premiership the previous month.

'Why not?' Alice demanded. 'He's solid, reliable ...'

'Stolid is the word I should choose,' Charles said. 'That pipe-smoking image is all very well, and that talk of reading books and keeping pigs ...'

'That was ages ago.'

'Yes, but he hasn't changed, and he never will. What is he now? Sixty-eight? Far too old.'

'I do not compute my age to the exact year, Charles, but I recall passing sixty-eight some few years ago.'

'My dear Alice, no stranger would believe that. However, you are not undertaking the burdens of Prime Ministerial office for the third time.'

'Arguing again?' Helen asked them brightly, as she entered, fanning herself with a copy of the *Tatler*. 'I'd have thought it was much too hot for that.'

Charles said, 'For my part, merely sounding a tocsin of warning about the policies, or lack of them, of dear old Baldwin. Peace and quiet at any price, so long as it keeps the voters happy, and never mind what Mussolini's up to.'

'*Much* too hot for that, dear,' Helen replied. 'Anyway, there are more important things. Such as this.'

She had opened the magazine at the page her thumb had been marking. She advanced it towards her mother-in-law, who peered at a photograph.

'Anne!' Lady Bourne exclaimed. 'With whom? "Sir Nigel Marsham, at the Eton-Harrow Ball at Hurlingham".'

'Well, well!' Charles said, coming over to look. 'So that's the young fellow she's been seeing so much of. Quite well set up, by the look of him.'

'According to Phyllis, they spent almost every evening last week together.'

'Who did?' Elizabeth asked, coming in with her father, anticipating tea.

'Anne and Sir Nigel Marsham, Bart.' Charles told her. 'Your future brother-in-law, perhaps?'

'Now, now, Charles!' Lady Bourne admonished him. 'No jumping the gun, please.'

'Well,' Helen said, 'there was a gossip piece in the *Express*, too.'

'They'll say anything to fill their columns. Remember when . . .'

Lady Bourne was surprised to be interrupted almost abruptly by her son.

'Just a minute!' Arthur was exclaiming over the photograph. 'Marsham. Nigel Marsham! Why didn't you say before?'

'Really, darling,' Helen said, 'I've been mentioning his name almost every other day since Anne went to stay with Phyllis and met him at that party.'

'But you never said he was Nigel Marsham.'

'Darling . . .'

'Not the *cricketer*. Look, "Former captain of Harrow, who has made two appearances for M.C.C. and several for Sussex this season . . .".'

Helen snorted, 'Oh, of course, that's the only thing that would really make you take notice of him. The fact that he might be asking to marry your daughter, one of these days . . .'

'First things first!' Arthur grinned waggishly. 'Marriage or no, it's my team against Halbury next Saturday, and if I can't raise a better turnout than last year, and the match is over at about three o'clock again, it might be the end of the fixture.'

'No bad thing, perhaps,' his wife retorted. 'It's sheer agony every year, your fussing over who you can get to play and who's going to be insulted having to go in last – not to mention the cost of the dance afterwards.'

The reference to the cost of the dance wiped the smile from her husband's face, but only momentarily.

'At least the club are going to stump up towards it this year,' he said. 'But I'm serious about the fixture. Father started the tradition of the Bourne Eleven v. Halbury and I've managed to keep it going. But if we can't make a good match of it, we can't expect the public to support us just for tradition's sake. They pay up cheerfully for the charity collection and they're entitled to a good game to watch in return.'

'It certainly wasn't last year,' his mother recalled. 'It was over *before* three.'

'And it had been rained off for an hour before lunch,' Charles added.

'You reckoned you had a strong side last year,' Liz said.

'We were – on paper. The whole team boasted of past achievements, but they were slow in the field, short-sighted – gone in the wind.'

'Haven't you picked better this year?'

'It's so hard to get a full eleven. The new vicar of Pembridge says he can play a bit, but he's an unknown quantity. There are the same four from the village ... But I've even had to fall back on old Admiral Graves, and it still only makes ten. If I could only get Marsham to turn out we'd be certain of a good game and his name might bring in a few extra crowd.'

His mother suggested, 'That nice young Dr. Harrington – doesn't he play cricket perhaps?'

'He used to play for Wolverhampton.'

'Well, then ...'

'Unfortunately, he plays for Halbury now – wicket-keeper – so he's with the opposition. No, Marsham's the chap I want, and with Anne coming down for the match there's every reason to invite him.'

Helen protested, 'That's all you care about their relationship, then? Using her as bait for your own devious purposes.'

'All's fair in love and cricket,' he grinned. 'Anyway, you know you're dying for a close look at him. I'm doing you a favour.'

Helen couldn't deny that much. Anne's natural magnetism for the opposite sex left her mother in little doubt that she would be the first of the three to marry, but she did rather wish for the appearance of some signs of a serious attachment. Brief flirtations, such as those with Gerald Hope-Langley and poor Rex Burton-Smith, were all very well as part of the exploratory stages of natural selection. The most durable relationship, with Michael Sherwood, was shadowed by his being a Catholic: for all Anne's insistence on her independence, Helen didn't believe she cared enough for Michael sufficiently to marry him as an act of sheer defiance.

179

Nigel Marsham was a more interesting prospect. Anne had been enthusing increasingly about him in her letters, and now even the Press were beginning to comment. He was well-to-do, young and good-looking, and – Helen had to admit to herself that it added to his attractions in her eyes – he was titled.

She acquiesced and telephoned Anne at Phyllis's flat; and Anne telephoned Nigel Marsham, and Nigel Marsham telephoned Arthur Bourne; and soon Helen was instructing Nanny that Admiral Graves, who was coming over from Cheltenham for the match, could have Vicky's room instead of the spare one, which would be occupied instead by Sir Nigel Marsham. Vicky was in Munich still, and, from the sound of her letters, fully recovered from the shock of Rex Burton-Smith's sudden death.

Phyllis drove Anne down the following day. There was an aura of excitement around her, and one of the first things she did after unpacking was to show Liz and Nanny a delicate silver pendant on a slender chain.

'Isn't he divine?' she asked.

'Has he ... actually proposed to you?' Liz asked. 'The *Express* seemed to be hinting.'

'Well, he hasn't gone down on his knees and that kind of thing. But I've met his mother and she likes me. And I've been invited to go down and stay with the whole family for Goodwood. So ... it's sort of ... unofficial, I suppose.'

Downstairs, Helen was asking Phyllis, 'Is it serious this time, do you think?'

Her sister-in-law shrugged. 'They're all serious, aren't they – while they last?'

Admiral Walter Graves, an old family friend, arrived on Thursday. On Friday came the visiting hero himself, driving a splendid Lagonda car. His time of arrival had not been put more precisely than 'sometime in the afternoon', so there was no reception committee. He came hesitatingly through the open front door, to find Lady Bourne having her post-prandial nap in an armchair and no one else in sight. But

Charles Ashley appeared on the staircase and recognized the tall, fair young man with the neat moustache from his photograph.

'My dear chap!' he greeted him, hurrying down. 'How do you do? You must be the hired assassin. I'm Charles Ashley, Arthur Bourne's father-in-law.'

'How do you do, sir?'

'Your host's out on the back lawn, loosening up in the net with one of our team. I'm surprised they didn't hear you arrive. Have you had lunch, by the way?'

'Yes, thank you, sir. I stopped at a pub.'

'Good. Come and meet another member of the family.'

Charles tapped Alice gently on the shoulder. She woke up at once.

'My dear, meet our young hero, Sir Nigel Marsham.'

'How do you do, Mrs. Ashley?' he asked.

'Oh, I'm not Mrs. Ashley,' she said shaking hands. Her immediate impression of him was excellent.

Charles explained, 'This is Lady Bourne, Anne's grandmother.'

'I'm so sorry, Lady Bourne,' their visitor apologized. He turned to Charles, 'Is Anne here?'

'Afraid not, at the moment. She went with her sister Elizabeth into Hereford. Some necessary shopping, I believe.'

Gates, aproned and hammer in hand, came in from the garden where he was working on the dais for the dance band. Charles hailed him to fetch in Sir Nigel's luggage from the car and take it up to the guest room. An extra large cricket bag was prominent amongst it when Gates passed through the hall again. Arthur, who had by this time come in with Admiral Graves and greeted his guest, eyed it appreciatively.

'I can't tell you how glad we are to have you here,' he said. 'Er, if you'd care for a net while you're waiting for Anne to come back . . .?'

The young man smiled. 'I think I'm in fair form, sir, thank you.'

'You certainly are if you're playing like you did at Lord's the other week,' Admiral Graves said. 'Against Scotland, you know,' he told Arthur.

'Thank you, sir,' Nigel answered modestly.

'I saw that innings of yours on the second day. You handled that leg-spinner like an old campaigner.'

'That's very kind of you, sir. Mind you, it was only against Scotland . . .'

'No, I won't have that. Some very passable cricketers have come out of Scotland. I'm a Scot, as a matter of fact. Played at Lord's once myself.'

'Really, sir?'

'Yes. 1898, for Eton against Harrow.'

'My school.'

'Of course! Someone did tell me. Yes, we were a useful side that year, '98. I scored 27 not out, batting at eight. I remember that innings vividly.'

Sensing that Walter Graves was going to embark upon a ball-by-ball account of it, Arthur took Nigel away to meet Helen in the garden, where she was supervising the contractor's men erecting the marquee and lights for the dance. Again, he made a splendid first impression, as he did also on Liz when she and Anne returned.

'I'm so glad you came, darling,' Anne said to him, as they strolled arm in arm round the cedar tree on the front lawn.

'I've been waiting for an invitation,' he answered, smiling down at her.

'But not to play cricket.'

'No, no.'

'But you don't mind?'

'Not at all. Sussex don't require me this week-end. And it is for charity, isn't it?'

'The Waifs and Strays Fund. I think it's wonderfully sporting of you, darling.'

He gave her her favourite smile. 'I think if Sussex had picked me I might have been tempted to cry off – for this.'

Anne squeezed his arm happily.

Despite the protests of the ladies, cricket dominated the conversation after dinner that evening.

'What sort of wicket do we expect, sir?' Nigel asked Arthur, after the protests had been shouted down.

'Oh, the Halbury wicket's one of the best in Herefordshire!'

'Really. I'm surprised this isn't more of a cricketing county, if everyone's as enthusiastic as you, sir.'

'Well, not everyone, I'm afraid. Tradition of this family, that's all. Anyway, the weather forecast's splendid.'

'And the opposition?'

'Nothing to worry you there.'

'Oh, Daddy!' Liz laughed. 'They've beaten you hollow three years running.'

'Ah, but not this year, I fancy,' her father retorted, with a wink at Sir Nigel Marsham.

'They're unbeaten,' Liz persisted, secretly standing up for the team for which Brian Harrington had been keeping wicket with consistent success. 'They beat the Gloucestershire police last week by an innings.'

Nigel Marsham chuckled. 'The Gloucestershire *police*! I say.'

Liz decided that she did not care for him quite as much as she thought she had done.

Great was the impression upon the household next morning when Gates came down the stairs carrying Sir Nigel's outsize cricket bag and was seen to have under his other arm no fewer than three bats, two of pristine whiteness, the other marked – all in the right area – with the red stains of the new ball. The owner, following behind, looked fresh and relaxed, in a double-breasted grey flannel suit, suede shoes and I Zingari tie.

Charles Ashley took him on one side, to say, 'Dear boy, before I forget, a word of warning about Admiral Graves. Don't call him for a short single. He doesn't hear too well and his days of scampering up the wicket are gone, I'm afraid.'

Nigel nodded smiling, understanding.

'Are you playing, sir?' he asked.

'Oh, no, no. Umpiring's my limit nowadays. Feeling in form, are you?'

'Thank you, sir. I'm one of those lucky people who don't get pre-match nerves.'

'No need for them today, anyway. Do it in fours and sixes, if you can. Please the crowd and they'll give more freely to Helen's Waifs and Strays.'

'I'll do my best, sir.'

'Ah, there you are!' hailed Admiral Graves, coming downstairs in cricket trousers of faded white, with an Old Etonian tie knotted for a belt, unbuttoned blazer and white choker. An old and much-used bat was under his arm.

'Good morning, sir,' the baronet greeted him deferentially. 'Carrying your bat, I see. That's a good omen.'

'Hope so. I had rather an interesting dream. Took a fifty off them. Particularly severe on a young chap they had sending down fast stuff. Takes me back to an innings I played in Singapore once, for a side called the Stragglers of Asia ...'

Up in Anne's room, Liz whistled at the sight of the gaily coloured dress her sister had chosen for the match.

'Are you sure about that?' she asked. 'It's rather ... sporty, isn't it?'

'It's a sporting occasion. And we have to take the collection boxes round and dazzle them into giving freely. Come to that, I don't think you look sporty enough.'

'It's all right,' Liz said, conscious that Anne was right. 'I don't want to draw attention to myself.'

'Oho! In case you're spotted with Brian.'

'Don't be horrible.'

'Sorry,' Anne laughed. 'It's funny, isn't it, our respective lovers being on opposite sides? Suppose they catch each other out?'

'Yes, first ball!' Liz laughed.

'Or a screamer from Nigel knocks out Brian's middle stump.'

Liz frowned.

'Preferably not,' she said, and meant it.

A few minutes later they were all off to the match – all except Helen, who had too much work to do, with Nanny and Mrs. Gates, preparing the refreshments for the dance. She had never been much interested in the game of cricket and preferred this backroom role, looking forward to the dance, though, and happy to know that on this day above perhaps any other of the year her husband put aside all cares, all concern about money, the estate, the future, and enjoyed himself playing a game at which he was not particularly good.

As Nigel Marsham had remarked, Herefordshire was not a county noted for its cricket. Most of its store of enthusiasm was exported to nearby Gloucestershire, the shire of the Graces and, in 1935, of the mighty Hammond. But Halbury possessed a neat little ground, with a trim white pavilion and a superb greensward, with a wicket that played hard and true on days such as this one, when the thermometer had been in the upper seventies for days and would certainly go over eighty by mid-afternoon. The Bourne XI charity fixture was one of those occasions which seem miraculously always to be blessed with fine weather and a responsive crowd. The last-minute inclusion in the local newspaper of a front-page item about the appearance of an M.C.C. and Sussex baronet in the Bourne side had actually boosted the gate by several score spectators, amongst them most of those who had declared after the previous year's debacle that they'd wished they'd gone to the seaside instead.

Sir Nigel lived up to the hopes of those of the crowd who had heard whispers of a romantic link between him and one of the Bourne girls. Every face turned towards the pavilion when the distinctive I Zingari cap was spotted (a Free Foresters one reposed in his bag as well, and he had had some difficulty deciding which to wear). He wandered out to the wicket, hands in pockets, and paced gravely along the length

185

of it, inspecting it keenly, before strolling back to the pavilion, nodding amiably to a few county folk whose deckchairs were in the most privileged place and shaking hands with the Revd. The Hon. Maurice Fuller and one or two other worthies who introduced themselves to him. Anne would dearly have liked to have taken that stroll to the wicket and back on his arm, for all to see; but decorum insisted that she sit with the family.

At a quarter past eleven Arthur and the Halbury captain came out to the front of the pavilion and tossed for innings. As almost invariably happened, Arthur lost. This was usually a matter of satisfaction to the crowd, for Halbury always elected to bat first and at least some entertaining play would be seen before the Bourne XI's customary collapse when their turn came. Today, though, there was some disappointment that Sir Nigel Marsham would not be seen in action early, though this was not shared by the purveyors of refreshment and the charity secretary. They knew that the longer the crowd had to wait for him to perform, the more money they would part with.

His presence ensured the Bourne XI an exceptionally warm handclap as they took the field, however, and those who knew about such things noted that he walked straight to the position of point, where good men go. The very first ball of the innings went to him, a couple of feet to his left. It was a hard, low crack, sizzling along the ground off the toe of the bat. Any other member of the Bourne XI would have made a token wave at it and let it tear past for someone further out to chase. As quick as a flash, Sir Nigel had stooped, shot out a rigid arm, snatched the ball up cleanly and hurled it back at the wicketkeeper so hard and accurately that the startled man had only just time to get his gloves in front of his stomach.

Applause rippled round the ground. The match had begun perfectly.

One spectator who had not applauded was Liz Bourne. Her heart had leaped uncomfortably at the dramatic piece of action, for the striker of that first ball had been Brian Harrington, promoted to Number One batsman for this match in the absence of the usual opener. The instinctive feel of a firm hit had sent him a few paces up the pitch before he realized that the ball was already hurtling back to the wicketkeeper. Had it hit the stumps directly he would have been out by yards. Had the Halbury wicketkeeper not been as much taken off guard as everyone else by such lightning fielding, and, in fact, almost knocked over backwards by the impact of the ball into his gloves, he would have had an even chance of running Brian out. As it was, Brian was able to hurl himself back into his ground, falling full length and acquiring grass stains on his flannels in consequence.

For a few seconds it had seemed to Liz that Anne's joking prophecy might have come horribly true. She sensed the menace of that lithe figure who stood, hands on hips, legs slightly straddled, staring implacably at Brian as he took guard again.

But Brian had learnt his lesson. After the shaking escape he played with a concentration unusual in anyone taking part in this charity fixture, moving right across his stumps whenever possible to enable him to play the ball back straight or to leg, ignoring completely anything sent down temptingly wide of the off stump. Very little more of the fielding went to Nigel Marsham, except when Brian's partner had strike. Sure enough, it was a good catch, low-down off an outside edge, which Nigel held to dismiss the other opener with the score at 32.

Brian met the incoming batsman and delivered a few words of advice concerning that lurking figure at point, as a result of which the score advanced steadily and with increasing rapidity. Nigel's brilliance in the field was anything but reflected by the other members of Arthur Bourne's team. True to form, they gave away runs galore by their slowness, their fumbling and their inaccurate throwing. In little more than an hour the hundred went up, with still only the one wicket down.

Anne's early jubilation at the performance of her particular hero was now eclipsed by Liz's at hers, although it was only to Anne that she dared express it. For Brian had reached his 50 and was beginning to score freely to most parts of the ground, except that segment guarded by Nigel. He was looking for runs now, aware of the need to force the pace before lunch. After it, the torpor induced by food and beer might well diminish the capabilities of some of his team mates who, he knew, regarded this match less as a contest than a day's fun.

This led him to begin to take chances, and when his score stood at 65 he took one too many and in the wrong direction. Trying to drive to mid-off he failed to middle the ball. It flew, at waist height, towards the non-existent cover-point and seemed a certain boundary. But Brian had failed to notice that Nigel Marsham had moved himself a pace or two to his right since the previous delivery. The ball was passing still well clear of him, but he flung himself to the right, arm at full stretch, and fell to the ground with the ball firmly grasped in his palm.

Justice had been done. The whole ground burst into applause, both for the excellent catch and for the end of a well-made and often entertaining innings. Liz and Anne exchanged a glance and a smile as they clapped their respective idols simultaneously.

Arthur had walked over from his own position at mid-on to congratulate Nigel warmly. They remained in conversation until the next batsman had almost reached his crease. The visible outcome of their discussion was that when the over ended Arthur tossed the ball to Nigel.

Arthur had occasion to curse himself for not having done this sooner. He knew of Nigel Marsham only as a batsman and hadn't thought to question him about his bowling. Indeed, Nigel had never bowled in first-class cricket, but he had at school, and with some success. At any rate, his slow leg-spinners had the Halbury batsmen in trouble from the beginning. Leg-spin was not a thing to which they were much used in that neighbourhood. Such spin as was encountered tended to come from the off, or, on any other pitch than Halbury's, from an irregularity of ground or an uncropped daisy.

Nigel might have had a wicket in his first over if Arthur himself had held the catch. It merely jarred his thumb and rolled harmlessly away to permit a quickly-run single. Nigel did get one in the second over, though, caught and bowled, and another in the next, clean bowled. Two more chances, one difficult and one any child would have been ashamed to have missed, were put down by fielders whose minds were now on the solace of the refreshment tent after a morning in the growing heat.

At last the clock granted them their wish. Charles Ashley removed the bails at the bowler's end and followed the less dignified progress of some of the others off the pitch. All round the ground hampers were being opened, carrier bags delved into, packages unwrapped, bottles and thermos flasks uncorked, and queues were forming at the two mobile refreshment stalls. The crowd was a happy one. It had seen almost 200 runs scored, six wickets taken, and at least two demonstrations of professional fielding at its best.

When play resumed at a quarter-past two the Halbury captain was conscious that he could not afford to bat for more than an hour or so before declaring. Normally, he would have been confident to leave himself two hours at the most to dispose of the Bourne XI. Today, though, the awesome prospect of what Sir Nigel Marsham might do to Halbury's competent but far from professional standard of bowling determined the captain that as many runs as possible were needed as quickly as possible. After that he could afford to follow a scheme for containing the star batsman to one or two strokes an over and steadily deprive him of partners at the other end.

Accordingly, he gave orders to the rest of his batsmen to go for the runs at all costs. On his part Arthur Bourne accepted Nigel's advice to set a far-flung field, for cutting off boundaries and allowing only one or two runs to each forcing stroke. Thus might Halbury be held down to no more than fifty or so runs in the time available to them, and they might be induced to offer catches in desperation to score more. Nigel himself took the ball as of right. He had impressed everyone at lunch by his refusal to drink more than one glass of sherry. He had eaten almost nothing. Anne, who had hoped to enjoy a relaxed chat with him, had found him silent, concentrated wholly upon the cricket match.

The striker awaiting the first ball after lunch was Halbury's Town Clerk, Mr. Bignell. He was not a regular member of the team. It was a pleasant custom for the mayor or one of his senior deputies to join the side for this fixture and Mr. Bignell had volunteered this time. He had not played cricket for several years, and before then only occasionally. He was a small man. Small men have a reputation for compensating for their lack of size by an aggressiveness of manner. While this is far from true of all of them, it certainly was of Mr. Bignell, who was noted for a complete absence of respect for persons or reputations. Moreover, as a late order batsman, he had had ample opportunity to dally in the refreshment tent during the latter part of the morning as well as throughout the luncheon interval. Purple patches could clearly be seen in the walls of his red neck as he strode to the centre, amidst ironic cheers.

Sir Nigel was seen to summon a man up to a close-catching position, evidently intending to trick Mr. Bignell into putting up a dolly off the edge of his bat. Charles Ashley gave Mr. Bignell a rudimentary guard and signalled for play to commence. Nigel ran in, an easy, economical half-stroll, and wheeled over his guileful arm with that deceptive twitch of the hand as it let go of the ball.

Mr. Bignell put the ball over the boundary ropes. He was facing up to the bowler's end again before it had even been thrown back.

Again Nigel bowled. Again Mr. Bignell lashed him over

the ropes, this time at the opposite side of the field. How he managed to do it, no one could make out. It all happened so swiftly. One moment there was the ball, arching gracefully towards a perfect length, and the next there was Mr. Bignell's threshing bat, and spectators scattering.

Mr. Bignell missed the next four deliveries completely. They also missed his stumps. Two of them missed the wicket-keeper and went for byes. Sir Nigel Marsham was seen to stand at the end of his run, hands on hips, while the batsmen ran around him. He seemed to be displeased.

Older members of the crowd were reminiscing facetiously about Gilbert Jessop, the Gloucestershire 'Croucher', and his epic feats of big hitting by the time Mr. Bignell had put the first ball of Nigel's next over into the tea tent, causing the lady volunteers to yelp with alarm. To hit the next one he expended so much furious effort that he almost finished up flat on his back; but the ball was ricocheting off walls in Halbury High Street. To the crowd's deep disappointment only one further six came off the over. At its end, Sir Nigel Marsham shook his head towards his skipper and retired to a fielding position from which he did not return to bowl again. The Vicar of Pembridge, put on in his place, bowled Mr. Bignell with his first ball, one which bounced twice before trickling under the heaving bat.

Halbury were able to declare at 285 for 9, in ample time to be able to dissect the Bourne XI. The 'hired assassin' could score his century, or whatever, if he didn't run out of part-ners in the process. There should still be a comfortable margin in Halbury's favour.

Traditionally, Admiral Graves opened the Bourne XI's innings. In earlier days he and Admiral Sir William Bourne had opened together and had generally been able to build a reasonable foundation upon which the rest of the team could crumble. Arthur, by no means the cricketer his late father had been, had not taken his place as an opener, preferring a much more modest role; but the surviving admiral's eye was not yet dim enough for him to mistrust the new ball and the fast bowlers. On this day as usual he strode to the wicket after the Halbury team had taken the field. Beside him walked Douglas King, Vicar of Pembridge. Arthur had consulted Sir Nigel Marsham about his own preference for position and had been told that No. 3 would be 'quite satisfactory'.

He might as well have gone in at No. 2 as it happened, for the vicar was out in the second over. The crowd buzzed with anticipation, and applause again sounded from every side as the elegantly athletic form, topped with the I Zingari cap, appeared from the pavilion doorway and descended the single step with a little skip on to the turf.

'Come on,' Liz said to Anne, who was staring fascinated at the firm but leisured progress to the wicket. 'Start collecting now.'

'But I want to watch him.'

'You can while we're going round. The more they're enjoying it, the more they'll put in.'

Anne had seen the truth of this demonstrated during their morning collection which had coincided with the Town Clerk's whirlwind mauling of Nigel's bowling. She had quite resented the enthusiastic generosity, only consoling herself that the Waifs and Strays would benefit from his humiliation.

She sighed and got up with her box, to set off along the opposite segment of the ground to Liz. She saw Nigel taking precise guard from the other umpire – Charles Ashley was at square leg – and then turning to note the position of every fieldsman. At length he stooped and began patting his blockhole gently as the bowler moved in.

The delivery was just outside the off stump. Moving into it unhurriedly, Nigel played it cleanly into the covers, his flashing white bat following-through in a graceful head-high curve.

His calm voice reached Anne as he called his partner for 'Just the one'; and he trotted leisurely up the pitch, watching a Halbury fieldsman closing on the ball.

Anne stood frozen, collecting box outstretched towards a spectator who, ignoring it, was staring open-mouthed. For Admiral Graves had not moved out of his crease. Although Nigel's call for the run had been heard by Anne, beyond the boundary, it had not penetrated the deafness of his fellow-batsman, less than twenty-two yards away from him. The admiral had been briefed by Arthur to let Nigel have as much of the bowling as possible, in the interest of rapid scoring, and had not expected him to give it away for a mere single at the very start of the innings. Nigel, on his part, had called and run with the instinct of a county cricketer who needs to bear no such considerations in mind unless up against a desperate situation where a tail-ender has to be shielded. There would be plenty of time for the fours and sixes as they came. He had made a pleasing stroke and there would have been no point in not getting off the mark with an easy single, rather than a hurried two.

The admiral sensed a commotion and turned from watching the fielder to see Nigel approaching his end. Horrified, he cried, 'Get back, young feller!' Anne saw Nigel hesitate. Cries and counter-cries of 'Run!' and 'Get back!' went up from the crowd.

Nigel by now had halted, waiting for his partner to run; almost supplicating him to. The admiral did not budge from his ground. He continued to wave frantically at Nigel. He had realized by now that he should have run, but it was too late to set off. The fielder had the ball. Admiral Graves knew he could never get down the pitch in time. His younger, fleeter-footed partner should be able to manage it.

Finding himself stranded, Nigel turned and fled. The throw-in was not a particularly good one, and the wicket-keeper, Brian Harrington, who had come up to the stumps to receive it, had to jump for it. There was a flurry of action as Nigel, bat outstretched and grounded, thundered into his crease as Brian swept off the bails and he and half the Halbury team roared their jubilant '*Howzat?*'. Every eye on the field and in the crowd swivelled to look at the square leg umpire, Charles Ashley. Slowly, he raised his right index finger. Nigel was out.

An audible groan went up from the crowd. The highlight of the day had been switched on and off again before they had had any time at all to bask in its luminosity. The batsman so many of them had come especially to see perform was walking back to the pavilion, head down, bat under arm, jerking off his gloves with unconcealed fury.

The most disappointed of them all hurried to meet him by the pavilion step.

'Oh, darling!' she said. 'I feel so wretched for you.'

He did not spare her even a glance, but strode on in. The visitors' dressing-room door was heard to shut with a crash. Some minutes later, the few people who happened to be in the vicinity of the back of the pavilion saw Sir Nigel Marsham, fully changed back into his ordinary clothes, carry his bag away to his Lagonda and get in, looking neither to right nor left on his way. He stayed in the car for the rest of the innings, which was no great time, for the usual Bourne collapse followed and the side was all out for 97 by half-past four, Admiral Graves carrying out his bat for 27. As soon as the last wicket fell Nigel drove from the ground alone. Anne, who had been his passenger on the way there, had thought it better not to approach him; and she had thought wisely.

At least, the charity secretary told his deputy, the star performer's presence had caused Halbury to bat on longer than they might have done. Some further profits had been made on teas which would not have been taken if the dreaded three o'clock ending had happened. And there had been that sparkling innings of Mr. Bignell's. If Sir Nigel Marsham's contribution to the day had been of an unfortunately negative nature, it had at least brought some benefits.

'Really, Charles!' Lady Bourne upbraided Charles Ashley when he came to her from the pavilion where he had taken off and hung up his white umpiring coat. 'He was quite clearly in.'

Charles had had an unhappy afternoon in which to question his own decision on the run-out. He defended himself with less than confidence.

'Oh, I didn't think so.'

'I tell you I was directly in line with the crease. His bat was over it.'

'It was ... all so close. And a frighteningly confident appeal ...'

'Of course there was. He was the scalp they wanted.'

'I'm not so sure about that. Their skipper came over to me later and said what a pity it had been. They were as keen to see him get going as the crowd were.'

'Then they shouldn't have appealed. That Doctor Harrington was loudest of all, and he was the one who did it.'

'Instinct, I suppose. Once you've appealed, you've appealed. I had to give the decision I thought was right.'

'Well, it wasn't. You ruined the match.'

Charles said miserably, 'I did warn young Marsham about Walter Graves and not calling quick singles.'

'It wasn't a quick single. There was plenty of time if the deaf old idiot had been looking. You really should have given the boy the benefit of the doubt, Charles.'

'Yes, dear. He told me as much on his way past me.'

'Really?'

'I attempted a word of commiseration. His reply was that the public had come to see him bat, not me umpire. Not a very polite remark, nor even original, but I see his point.'

The atmosphere back at Larkfield Manor early that evening was not of the best. Nigel was coldly polite but markedly aloof. To the sympathies he had been offered earlier he had replied with a thin smile that if there were two things a professional batsman feared more than any bowler they were irresponsible appeals and umpires who could be browbeaten by them. Liz flushed when he added that an unscrupulous wicketkeeper was a notable additional hazard.

'He's a rotten sport!' she declared to Anne, as they dressed for the dance. 'I suppose he'll sulk all evening.'

'He isn't sulking,' Anne defended him. 'He'd every right to be annoyed.'

'He'd no right to say what he did to Grandpa.'

'Well, I don't blame him. It was jolly decent of him to come in the first place.'

'I thought he accepted because of you. I don't notice him exactly falling over you since it happened.'

It was true. He had presented the cold shoulder to Anne as much as to any of them.

'He'll thaw out,' she said confidently. 'That stupid old admiral!'

As soon as she had finished dressing and making up she slipped the chain of the silver pendant round her neck and hurried along to the guest room. Nigel answered her knock and she went in. He was tying his black bow tie.

'Look,' she said. 'I'm wearing your pendant.'

He did not return her smile.

'So I see.'

'Do you think it looks nice?'

'Naturally. I bought it for you.'

She tried again.

'You mustn't worry about it, darling.'

'Worry about what?'

'The silly game. Nobody minded. The Waifs and Strays did really well.'

He turned round to face her. 'Look, I came a long way to play what I thought was going to be a serious game of cricket – which turned out to be a complete farce. The fact that "nobody minded" is neither here nor there. *I* minded – that's the point.'

She looked into his angry eyes.

'I . . . I'd hoped you'd really come to see me,' she ventured. For a moment she feared that he would make some reply which would hurt or insult her. He bit his lip, then managed a smile.

'Of course I did. I'm sorry. Of course I came to see you.'

He kissed her. She said, relieved and happy again, 'If you're ready, let's go on down.'

The band was already playing in the marquee, saxophone, drums and piano predominating. There were more people in the main hall of the house, though. The drinks and buffet there were proving to be the chief attraction for the time being.

'There aren't enough dancing,' Helen said to Liz. 'Go and set an example, will you?'

Liz was only too glad of the chance. As soon as her mother had moved on she went to Brian Harrington, who had been talking to a man she had seen on the cricket field with him.

'Dr. Harrington,' she said formally, 'my mother wants me to go and dance. Could you bear to partner me?'

He smiled. 'I'd be delighted, Miss Bourne.'

Not touching one another, they went off through the french windows towards the beckoning lit mouth of the marquee. In the space of dark lawn intervening they paused to exchange a quick kiss and hold hands for a few moments.

'Now I can congratulate you on your innings,' she said.

'Thank you. I felt dreadful about that run-out, though. I could have bitten my tongue off for appealing.'

'Was he really in?'

'I think so, now. It was the excitement of the moment. I suppose Anne hates me for it.'

'She wasn't pleased. But I think he was the one really upset.'

He shrugged; then said, after a pause. 'Is Anne . . . serious about him?'

It was Liz's turn to make a gesture of uncertainty.

'I don't know. He's not exactly . . . Do you think I should talk to her?'

'No. Let her sort it out.'

Some more people were coming from the light of the hall.

'Anyway,' he asked, giving her hand a last squeeze, 'who are you to talk about unsuitable young men?'

'I think, dear,' Aunt Phyllis said to Anne some time later, 'you really ought to go and commandeer your baronet friend.'

They were talking in the hall, where Anne had come to fetch Nigel and herself drinks and had lingered to chat with some people.

'What do you mean?' she asked. 'I've just left him in the marquee. I'm getting us drinks.'

'Well, in your brief absence he's managing to make rather an ass of himself with that local girl of yours, Peggy Short – I mean, Chapman – who's helping with the trays. I don't think she's welcoming his attentions.'

Horrified, Anne hurried back to the scene of the dance. At the entrance of the marquee she passed Peggy, coming out red-faced and walking with angry haste, her tray hanging from her hand.

'Peggy ...' she said, but the girl hurried on. Anne went into the tent. The band was wailing away and a few couples were dancing languidly. The atmosphere was anything but festive. Nigel was leaning against one of the supporting poles, his arm draped around it. He seemed to be sagging. His eyelids certainly were.

'What's the matter?' Anne asked, holding out his drink.

'Nothing's the matter. Thanks. I'm thirsty.'

'Would ... would you like to dance again?'

He roused himself. 'What another bloody Paul Jones? For God's sake, why can't they play something up to date? A Rumba. What about a Rumba?'

His voice was rising. Anne said hastily, 'Darling, don't you think you've had enough?'

'Enough? Me? By God, I've barely started. Oh, these country hops. What a bore they are!'

He threw back his drink. Looking blearily round he caught sight of Liz and Brian Harrington, heads close together in conversation. He pointed with his glass.

'What are those two up to? Secret lovers, I bet. Drooling over each other all evening.'

Brian and Liz caught sight of them looking towards them and decided it would be prudent to come over and chat. Unfortunately for everyone, Admiral Graves chose the same moment. He was not a man renowned for his tact at any time.

'Ah, Marsham!' he said. 'Extraordinary coincidence. Only just thought of it. That 27 not out of mine – exactly the same score as I made against you people at Lord's in '98.'

Nigel regarded him cynically.

'You amaze me!' he said at length.

'Eh?' the old man said, not recognizing a deliberate insult. 'Ah, yes. Well, er, pity about the, er, misunderstanding this afternoon, eh? Mistake to commit yourself before you know your partner's coming, you know.'

'Is it really?'

'Oh, yes. Cardinal rule. Don't mind my saying so, Marsham, but rather a rash call, that.'

'Yes. I called a single. I should have called two. There was ample time.'

The admiral goggled, sorting out the implication. Liz couldn't restrain herself from saying to Nigel, 'Oh, not still sulking!'

He looked at her patronizingly. Anne snapped at her sister, 'Of course he's not. Leave him alone.'

Brian Harrington put in, 'It was bad luck, that's all. You get unlucky decisions in any game.'

Nigel turned his head deliberately to regard him.

'Unlucky?' he echoed.

'I think so. You may have been in.'

'Then, why did you appeal?'

'Oh, you know – the general excitement, I suppose . . .'

'Yes. Well, I'm not accustomed to playing cricket with cheats.'

It was Liz again who flared back, 'There was no cheating about it. How can you say such a thing? Anyway, it was my grandfather who gave you out. He wasn't on their side.'

'I'm not accustomed to playing cricket with grandfathers, either,' Nigel told her. 'Or deaf admirals.'

He looked at their appalled faces in turn and then addressed himself finally to Liz.

'Miss Bourne, I don't give a fig for your opinion of me, or your family's. I was invited here under false pretences, and if you'll now excuse me I mean to make the most of what remains of a thoroughly disagreeable evening.'

He released his hold of the tent-pole, wavered slightly, then wove away. Anne made no move to go after him. She just wished the band would shut up and everyone would go home.

Liz took her arm and they wandered away towards the lighted house. Anne said, as they crossed the dark lawn, with the sound of the band receding behind them, 'I don't know what's come over him. He was never like this in London.'

'Dear child,' Liz comforted her, 'you've never seen him as a loser in London, have you? It's those who know how to lose who win in the end – isn't it?'

'Oh, what do you know about it? You're a fine one to talk, you and your unavailable doctor. At least Nigel's ... available ... and ... and ...'

'And what?' Liz asked sincerely. There was no reply.

When they all came down for breakfast next morning it was discovered that the Lagonda was gone from the drive and Nigel's things from his room. No note of farewell was to be found.

'Extraordinary fellow!' Admiral Graves declared. 'If that's the way their temperament turns I'm glad I never turned professional. Mind you, I had every chance, you know. I well remember, after that knock at Lord's in '98, a chap seeking me out in the pavilion and saying ...'

CHAPTER ELEVEN

THE other annual public festivity centred upon the Bourne family was Winchley church fête. It was held towards the end of summer and embraced the big lawn at the back of the manor, the smaller one at the front in which the cedar tree stood, and the house itself. It was traditionally a time of much coming-and-going, commotion and general upheaval. Unlike the cricket match, it did not enjoy invariable help from the weather. The late Admiral Bourne had been known to remark more than once, his clothes and white hair soaked by a downpour, that it was a pity they had chosen God's day off on which to try to raise a bit of money for Him.

A full muster of the family was needed to cope with the occasion. Lady Bourne and Charles Ashley would be attending this year as usual.

The 'Universal Aunt' was coming down from London. And Vicky was home, for the holiday before her last spell in Munich. She had brought with her Klaus von Heynig, who had turned out to be a polite, correct and rather stiff young man, of pallid countenance with eyes which smiled only formally or, more rarely, when a broadly applicable joke overrode his cautious reserve.

It was perhaps as well that he left for home before the time of the fête. Or a pity. There has always been much to be learned by perceptive outside observers from the behaviour of the British under the influence of society rituals.

'My husband has agreed to run the children's sports again,' Helen Bourne informed a meeting whose quorum consisted of herself, the Reverend the Honourable Maurice

Fuller, and a physically and opinionatedly top-heavy lady named Mrs. Hedges, a pillar of the Mothers' Union. They had moved into occupation of Arthur's study and were stimulating their deliberations with coffee and biscuits.

'Liz will take on the pony rides,' she added, 'and Anne thought she might tell fortunes.'

Mrs. Hedges growled, 'Can't do that. It's illegal.'

The rector smiled. 'I feel sure P.C. Rumbelow will be indulgent. After all, it is in aid of the restoration fund, and he does sing in the choir.'

Helen went on, 'And I'm asking Vicky to take turns with Doreen Williams at sitting under the bucket of water.'

Again Mrs. Hedges objected. '*Must* we have that particular sideshow? It is so very vulgar. And that Williams girl is getting so well developed.'

'And very popular,' the rector said, thinking of his fund.

'And now,' he resumed, 'that seems to be the duties all apportioned. It only remains for us to choose an opener. Poor dear Lady Cartwright, who had accepted, won't be available because of her stroke, so if either of you has a bright idea ...?'

Mrs. Hedges was ready. 'The very person, Rector. Our Member of Parliament, Sir Wilfred Hatton-Jones, happens to be playing golf with my husband only the day before.'

'Oh, but, surely better not. I mean, mixing politics and the church.'

'I fail to see ...'

'I do,' Helen said. 'Put his name on the posters and all our Liberals and Socialists would stay away.'

'And a good thing, too!'

'Not for our fund,' the rector reminded Mrs. Hedges warmly. 'Mrs. Bourne, I was wondering whether your mother-in-law, Lady Bourne ...'

'Oh, but she's done it so often in the past. Surely, someone fresh ...'

'I was looking at the records, Helen, and, do you know, it's coming up to twelve years since Alice did it. Twelve years!

Shows you how time flies. I mean, when old Billy was alive she was up and down on our platforms like I don't know what. She must feel we've been neglecting her dreadfully.'

'Oh, I doubt that. She isn't exactly a local any more.'

'Then all the more reason for inviting her again. Don't you agree, Mrs. Hedges?'

Mrs. Hedges didn't. The rector's familiar manner of communing with the Bourne family was not to her taste at all. Why was it, for instance, that he was not on Christian names terms with herself or any other member of the Mothers' Union? She could not understand it. On the other hand, she could recognize the value of a titled name on a poster; and since one such name was not available another might be useful. After all, the M.U. stall was, from long established custom, allowed to keep half its profits, and the new banner was becoming an urgent necessity. A bright new image was needed for the cause. Let these liberal-minded people help provide it, then.

'Very well,' she shrugged. 'If it won't be too much strain – at her age.'

If that comment had been reported to Lady Bourne when the rector approached her a few minutes later she would have accepted like a shot, on principle. As it was, though, she demurred.

'Oh, come, Maurice, I'm old hat. Surely you can find someone more interesting.'

'My dear Alice, if we could we ... Oh, dear, I don't mean it like that at all. I mean, we need a name for the poster, and, remember, plenty of new people have moved into these parts since twelve years ago.'

'Well, I'll do it if you really wish. But I think people who'll pay to come into a fête are entitled to someone more interesting than the widow of the late owner of a house that probably needs more doing to it than any of their neat little bungalows. But don't repeat *that* to Mrs. Hedges.'

The Hon. Maurice smiled. 'She might have it embroidered on her banner.'

Vicky said to Anne, when the news reached them, 'No offence to Granny, but we need a real name to get them in.'

'Yes,' Liz agreed. 'Like Nigel Marsham's, at the cricket match.'

'Pig!'

'Well, it worked – for the Waifs and Strays.'

'And that's about all!'

Vicky had been absent from that unfortunate occasion, but had been regaled with varying accounts of it. The hottest and most lurid had come from Anne, who had exaggeratedly foresworn the companionship of young men for ever more. In other words, Michael Sherwood was still at a geographical distance, unattainable, and no one else of interest was in the vicinity.

The three girls sat under the cedar tree next morning. The early September air was still a pleasant temperature, but there was in it the first tang of autumn. The drifting smoke from Gates's bonfire bore a fragrance no perfumier's artifice could ever hope to capture.

Presently, Vicky leaped up and almost skipped off into the house. The other girls heard the distant ping of the telephone but continued to chat idly and incuriously. Then Vicky came back.

'Right,' she told them. 'It's fixed.'

'What is?'

'Earl Mulligan. To open the fête.'

Her sisters stared at her.

'Earl Mulligan!'

'The film star. I told you, the Universal Aunt is coaching him to mime playing the piano for the film he's making at Denham. So I rang her, and he just happened to be there, and he said yes. Now, who's clever?'

'You mean ... a real Hollywood star ... to open our tinpot little fête.'

Vicky smirked triumphantly.

'What you might call a *fête accompli* – eh?'

'Whew! Have you told Granny? I bet she was relieved.'

'She and Mummy aren't back from Halbury yet, and Daddy's over at the farm giving Frank Chapman a hand with something or other. I'll tell them all at lunch.'

'I don't believe it!' her mother ejaculated when the news was broken. 'Earl Mulligan coming *here*!'

'We'll have half the county invading us,' Arthur said, thinking that the annual mutilation of his lawns, especially when it was wet, as it usually was, was bad enough after an attendance of only a couple of hundred.

'Wasn't I clever?' Vicky demanded. 'I remembered Auntie Phyl was teaching him the piano . . .'

'He must be a very quick learner,' her father said.

'No, Daddy, he doesn't actually have to play. They get a proper pianist to do that, but the actor has to make it look realistic on the screen.'

'Ah.'

Helen said, 'I think Maurice Fuller should have been consulted. It is the church fête, after all.'

'Oh, he'll be tickled pink,' Vicky said. 'Everyone's heard of Earl Mulligan. Anyway, Mummy, you said the rector wanted a title. Well, what could be better than "Earl"?'

'Certainly not just plain "Lady",' they were all surprised to hear Alice Bourne put in, speaking for the first time. 'And nobody's heard of me.' She was looking far from amused.

'Oh . . . Granny! I . . . I thought you'd be glad of the reprieve.'

'Really?'

Anne said, 'She thought she'd be doing you a favour, Granny.'

'Well, she wasn't. Once I'd accepted the invitation I'd started to look forward to it. Quite like old times. I've been working on my speech.'

'Mother . . .' Arthur tried to console her, but the old lady was stoking up her indignation.

'I thought it would be a nice chance to say something publicly to a few dear old friends who're bound to attend.

After all these years ... And who knows that I shall ever get another chance ...?'

She got up quickly, putting her napkin down on her plate. 'I think I shall take a stroll in the garden to settle myself. No, none of you need come.'

But Charles Ashley did, leaving the rest of them in disarray.

'Oh, how awful!' Anne exclaimed. Her mother turned to Vicky.

'It was a dreadful thing to do. See how upset poor Granny is.'

Vicky herself was near to tears.

'I thought she was being pushed into doing something she didn't want to.'

'She was a little reluctant at first, that's all. You should have asked me.'

'You weren't in. And it was just a fluke that he was actually with Aunt Phyl at that moment.'

Liz added, 'And it just happens that he'll be filming on location in Wales just at the time of the fête and he can easily nip over. It all seemed too good to be true.'

Arthur explained, 'Granny's a Victorian by upbringing, remember. It wasn't considered ladylike to show undue eagerness. She'd probably been hoping these last few years that we'd ask her to open the fête again, but it never occurred to any of us.'

'Oh, I could die!' Vicky moaned.

'That wouldn't help,' her mother pointed out. 'You'll simply have to ring Phyllis back and tell her ... there's been a mix-up. She can apologize to Mr. Mulligan and put him off.'

But Arthur said, 'No, Helen, I don't think so.'

She looked at him surprised.

'But of course she must.'

'I don't agree. It's very unfortunate about Mother, but I don't think we've any right to take this thing personally. The fête is held in our garden because it always has been, but it's supposed to be for the glory of God, not of the Bourne family. Now, this Duke Mulligan . . .'

Anne gave a relieved little giggle. 'He's only an Earl, Daddy.'

'Well, at least I've heard of him and that means everyone else in the neighbourhood is bound to have.'

'No doubt of that,' Liz agreed. Her father was a renowned non-picturegoer.

'So you see, it's the church that's going to benefit if more people come to see him.'

Charles came back at that moment. To everyone's relief, he winked.

'She'll soon get over it,' he said, sitting down to resume his meal. 'Actually, I think she's quite looking forward to meeting Earl Mulligan herself.'

'Oh, Grandpa, you've made me feel so much better,' Vicky said.

'I think it would have broken my heart if we'd had to stop him coming,' Anne said.

Charles asked quizzically, 'Is he on your long list of loves, too?'

'Oh, no. He's much too old. Thirty-five at least.'

'Nearer forty,' Liz said.

'Poor old chap!' their grandfather said. 'I hope he'll have strength enough to get here at all.'

Sheer hunger drove Lady Bourne back in at length. She kept up an offended pose, but it could be seen by everyone for what it was. It was confidently believed that the matter was settled. The rector was informed and expressed himself delighted. He added that he felt they could positively promise Lady Bourne that she should officiate next year. Personal preparations went ahead.

'I think I'll call myself Madame Scorpio,' said Anne, who was going to tell fortunes.

'That's not your sign,' Liz said.

'I know. But Madame Virgo would be a contradiction in terms.'

They giggled.

'I think we ought to cut out the egg and spoon race this year,' said Anne. 'It caused a lot of bad feeling last time.'

'Yes, it did. The girls played fair, but the boys kept on kicking their eggs after they'd dropped them. Hullo, Mummy.'

'How do I look?' Anne asked her mother. She was trying on the fortune-teller's robes.

'All right, darling. You'll have to do something about your hair, though. That was Mrs. Hedges on the telephone.'

'What now?'

'She's heard about Earl Mulligan. Apparently Maurice Fuller forgot to tell her himself and it reached her via the post office counter.'

'Oh, no! That'd make her furious.'

'It has. Not only for not being consulted, but for our inviting Earl Mulligan at all.'

'Didn't you give her father's line about the church benefiting?'

'It's not a "line", Vicky. But you can hardly expect the president of the Mothers' Union to approve a man who's been married four times.'

'*Four*! I thought it was twice.'

'Even that would have been bad enough for the M.U.'

'Well,' Liz pointed out, 'even if they stayed away en masse they'd be made up for several times over by those who'll come flocking. As it is, we'll probably be swamped.'

'They'll come, don't worry,' Anne said. 'Four marriages is even better than two when it comes to a Hollywood star. They'll all want to get a close look at him.'

Helen smiled. 'Four divorces in the near future, I hear. I must say, Mrs. Hedges is remarkably well informed.'

'Takes her job seriously. I bet they keep charts.'

'That will do, Anne. The M.U. mean well.'

Aunt Phyllis arrived two days before the fête. She was eagerly questioned by the girls about her glamorous and celebrated pupil, but disappointing by having to say she had not been out with him. Their relationship had been confined to two hour-long sessions of hard work in her studio. She had no personal gossip to pass on. Earl Mulligan was apparently agreeable and very professional.

The weather had turned a little colder and a gusty wind seemed to be establishing itself. Gates was told to keep a sharp eye on the moorings of the marquee and tents which had now been put up on the lawns. It seemed likely that the elements were brewing up the usual concoction for the day of the fête.

Worse than the threat of bad weather, though, was the arrival of the evening newspaper on the day before the event. It came first into the hands of Liz, who glanced idly at it, stared, then ran to where Anne was sewing the last spangles on to Madame Scorpio's gown.

'Look!' she shrieked, pointing to a photograph and big headline.

'Oh, my God!' Anne responded, having done so.

'Whatever is it?' Vicky asked, chancing to come in just then.

'It's him!' Liz answered. ' "FILM STAR IN NIGHT CLUB BRAWL" ...'

'Oh, no!'

'Listen. "Police were called to a London night club early this morning to quell a disturbance involving Earl Mulligan, the Hollywood star now making his first film in England. A fight, which started when Mulligan claimed he had been insulted, led to tables being overturned and several persons sustaining minor injuries. The same star figured in a similar incident in Los Angeles last July ..." '

She broke off.

'Who's going to break it to Daddy?'

Arthur and Helen were predictably shocked to receive the news, and there was something of an 'I told you so' air about Lady Bourne when the rest of them were told. Mrs. Hedges was on the telephone in a matter of minutes. Arthur took the call. The girls were relieved to hear their father answer her torrent of words with a calm reminder that no criminal charges had been made, that no imputation had been made that Earl Mulligan was anything other than the aggrieved party in the quarrel, and that there was no question of asking him not to come, since so much excitement had been engendered locally by the appearance of his name on the posters.

'Good for you, Arthur,' Charles Ashley said. 'But you'll have even more coming now. They'll be hiring charabancs.'

Arthur groaned and went to the window, to look first at the sky and then at the flapping canvas on the lawn.

The wind was still blowing strongly when they all went to bed that night. Arthur make a torchlight round of the moorings and looked anxiously at the stars. The wireless weather forecast had been too generalized to be helpful. In any case, the district was one of those whose weather often varied dramatically from that of quite nearby ones.

When he woke early he was relieved to hear no wind. His sailor's instinct told him what the alternative might prove to be, though, even before he had got out of bed and looked out. The sky was a solid mass of cloud. But it was not raining and the light was fairly bright.

'What's it doing?' Helen asked, fearing the worst.

'I think we'll manage,' he said.

The morning was a busy one for everyone, equipping stalls and sideshows, festooning the ceremonial platform and the tents, endlessly fetching and carrying between the kitchen and the marquee. Male and female helpers from the village were everywhere underfoot and the telephone almost needed a permanent attendant.

It was lunchtime before Phyllis, as she gladly accepted a gin and orange squash from Arthur, asked, 'No word from Earl Mulligan?'

'Good heavens!' Helen said. 'I've been so busy . . . Did you say anything to him about lunch?'

'I said you'd probably be too busy for anything formal, but there'd be plenty of bits.'

'He's probably stopped at a pub, then.'

'Several pubs perhaps,' Arthur speculated gloomily. 'Nothing's going to surprise me.'

'I am.' It was the voice of the monumental Mrs. Hedges, striding in from the front door, to announce dramatically, 'Your film star has arrived. The rector and your gardener are carrying him in.'

'Carrying!'

'Don't say he's drunk!'

Mrs. Hedges shrugged expressively.

'All I can say,' she reported, 'is that I found him lying in the drive and claiming he was run over . . .'

'Oh!'

'. . . by a pig.'

Several voices simultaneously echoed, 'A *pig*?'

'That's right,' they heard a cheerful American voice saying from the doorway. 'Say, you need a notice on the gate, "Beware of the Pig".'

The owner of the voice was immensely tall, immensely broad in the shoulder, immensely tanned. His big face was square and homely, rather than handsome, with lines in the forehead and around the eyes which were almost his trademark, adored by women all over the world. He was smiling ruefully and rubbing a knee, while the rector and Gates looked on anxiously from behind. What, to Arthur's relief, he obviously was not was drunk, and he was standing unsupported.

'Hi folks!' he grinned. 'How's that for an entrance? Parked my car over the way so's not to take up space and was just walking up your drive, doing no harm, when this hog got me.'

Gates explained to Arthur, 'It ran away, sir, just as Frank Watson was unloading it.'

Helen said, 'I'm truly sorry, Mr. Mulligan. Bowling for a pig is a traditional sport at these country fêtes.'

'Well, this time the pig did the bowling.'

They all laughed and even Mrs. Hedges simpered. The

unspeakable debauchee and divorcé seemed amiable at least.

'I'll go and see to the pig, sir,' Gates said to Arthur, and hurried away. To Anne's envy, Liz asked Earl Mulligan, 'I'm medically trained, if you'd like me to look at your leg?'

He rubbed his knee, grinning.

'I'd be cheating. Just a bump, but it was on my sore spot. I injured myself making a Western. I was one of the baddies chasing Gary Cooper. Ran out of a saloon, sprang on my horse, and – ouch!'

'Well, I'm sure you need a drink,' Arthur offered, when belated introductions had been made. 'What can I get you? Gin, whisky, er, sherry . . .?'

'I'll settle gladly for a glass of your country milk,' was the unexpected answer. 'I only touch the hard stuff between pictures. When I'm working it's nothing stronger than coffee or milk. You heard about my little fracas in the night club this week? That was over me drinking milk.'

'How on earth . . .?'

'Guy at the next table saw them fetch me the milk and made some uncalled-for remarks to his party. When I told him to mind his business he insulted my mother.'

Mrs. Hedges bristled. 'You took your mother to a night club!'

'No, ma'am. My dear mother passed on five years back. It was the name that guy called me – I won't repeat it – that reflected on her memory, and that was something I could not accept. It was all very unfortunate.' He dusted ruefully at his clothing. 'Guess I'm what they call accident-prone.'

'Well, if there's really nothing we can offer you, Mr. Mulligan . . .'

'Earl, please.'

'Thank you. I'm Helen and my husband's Arthur. Darling, if you'll show Earl up to the bathroom and get him a clothes-brush and so forth, we'll be in nice time for the opening ceremony. The stalls aren't allowed to start until the opening's over,' she explained to the visitor.

'I get you. Whenever you say, Helen.'

'Just a few minutes to get everyone assembled and the band ready. We wanted to play "The Star-spangled Banner" as you walk out, but they're only our village band and I'm afraid they don't know it. So we've settled instead for "Marching Through Georgia".'

They were disturbed to see the grin vanish from the American's craggy face.

'Anything but that tune, please,' he begged. 'Georgia happens to be my home state.'

'Then, isn't it appropriate?' Anne asked.

'I see I'll have to teach you some American history, young lady. That was the song of Sherman's Yankees when they marched through our state burning and pillaging and ra ... behaving roughly with the ladies.'

'Good heavens! They'd better stick to something English, then.'

'Thank you. Say, I meant to ask, is that your church I passed about a half mile back – Perpendicular period with a Decorated tower and rose window?'

They stared wonderingly at this remarkable man of contrasts.

'Yes it is,' the rector managed to reply. 'But, I fear, badly in need of some restorations. We're grateful to you indeed, Mr. Mulligan. We've already taken more at the gate than ever before, and they're still flocking in, by the sound of it.'

The celebrity was played to the platform soon afterwards, to the tune "Country Gardens", rendered unevenly by the Winchley band but considerably more effectively than their version of "Marching Through Georgia" would have been. A great cheer – a thing unprecedented in all the history of Winchley Church fêtes – went up when the idolized features were recognized. His brief speech was rendered almost incomprehensible to all but a few by his accent and the buzz of admiring murmurings, but was warmly applauded just the same. Then half the crowd rushed at the stalls and sideshows while the rest rushed at Earl Mulligan, brandishing autograph books, scraps of paper, backs of envelopes and anything else upon which he might be persuaded to scrawl his name. He obliged freely, but had taken the precaution to get the rector to place a collecting box in front of his position at the front of the platform. Anyone requesting a signature without first contributing was stared at blankly and the box tapped with a significant finger until the nerve of the supplicant broke, or the queue behind grew too vociferous to be ignored, and a coin was inserted. Then the grin was switched back on and the signature given, with a word or comment to be treasured for years afterwards. The box had to be replaced twice before the demand petered out.

The rest of the household worked equally hard. Anne, splendidly transformed into Madame Scorpio, enjoyed a steady trade and learned enough intimate secrets to keep her sisters regaled for hours. Vicky, in her bathing costume, suffered soaking after soaking as she sat under the bucket-shy. Arthur supervised the races, landing himself in dispute with the rector for disqualifying the winner, a choirboy who had indulged in the most outrageous bumping and boring while the rector's back was turned. Earl Mulligan mediated effectively by signing his name five times for the disappointed cheat, telling him that five Mulligans would be almost certain to buy him one Gable on the open market.

Unnoticed by anyone, the clouds had been consolidating and darkening. A flash of lightning and an almost immediate clap of thunder were the first intimation that Winchley Church fête was in for it again. But the rain which descended was so sudden and heavy that none of the crowd had time to leave. Instead, they all herded somehow into every possible marquee, covered stall and sideshow, and great was the trade thereby.

The only real losers were Mrs. Gates, Arthur Bourne and Charles Ashley. As usual, Mrs. Gates had baked the giant cake. So large was this grotesquely swollen confection, whose weight had to be guessed, that it had to be carted about in an old pram. When the storm struck the pram was standing momentarily unattended. Its minder, briefly absent, instinctively made for cover. By the time she remembered her charge, and retrieved the pram, the cake was a soggy, crumbling mess.

Charles Ashley lost his panama hat, for which he had paid a guinea only the week previously. He had lain it on Mrs. Hedges's jumble stall while he went to get a cup of tea. During his separation from it it had been sold, for sixpence, to the postman.

Commander Bourne was the principal loser. Upon the discovery of the ruin of the great cake – which had, in any case, been constructed from Bourne-bought ingredients – Helen sent Vicky to the cellar to fetch a bottle of wine, to be drawn for by all those who had paid to guess the cake's weight and whose entries could no longer be judged. Little versed in the matter of wines, Vicky chose a dusty old bottle which, from the state of its neglect, seemed to her to be one her father could well dispense with. She wiped it clean and took it upstairs.

'Earl,' Helen asked that endlessly obliging man, 'will you draw the number for us, please?'

'My pleasure, Helen.'

The hat full of slips was advanced and the number drawn.

'Forty-seven.'

'Oh, no! That's Lady Bourne, my mother-in-law. We can't possibly let it go to one of the family. Quickly, Earl – draw again, please.'

'Eighty-two.'

'Eighty-two? That's better. Fred Stevens. He's the fat man playing the drum in the band.'

'Like me to take it out to him?'

'Would you? He'll be thrilled if you present it. The rain seems to have stopped.'

It had and the throng was milling again. Earl disappeared into it. A few minutes later Arthur Bourne came into the house, looking hot, damp and angry.'

'Who's been at my cellar?' he demanded in uncharitable tones.

'Only me, darling,' Helen said. 'I sent Vicky down for a bottle of wine to make up for the cake. It got drowned, you know.'

'Well, that bottle of wine is one of my best Napoleon brandy. Only three left – two, now.'

'No!'

'Yes. And it's gone to that beer-swilling Fred Stevens. It's worth £20 if it's worth a penny.'

'Offer him a fiver for it,' Charles Ashley suggested. 'That's the equivalent of – what? – a hundred-and-fifty pints of beer.'

Arthur went off, muttering, to do so. 'At least,' Charles mourned, 'he'll get his brandy back untouched. But my panama hat – have you seen that postman's hair-oil?'

With these and other little crises the afternoon wore itself down. The long-delayed results of raffles for produce, bottles of sherry, home-made cakes, arrangements of flowers and baskets of fruit were read out by Earl Mulligan, whose patience and good humour had never dwindled. The crowd at last began to drift homeward.

'I think you're marvellous, Earl,' Liz said.

'I love you too, baby.'

'No, but you're such an ... unexpected person. Drinking milk, and minding your language, and knowing all about church architecture ... All that stuff about Perpendicular towers and the Rose window ...'

'Honey,' he said conspiratorially, 'I don't know the first thing about church architecture. Your Auntie Phyl asked me if I'd do a little job for Winchley Church in Herefordshire, so it was no trouble to have a kid at the studios look it up for me.'

'You mean, you took all that trouble – to memorize it?'

'Hell, I'm an actor. Memorizing's my business.'

'But you do all these nice things, and then we read you raise hell in night clubs and break up furniture and hit people for six ...'

'I explained about that.'

'Yes, but it said in the paper you did the same recently in Los Angeles.'

'I know, I know. And that wasn't the first time, either. Okay, I'm no angel. I have a quick temper, and between pictures I abstain from milk. But when you play a tough guy in movies, every other drunk you meet has to try to prove he's tougher. I only like to fight when I'm paid to – but turning the other cheek gets a little hard when there's some stranger calling you dirty names.'

'I suppose so.'

'*And* not having a real home these days. My parents split up when I was a kid. I've never stayed married long enough to make a home and raise a real family.' His eyes brightened and he tugged out his wallet. 'I do have a little daughter, though. Here's her picture.'

Liz took it. The child was Shirley Temple-like, unmistakably American in her sophisticated blonde hair-do and chequered apron dress. There was something appealing about the burnished innocence.

'She's sweet,' Liz said genuinely. 'What's her name?'

'Lucy May. She's four.' (Liz had guessed six.) 'You know what? I gave her a Dalmatian pup for her last birthday. Lucy May was over the moon about him. And then my bitch of a wife – pardon me, I'm not minding my language now – she said she wasn't having a dog in her apartment, and when I was away she sent it to the vet's to be put down. Now, how about that?'

'It's . . . terrible!'

'So, divorce number four. Lucy May was still crying over that poor dog the last time I saw her.'

Liz asked thoughtfully, 'Are you able to see her often?'

'Whenever I'm in New York. I can't have custody of her. I move around too much.'

'Wait here, Earl.'

She ran off upstairs and shortly afterwards was down again, carrying something small. She showed it to him. It was a toy Dalmatian, worn from years of fondling, but still recognizably of its species. She put it into the wondering American's hands.

'I want you to have this – for Lucy May, from us all,' she said. 'As a token for all you've done for us, and as something for her, in place of . . . the other.'

He stared down at the worn markings of the scruffy toy in his big hands, swallowed, and said, 'But you must have had this since you were a kid, too.'

'Never mind. I'm a big girl now. I'm afraid poor old Dilly Dally's rather old and moth-eaten. And he's lost a bit of one ear . . .'

'No – that's why he'll mean so much to her. I could go into the biggest toyshop in New York or London and I daresay find her a new Dalmatian toy. But this li'l fellow has been loved – really loved, and for a long time. Kids can sense that sort of thing.'

'Then take him to her, Earl.'

He leaned across and gave her a chaste kiss on the cheek.

'You're a lovely girl, Liz,' he said. 'I only wish I was half my age and living in Winchley, Herefordshire.'

Half an hour later, Vicky and Anne came storming up to Liz.

'Liz!' Anne burst out. 'Did you give Dilly Dally to Mrs. Hedges for her jumble stall? Because I didn't, and Vicky didn't, and Mummy never would have. But there he was – *and* he's got a "Sold" tag on him.'

'I didn't give him to Mrs. Hedges,' Liz answered, aghast. 'I gave him to Earl Mulligan.'

'You *what*!'

The circumstances were explained. Even then, Liz's sisters could not come round to forgiving her. The family toys, even the shared ones, were the most treasured things in Larkfield Manor to them.

Anne demanded, 'Then, what's poor Dally doing on that woman's stall? I know. Your precious Earl didn't like to refuse your offer, but just went out and dumped him on the stall.'

Vicky said, 'He could at least have had the decency just to leave him behind in the house.'

'Just a minute,' Liz stopped the tirade. 'Here's Mrs. Hedges coming in – and she's got Dally with her.'

Mrs. Hedges, with an obviously heavy shopping basket over one arm and Dilly Dally in the other hand, came into the hall beaming.

'Sold out!' she cried. 'Every single item. The first time ever.'

'Who bought our dog?' Vicky asked rudely.

'Why, the film star. Mr. Mulligan. Not that he had to, because he said you'd given it to him already. But he said it would be wrong for the church not to benefit, so he gave it to me to sell to him – for *ten pounds*. It put me nearly twenty pounds up on last year's takings. I must say, in spite of ... well, I think he's a dear, dear man.'

The others came crowding in, carrying the takings in boxes and biscuit tins, which they piled on the grand piano. Earl was with them, grinning happily. Arthur said, 'Well, it's been a long and tiring day. I think we can all do with a drop of consolation. What may I get you, Mrs. Hedges?'

'A glass of sherry would be very nice, thank you, Commander Bourne.'

'Whisky and soda for you, Maurice?' Arthur asked the rector, knowing his uncomplicated tastes.

'Thank you, Arthur.'

'And you, Earl? Won't you break your rule just this once?'

'Thanks, but no thanks. It's time for me to be moving on. I have a long drive ahead.'

'Not even a glass of milk?' Helen urged him, and Liz said, 'We'll promise not to make any rude remarks.'

'Not even that. Folks, dear kind folks, I just wanna say one thing before I go. You've given me a day I shan't forget. The kinda day that renews a guy's faith. Saint Paul wrote in his Epistle to the Corinthians "God loveth a cheerful giver", and that tells me the Almighty is sure smiling down on you here today, because of the joyous way you have worked for the greater glory of His house. Sorry, Reverend. I seem to find myself trespassing on your pastures. But now it's good-bye and thanks a million to you all.'

After the handshakes and farewells which followed this unexpected speech he went away to his car, escorted by Phyllis and Liz.

Maurice Fuller looked into his second glass of whisky, cleared his throat, and said, 'He has made me feel very humble.'

'In my case, rather ashamed,' Arthur said. 'Losing my temper over a mere bottle of brandy.'

'I can't forgive myself for saying such uncharitable things about him,' Mrs. Hedges said.

'What's the matter with you?' Helen demanded of Anne, who was shaking with laughter.

'Didn't any of you see *The Whited Sepulchre*? It was at Halbury cinema about six months ago.'

None of them had.

She explained, 'Earl was the star in it. He was a bogus preacher, and he had one speech that was almost word for word what he said to us just now. What an actor!'

'He's as big a humbug as the rest of us,' Liz laughed.

The rector beamed. 'Humbug or not,' he said, 'if ever I met a cheerful giver, Earl Mulligan is his name.'

CHAPTER TWELVE

THE entire family mustered once again in the Autumn, to go over to Ludlow for the wedding of the girls' first cousin Penelope Bourne to a young stockbroker. A spell of perfect weather favoured the occasion.

'A marriage from this house. That's what I'd like to see,' Lady Bourne remarked as she sank thankfully into an arm-chair in Larkfield Manor hall afterwards. Charles Ashley, Phyllis, Arthur and Helen were with her. The girls were out of earshot upstairs.

'Wouldn't we all?' Helen agreed.

Her father-in-law asked, 'Any chance, in the not too distant future?'

'Well, Anne still seems quite keen on Michael Sherwood. But he hasn't been down for ages. They hardly ever meet.'

'Goes flying at week-ends, you know,' Arthur explained. 'Auxiliary Air Force.'

'Ah, yes, I remember.'

'That's what I'd have gone in for in the next show if I'd been his age,' Arthur went on. 'Flying. Preferably Naval flying, I think. Best of both worlds.'

' "Next show"!' his mother snorted. 'Don't be so morbid, Arthur.'

He shook his head doubtfully. 'I hope I never have to say "I told you so", Mother, but there are those of us who agree with Churchill. All this appeasement of Mussolini and Hitler is just playing into their hands. This invasion of Abyssinia is an early dress rehearsal.'

'Never mind Churchill. He likes drawing attention to himself. What about the Peace Ballot? Eleven and a half million people took the trouble to vote, all over the country. An overwhelming majority for international disarmament. With opinion like that to back it up we've simply got to support the League of Nations at last, and stop paying mere lip-service to it.'

Charles said, 'I somehow doubt whether Messrs Hitler and Mussolini will pay much attention to polite notes from the League, threatening them with a hundred lines apiece if they don't stop misbehaving in class.'

Helen said anxiously, 'Father, you're sure it's all right for us to send Vicky back to Munich tomorrow? I don't like the sound of all these incidents – against Jews. She even saw one of them chased and beaten.'

'Then she's learned a useful lesson in life she wouldn't have had from staying here and reading *The Field*,' Charles answered unhesitatingly. 'I know that sending girls abroad to be finished – a term I've always found repugnant – is just a movement in the ritual dance into womanhood. But if it succeeds in providing them with some real insight into other people's lives, then it's more valuable than I've ever believed it to be.'

'Hear, hear!' Phyllis agreed. 'In years to come they'll wonder why we ever half-bankrupted ourselves to do anything so archaic.'

'It didn't do you any harm,' Lady Bourne retorted. 'Think of all those helpful musical people you got to know in Germany.'

'Oh, I agree. But that was because I used my exile as a working year. I didn't spend half my time going skiing and social gallivanting like Vicky and Anne.'

'Vicky is working hard at her music, isn't she?'

'When she's nothing else to occupy her. She doesn't practise anything like enough for someone who wants to turn professional.'

Arthur asked, 'I often wonder whether she really does? Do you think she's got it in her, Phyl? Honestly?'

His sister glanced at the stairs to ensure she wouldn't be

overheard by any of the girls coming down, before replying, 'Frankly, Arthur, no. If she were one of my pupils I'd put her in the very talented amateur category. If she really were to buckle down to it for several years hard she might make a professional. She has style, and unless one has that there's no question of it. Her technique is competent, but more than that I couldn't say for it. I don't want to disappoint you, darlings . . .'

'No,' Helen agreed with Arthur, glancing uneasily at him. 'We had better hear the truth.'

'Well, there's a terrific gap between clever amateurism and professionalism. Very few get across it.'

'You're a professional,' Lady Bourne reminded her daughter. 'I've heard you praise Victoria for playing pieces better than you could have done.'

'That's true, Mother. At her best, she's good. As for me, I'm a teacher, not a performer. I know my limitations. I'm sure the last thing Arthur and Helen would want would be for her to be a teacher.'

Helen answered, 'With all due respect to you, Phyl, dear – no.'

'So you see? Now you be honest, and admit you'd sooner have her married – all three of them, come to that.'

It was something Helen could not deny. Her father said, 'I thought there were hopes of this von Heynig boy.'

Arthur rubbed his chin. 'Not serious ones. He seems decent enough. Only . . . Well, apparently even the von Heynigs have started to blame the Jews for almost everything. There seems to be something . . . infectious about it. We'd hate Vicky to catch that particular germ.'

'I agree,' Charles said; 'except that she wouldn't. She's not at all the kind of person. No, my dear,' he said to Helen, 'One more term is unlikely to do her any harm. But I should definitely make it her last.'

'No fear about that,' Arthur assured him. 'A definite policy of retrenchment before long, believe me.'

Up in Elizabeth's room the other two daughters were discussing their own prospects.

'Sort of love letters are all right up to a point,' said Anne, who had received one that day. 'But it would be a jolly sight nicer to see the chap from time to time. Flying his wretched aeroplanes . . .'

'He's obviously very fond of you,' Liz consoled her. 'At least he follows up each excuse for not coming down with one of his romantic effusions.'

'Oh, yes. He writes jolly well. But it's not the same as having him here. At least you see yours.'

Liz glanced instinctively at the closed door.

'Well, you do,' Anne reiterated. 'I know it's hopeless, and all that, but at least you get a bit of fun out of it.'

'Fun? Hiding in a cold two-seater up on the common? Meeting at The Copper Kettle by carefully arranged co-incidence? Miss Pringle could run a pretty line in blackmail if she wasn't so unobservant.'

'Does everyone know that he's separated from his wife?'

'They must by now. Ever since old Croppy left and she hasn't moved in with Brian.'

'Do Mummy and Daddy ever talk about it? I've never heard them.'

Liz shrugged. 'They never have to me. It's the one proof I cling to that they haven't . . . found out. Anyway, it's worse for us than for you and Michael. At least he hasn't a wife.'

'No. But he's an R.C., too.' Anne made one of her defiant grimaces. 'Not that that would stop me if I wanted to marry him. I'd convert.'

'You wouldn't!'

'Wouldn't I? Oh, I know Daddy wouldn't like it, but I'm sorry, too bad. I mean, it's not as if we were a really religious family or anything. It's all just convention, like going abroad to be finished and that sort of thing. Poor Daddy, worrying over his bills, and Vicky could just as well have stayed at home or at school.'

Liz sighed. 'Ah, well . . . Who knows? I hate Autumn. It's so depressing . . . everything running down.'

'I love it. Summer makes you so . . . floppy. There's a sort of excitement to Autumn. You feel you've had your long laze about and it's time to be up and doing things. Speaking of which,' Anne concluded, glancing at her watch and then getting up, 'it's time we were changing for dinner.'

Liz sat on for some minutes after her sister had left the room. Then she bestirred herself, washed, changed, made herself up and did her hair, thinking all the time. Even when she was ready she sat looking at her reflection in the dressing table mirror for a full five minutes before making the effort to go downstairs. Her grandfather was alone in the hall, looking at his newspaper. He smiled up at her.

'Nights drawing in, Liz, my dear.'

'Yes. It's quite chilly.'

'The price to pay for a beautiful day. Autumn again, though.'

'I know. I hate it.'

'Well, I know what you mean. The dying of the year. My word, though, on days like today one can't help thinking that Nature knows how to die gloriously. I'm afraid that some of the dying that's going on in the world just now is anything but magnificent.'

'Grandpa – please! I'll get the shivers.'

'I'm sorry, my dear. Association of ideas, due to old age, no doubt. D'you know, though, I was standing at the window, watching it get dark and looking at the cedar tree. And I thought to myself how much we take that fine old chap for granted. He was old before even I was born, and he'll outlive me by a century.'

'Like this house,' Liz said, glancing around the taken-for-granted room.

Her grandfather nodded. 'The Georgians built to last, but Nature doesn't. Not even something so long-lived as that tree. I worked it out – if a year of a dog's life equals seven of

a man's, and assuming a life-span of three hundred years for
Cedrus Lebani against, say, seventy for *Homo Sapiens,* then
for every year the man lives . . .'

'Grandpa,' Liz broke into this abstruse equation. 'Can I
ask a favour?'

'To shut up? I'm sorry, my dear.'

'Nothing like that. Will you back me up against Mummy
and Daddy if necessary?'

Charles Ashley's expression changed to seriousness. He
searched her face.

'It would have to depend,' he answered cautiously.

'Well, you know – I know – they'd like like me to marry.
They want all of us to. I've been thinking about things for
these past months, and trying to decide whether to go on
with medicine or just stay here and, well, wait for the inevitable. But now I've suddenly decided I want to go back to
London, take my final M.B., and go on with my career.'

'Oh, I see. Has . . . anything made up your mind for you?'

'Not really. A . . . friend I have, in the medical profession,
warned me not to leave it too long before going back if I was
ever going to. He . . . he said you can quickly forget things.'

'I quite agree.' Charles tapped his newspaper. 'It's like
cross-words. Do them regularly and you get to know how the
compiler's mind works. Leave them off for a while and you
have to start getting to grips with him all over again.'

'That's what I'm worried about.'

'Then you definitely *want* to be a doctor?'

'I want to be *something,* Grandpapa. I'm not the kind of
girl who could be content just running a home, like Anne or
Mummy. I want to be useful outside the family – to complete strangers.'

He smiled. 'Yes, I understand that. You know, we're
rather alike, Liz. All those boys at Eton . . . they come to one
as complete strangers – suspicious, fearful, reluctant. And
yet, in the end, one believes – one *hopes* – they go away
feeling grateful that one has done something useful for
them.'

226

'That's exactly what I feel. You were talking about the cedar tree. Well, I imagine it as some sort of magnetic pole, holding us all here. And it's very comfortable, too; only I think I've got to pull myself away from it.'

'Quite right, my dear Liz. But why ask to be backed up? Your parents aren't going to throw fits, are they?'

'I just don't want them to think I'm rejecting them.'

Charles smiled again and patted her arm fondly.

'Glad to see the back of you, I shouldn't wonder,' he said. He had lowered his tone, though. All the others were coming downstairs, still chattering about the Ludlow wedding.

In fact, when the subject of Liz's decision came up at last, after dinner, it was her Aunt Phyllis who came out most vociferously in her support, both publicly amongst them all and privately to Helen in the kitchen afterwards.

'Oliver Horner!' she scoffed. 'You can take my word for it, dear, he may be "such a nice suitable boy", as you put it, but he isn't for Liz. In fact, you and Arthur had better both make your minds up to it – Elizabeth will never in this world find anyone remotely suitable on the hunt ball circuit. If you really want to marry her off, she's much more likely to meet her soul-mate tramping some hospital ward.'

'Really, Phyllis! We're not trying to marry her off at all.'

'Of course you are. Don't deceive yourself. You can only see one recipe for a happy life – your own. And who shall blame you? But we're not all cast in one mould, like lead soldiers. I'm just a little sick of watching this endless match-making, as if we were living in Edwardian times.'

Helen defended herself weakly: 'Arthur can't afford to go on supporting three grown girls.'

'Heaven forbid that he should! Any girl worth her salt can take her place in a man's world today. Elizabeth will. Vicky could, if she tried. And Anne will marry a county booby and provide you with enough grandchildren to satisfy the most avid appetite.'

This, on top of her own father's careful persuasion, was more than enough to demolish Helen's instinctive resistance to Liz's wish. Lady Bourne set the cap on it all when her opinion was sought.

'Good for her! Means I can see something of her in London. Introduce her to a few dashing fellows.'

Helen's hopes rose again, and her spirits with them.

Vicky departed next morning in much the same frame of mind as she had been when she had made her last homecoming from school; looking forward to seeing the von Heynigs, and especially Klaus, again; regretful that this was to be her last spell with them; yet thankful that, after it, her home really would be her home. The cedar tree's magnetic pull was as strong upon her as it was upon Elizabeth, only Vicky was the more willing to submit to it.

Immediately afterwards Liz and Anne went out for a walk with the dogs, making themselves scarce while preparations were completed for the further exodus – that of Lady Bourne and Charles Ashley. Phyllis had offered to drive them to London and Mrs. Gates had packed a picnic lunch for them all to eat en route.

'You'll drive carefully,' Nanny Benson tactlessly demanded Phyllis within both the old people's hearing.

'Of course I will. I always do.'

Charles said, a touch pitifully, 'I always look forward to eating in the train dining-car.'

Lady Bourne, as apprehensive as ever about her daughter's driving, mocked him. 'You're nervous, Charles.'

'Oh, not at all. I . . . I had just devised a little experiment, that's all.'

'What was that?'

'I . . . I had planned to work out the actual speed of a dining-car attendant advancing with the vegetables in the contrary direction to the train. Odd thought, you know, a waiter with a tureen of cauliflower walking through Reading at, say, two miles per hour, whilst being carried the other way by a train travelling at seventy miles per hour . . .'

'Pure nerves!' Alice Bourne scoffed, and carried herself off to the waiting car like an aged *duchesse* preparing to clamber into the tumbril.

Anne and Liz had come back in time to say good-bye to them. When the car had gone round the drive and out of the gate the remnants of the family turned back into the house.

'Four gone in one morning,' Arthur remarked. 'And I must make myself scarce, too. Frank will be waiting for me at the dairy.'

He put on his wellington boots and plodded off across the pasture. Helen said, 'Oh, Liz, there's a letter for you. And Dr. Harrington telephoned.'

Anne watched with curiosity as her sister asked cautiously, 'Dr. Harrington? What for?'

'Some book of his you have. He needs it back urgently.'

She went to the telephone pad.

'I've written the title down. I can't pronounce it. He had to spell it out for me. By the way, I told him you've decided to go to London and study again. He sounded rather surprised.'

Liz said, 'He probably thought I was lost to the cause. I'll ... take his book in straight away.'

'Oh, I don't suppose it's as urgent as that.'

'It's all right. I ... I was thinking of going into Halbury.'

'Well, do telephone if you won't be back to lunch – though it's only cold, anyway. Here's your letter.'

One glance at the envelope was enough to tell Liz who it was from. 'I'll just go and put on something a bit more respectable,' she said, and hurried off to her room. A few minutes later Anne, who had recognized the handwriting, too, and had had her curiosity thoroughly aroused by the combination of letter and telephone call, went to look for her. She was surprised to find her sister standing in the middle of her room, staring at nothing, one arm hanging limply down by her side with the letter in the hand.

'Liz!' Anne exclaimed, shutting the door quickly behind her. 'What is it?'

Liz turned to her, looking dazed.

'It's from Brian,' she said in a remote tone.

'I know that. I recognized the handwriting.'

Liz made no move to pass her the letter to read. Instead she said, 'Something . . . very odd has happened. It's his wife. She was in a terrible motor accident. She died in Wolverhampton Hospital.'

The shock of the news had its impact on Anne, too. It was some moments – during which her mind raced itself back from numbness – before she could ask, 'Are you . . . still going to see him?'

Liz had come alive again. She began to change from her thick jersey and old skirt into a suit and blouse.

'Yes, I must,' she answered. 'That must be why he telephoned. I think he wants to see me urgently. Anyway, since Mummy's spilt the beans about my going to London I want to explain.'

'But . . . will you go to London – now?'

Liz paused to stare at her.

'I hadn't thought. I don't know.'

'Supposing he proposes?'

'With his wife just killed?'

'No. Of course not.'

Liz resumed her dressing.

'I can't take it in. What an awful thing to happen, in spite of . . . Oh, hell!'

Anne said tentatively, 'You'll have to consider it, though. I mean, at least he's free now.'

'That's why it's so hard to grasp. Can you imagine suddenly being able to have something you've always wanted – well, for ages, it seems? One moment it was impossible. The next – wallop! It's there in your arms.'

Anne shrugged and replied, 'That's how it is in the fairy stories.'

'There are bad stories, too. The keep-you-awake Brothers Grimm kind.'

'But this isn't. I mean, *he* hasn't been killed.'

Anne was startled by the passion with which Liz retorted to this.

'No. And that would have resolved the whole matter much more neatly, wouldn't it? I'd have known exactly where I stood then. But how can a woman's death, miles away, suddenly make everything all right, when it was all wrong before? How can what Brian and I feel about one another be a sin one moment and blessed the next?'

Anne said sincerely, 'I don't suppose I'd think about that, if it were me.'

'What would you think, then?'

'I'd just think "He can be mine now. All mine." That would be everything. It's what I meant when I said I'd convert to R.C. for Michael, if it came to it. I wouldn't let anything stop me.'

Liz shrugged. 'I suppose that's the Eternal Feminine in you.'

'There's nothing unfeminine about you, Liz. Look, it seems clear as daylight to me. You want him. He wants you. Something made it impossible. Now something's made it possible. Q.E.D.'

'But those "somethings" ... I mean, if there were something *I* could have done to make it possible. Some sort of sacrifice ... But for it to have to depend on that poor woman's awful death ...'

'You didn't know her.'

'But it's soured everything.'

'Well, more fool you, if you let it. Sorry, darling, but that's how I see it. Anyway, it's up to you – and him. You go and talk to him. As you say, it probably won't arise so soon.'

Her elder sister kissed her cheek.

'Thanks, darling,' she said. 'You're quite a realist underneath, aren't you?'

'Maybe. Enough to know that if you're still going to London I'm not staying mooching about here all on my own.'

Liz was making for the door. Anne added, 'Also realist enough to point out that it would look better, if you meet

Mummy on the way out, to have that medical book of his in your hand.'

'Oh, lor'!' Liz exclaimed. 'Thanks. Actually, there isn't one. It's a message we'd arranged if ever he wanted to see me urgently.'

'Then take one of your own. Mummy would never remember that title. And good luck, Liz.'

Liz stopped her car on the way into Halbury and telephoned from a kiosk, guiltily ready to give a false name with a muffled voice if his receptionist should answer. Luckily, though, Brian picked up the telephone himself. They spoke briefly and arranged to meet in The Copper Kettle as soon after noon as his morning surgery would permit. He was by now well established in Dr. Cropper's place and popular for the part he played in local sporting activities. It had indeed become common knowledge that he had a wife somewhere, but that they were living apart. Only the Mrs. Hedges and her kind of Halbury held it against him.

When they had got over the formal greetings, for the benefit of Miss Pringle, and had ordered coffee, and had finished the more private business of explanation and commiseration, Brian Harrington asked, 'What's this your mother said about your going to London?'

'I decided to go back to medicine. It's what you advised.'

'A long time ago – it seems now. Weren't you going to tell me?'

'Of course I would have done. I've only just made up my mind. Brian, it all seemed so hopeless. You know that.'

'But now I'm free.'

Liz shivered involuntarily. He nodded. 'I know what you're thinking. Profiting from her awful death. But we can't wish that undone.'

'No. But there's the other thing – the religious one . . .'

He raised his eyebrows. 'Even a Catholic is allowed to marry if his wife dies.'

She said, 'That's what I mean. If it was all wrong to marry

again while she was alive, why is it suddenly all right now she's dead? I'm afraid I haven't gone deeply into the niceties of your religion. The good old C. of E. is something one wears so lightly, one doesn't imagine having to toe the line.'

'Not *having* to, Liz. I do take my religion seriously. You can't blame me for that. It's just that while Kaye was alive I could never hope to re-marry. Now I can.'

'If I'm prepared to step into a dead woman's shoes? That was never part of my dream.'

'There couldn't be any other way. We both knew that.'

Liz shook her head. 'Yes there could, Brian.'

'What?'

She watched him intently as she said, 'If you really cared for me, you could have given it up – become a Protestant, or nothing at all, if you preferred. Got a divorce and set yourself free.'

As she had feared, the suggestion appeared to horrify him. He answered, 'You don't know what you're asking. For a Catholic, that would be tantamount to self-damnation.'

'Yet you want to link yourself for ever to a Protestant, who's presumably automatically damned?'

'You could change, Liz. There's nothing in your church to stop you.'

She felt a flush of anger in her cheeks.

'Thank *you*. But being a Protestant happens to suit me. Why should I change?'

Her voice had risen and Brian glanced round, afraid that someone might overhear. The Copper Kettle was filling up for its lunchtime trade. He noticed Miss Pringle look their way, then up at the clock. She would be wanting their table.

'Darling,' he said urgently to Liz. 'You do love me, don't you?'

She hesitated before replying, 'I don't know any more. Honestly. I'm sorry, Brian. It's all come as such a shock. Anyway, I must be getting home now.'

'Just a minute longer – please. Look, I've handled this badly. I've talked to you too soon. I should have left it at

233

that letter, only I just had to telephone as well. And then hearing you were going away . . .'

Miss Pringle was obviously writing out their chit. Liz picked up her handbag from the floor. Brian almost begged, 'Look, we need time to think things out. Let our feelings develop. All that secrecy, and hiding, and lying . . . it's been an artificial atmosphere.'

But Miss Pringle had brought the bill and was waiting. He paid and they left the cafe. When they were out in the street he wanted Liz to go back to the surgery and talk, but she insisted on going straight to her car and driving home.

'Well?' Anne demanded, when she had managed to get Liz to herself, in the security of Liz's room.

'It was dreadful,' her sister answered unhappily. 'Dreadful.'

'I thought you looked pretty down at lunch. I don't think Mummy and Daddy noticed, though. You poor old thing!'

'It was as if we were drinking our coffee over that poor woman's grave.'

'Ugh! Don't! What did he say?'

'I hardly remember.'

'He didn't propose, then?'

'Anne, you're as ghoulish as he was – carrying on about being free. Taking it for granted that I'd be as thankful as he is.'

'Well, aren't you? It's what you've both been wanting.'

'I can't help thinking of her – his wife.'

'Liz, I simply can't understand you. You can't change what's happened, but everything's been changed for you. Instead of sneaking about with another woman's husband, you can be all above board now – in anybody's eyes.'

'Not in mine,' her sister said. Anne made a gesture of exasperation.

'Look, you won't like this,' she said, 'But I don't think you really love him at all. I don't think you ever really loved him.'

234

Liz looked at her, astonished.

'How can you say that?' she demanded angrily. 'Are you making out that I'm some sort of a ... a ...?'

'I'm trying to say that you *thought* you loved him.'

'But that would mean I was totally irresponsible – grasping, selfish ...'

'Oh, Liz, you're *Liz*. Stop putting yourself and everything under a microscope.'

Anne impulsively took her hands.

'I'm sorry,' she said earnestly. 'I didn't mean to upset you and make you cross. But suddenly I think I can see it all clearly and I must say it before I lose sight of it again. I think ... I think you've been playing safe all this time.'

'Safe? All that hiding and deceiving safe?'

'You were acting out a kind of charade. You knew it couldn't end in anything real. So, deep down, you felt safe. The perfect excuse to yourself for putting off going back to London and back to your career.'

'That's not true. I was so miserable I wanted to go to London and forget him. I did it once, and I was just on the point of it again.'

'Not to forget him, Liz – to challenge him. Force him to do something about it, if he was ever going to. See if he was only play-acting too.'

There was a silence while Liz let her mind turn over this proposition.

'You're a very wise old owl suddenly,' she said at length.

Anne grinned and gave her hands a squeeze. 'I has me moments. Anyway, *are* you still going to London?'

Liz thought again, then shook her head. 'Not for the time being,' she decided. 'It'd mean committing myself, and it's too soon. But I must get away from here for a while. I don't want to have to keep talking to him.'

'Why not go to Wales again? Your pal will always have you, won't she?'

'Just what I was beginning to think.'

'Marvellous! Then I can tell Mummy I'm bored on my

own and she'll let me go to the Universal Aunt. I could just do with some theatres and dances and things.'

'Scheming little devil!'

'I just know what I want, that's all. I'm not clever like you. I haven't any kind of vocation. I just want to enjoy it all until the irresistible comes along and pops the question, and then I'll be quite content with the inevitable.'

'You're cleverer than you think,' Liz smiled affectionately. 'As for a vocation, I think perhaps you've got the best one of all.'

The following evening, after dinner, Arthur and Helen sat alone in the hall. The only other person in the house was Nanny, up in her attic. Mrs. Gates had finished the dishes and the tidying up and had gone home to the lodge. Apart from the little stirrings of the log fire the house was silent. Arthur had allowed himself the port decanter and a meditative cigar. The newspaper lay unopened on his chair arm. Helen was sewing, for once something decorative rather than functional.

At length Arthur said, 'And then there were two.'

'Not for long,' she reminded him. 'There'll be plenty more of coming and going before we're shot of them for good.'

'Would you want to be?'

'Well ... it's quite nice to have the place to ourselves occasionally.'

Arthur nodded. 'At least it's more peaceful. Makes the old place more like a ship than ever.'

'A ship?' Helen echoed, surprised.

'Yes. Far out at sea and away from all the busy shipping lanes.'

'You're surprisingly rich in metaphor, darling.'

'No, no, it's true. D'you know what it was made all those chaps in sailing ships go back and back to sea, in spite of the hardships and the dangers?'

'The Press Gangs, wasn't it?'

'Apart from that. It was to escape from life ashore, because that was made even worse by so much squalor all round them. When your entire world is a ship, out of all sight and sound of the world's tumult, you know a kind of peace and dignity that can be completely lacking ashore.'

'You're not suggesting that we're surrounded by squalor!'

'It's a squalid world just now, and we're very insulated from it here. We have our worries ... By the way, I've decided definitely to re-mortgage the house. We still have three girls to keep. We must spend something on the estate, and we can't go on always being short of liquid cash.'

'I think you're right,' Helen said, relieved. 'None of us can go on never having any new things, either. Just so long as the liquid cash doesn't go like liquid. But what were you going to say?'

'What? Oh, just that we have our share of worries and domestic ups and downs. We have our responsibilities to people who rely on us – Nanny, the Gateses, the two Chapman families, and the hands ...'

He tapped the newspaper. 'But this chronicle of woe, and the wireless, are about the only points where outside life touches us. Our preoccupations are with keeping things going in the same old way. Our future hopes are almost entirely with the girls' futures ...'

Helen had listened quite astonished by this uncharacteristic monologue. He caught her look and laughed self-consciously.

She said, 'You should take to port-drinking. It really does bring you out.'

Arthur picked up the newspaper at last, opened the first page, then shut it again and tossed it aside.

'No, I'd sooner stay afloat in our ship for as long as we're allowed,' he said. 'You can't sail on for ever without hitting shore eventually. Destination unknown. Meanwhile, I'm enjoying a happy passage. I hope you are, darling?'

Helen smiled back. 'Couldn't be better. Now, do have some more port and put another log on the fire. I haven't been so cosy in the evening for years.'